To Je...

Prepare ...

BOOK 2 OF
THE YELLOW HOODS

BREADCRUMB TRAIL

[signature]

AN EMERGENT STEAMPUNK SERIES
BY ADAM DREECE

ADZO Publishing Inc.

Calgary, Canada

ADZO Publishing Inc.
Calgary, Alberta, Canada
www.adzopublishing.com

Edited by: Jennifer Zouak, Chris W. Rea
Printed in Canada

This is a work of fiction. Names, characters, places, and incidents are a product of the author's imagination. Locales and public names are sometimes used for atmospheric purposes. Any resemblance to actual people, living or dead, or to businesses, companies, events, institutions, or locales is completely coincidental.

Library and Archives Canada Cataloguing in Publication

Dreece, Adam, 1972-, author
 Breadcrumb trail / by Adam Dreece.

(Book 2 of the Yellow Hoods : an emergent steampunk series)
Issued in print and electronic formats.
ISBN 978-0-9881013-3-3 (pbk.).--ISBN 978-0-9881013-5-7 (pdf)

 I. Title. II. Series: Dreece, Adam, 1972-. Yellow Hoods ; bk. 2.

 PS8607.R39B74 2014   C813'.6   C2014-905593-5
                                     C2014-905594-3

3 4 5 6 7 8 9 2016-07-26 66,423

DEDICATION

To my daughter, who is my muse,

To my sons, who remind me what raw,
simple, awesome imagination is about,

To my wife, whose support continues
to make these books possible,

and

To the fans of Book 1 and Twitter
supporters of @AdamDreece,
who make me
smile, laugh and feel appreciated.

EORTHE

Cartographer: Driss of Zouak, 1793
Created at the behest of the Council of Southern Kingdoms

CHAPTERS

CHAPTER ONE

CRUMBLED PLANS

The Hound stood back up and rubbed his head as a dark April rainstorm beat down. He'd landed hard on the slick stone rampart, yet had managed not to slip off or black out. Rain poured off his brown and beige leather long-coat.

For a moment, he looked concerned. He glanced at the control boxes on his forearms and the connections to his oversized, metallic, gear-covered gloves. He hoped rain wasn't getting in. Satisfied, he turned up the dial on each forearm's control box. Electricity started to jump and crackle between his fingers. He then turned his attention back to the Yellow Hood at his feet.

The yellow-hooded Tee dangled below the half-built rampart, desperately clutching her slingshot. When she'd slipped, its leather strap had caught between two of the moss-covered stones. She could feel her hands slipping as the rain wormed its way between her fingers to moisten the slingshot's wooden handle. She looked down and swallowed hard.

The plan sounded bad from the start, but they had

trusted the leader of the Tub. It was bad enough to be asked to go deep into the Red Forest, to an open area with an unfinished, crumbling castle tower and half-built rampart wall—never mind the leader's unwillingness to tell them why they were going there in the first place. Once the opposing secret society's coach had arrived and the representative for the Fare had stepped out, the plan fell apart.

Tee shot a glance around to look for her fellow Yellow Hoods. Elly, with her gray metal shock-sticks in hand, was dodging and blocking a red-hooded swordsman's thin blade. Richy couldn't be seen.

"Lights out, kid," said the Hound. His gloves crackled and electricity danced from finger to finger.

Tee took a deep breath. She could only think of one option, and it was risky. She freed one hand to delve into her yellow cloak's hidden pockets. Pulling out a shock-stick, she pressed its activation button while staring into the Hound's eyes. He hesitated.

"You've *enjoyed* this before, haven't you? Care to do so again?" Tee said menacingly. She wasn't sure if she was willing to risk the fall to the cobblestone below.

Suddenly, Tee's pinky finger slipped off the end of her slingshot. She could feel the other fingers slipping, too. Then, a glint of steel from an arrow aimed at her from less than twenty feet away caught her eye.

The red-hooded archer smiled and said, "Goodbye, little yellow birdy!"

CHAPTER TWO
THE MAN IN THE CRIMSON COAT

Four months earlier, Nikolas Klaus buried his hands in the comfortable pockets of his crimson, full-length coat. Enjoying a deep breath of crisp air, he looked around at the newly fallen snow. He loved December. There was something honest, something innocent about December. Perhaps it was the Solstice celebration, just hours away, that made the month so special to him.

Once again, he checked the skids on his sleigh, and the reins that awaited the horses. Everything was ready.

"I already checked everything, twice, Monsieur Klaus," said Bakon, coming up behind Nikolas and laying a friendly hand on his shoulder. Bakon's brothers, Squeals and Bore, both smiled.

Bakon sported a well-worn brown leather and fur coat, and a fur winter hat. His brown hair peeked out from under his poorly stitched hat, just below his ears. His soft, brown eyes were in contrast to his rough, yet good-looking face.

His brothers were similarly dressed, but rather had blond hair poking out from under their fur hats. Whereas Bakon was five feet and ten inches, Squeals was six feet tall, and Bore, a massive six-foot-five.

Bore remained, as ever, a gentle giant, but Squeals and Bakon had changed in recent months. Egelina-Marie's presence had softened the edges of Bakon's personality, and Bakon gave Squeals more room to prove himself. Squeals, having helped save the lives of the Yellow Hoods months ago, had seemed to finally be finding his adult footing, at the tender age of twenty-four.

Nikolas nodded his approval and appreciation for the brothers' help. It was great to have them back. Since he and his late wife, Isabella, had taken in the abandoned Cochon children, the boys had been there, along with the rest of the Klaus children, to help prepare for the winter Solstice celebrations, until Isabella's death ten years ago. She'd always said that Solstice was the best way to chase away winter and make way for spring. Nikolas missed her deeply.

"Bore gave the sleigh a good shake, and nothing moved," said Squeals.

"I've got the last bag of toys here, Monsieur Klaus," said Egelina-Marie, arriving on the scene to heave the bag on top of others already in the sleigh. Her blue eyes were filled with the joy of feeling like a kid again. Her shoulder-length, dark brown hair framed her heart-shaped face. She had fond memories of seeing Monsieur

Klaus come into town in his red coat, followed by screaming children. The adults would follow with food and drink to share with friends and neighbors.

Nikolas looked sternly at Bakon, his old-fashioned values showing themselves.

"Hey—! Eg insisted she carry that last bag," said Bakon, defending himself, hands up.

Egelina-Marie chuckled and Bore started to laugh, covering his face with his enormous hand. Until a couple of months ago, Bore had almost never seen Bakon smile. Now, he saw it on occasion. He liked that. He liked Egelina-Marie very much, too.

"Mister Nik, we all done?" asked Bore, his voice deep and simple-sounding.

"Almost, Boris, almost. You did good, very good," Nikolas said. His eastern kingdoms heritage was evident in his heavy accent. He reached over and gave Bore an affectionate slap on the arm. "Now, where are my granddaughter and her friends? They are a bit late. We need to get down to Mineau for six o'clock. Squeals, will you fetch the horses, please?"

Squeals nodded and pulled Bore along. "Come on, big guy, let's go see the horses." Bore loved horses.

Nikolas snapped his fingers, remembering the brass tube with design plans that he wanted to bring. "I'll be back in a moment."

"Oh, Monsieur Klaus, my father wanted me to tell you that he'll meet you at the gift-giving ceremony. He has a couple of things to attend to before that," said Egelina-Marie.

Nikolas' eyes went wide as he realized he hadn't taken care of something important. He rubbed his short, salt-and-pepper beard. To avoid his usual clumsiness with words, he'd typically take his time to smooth out thoughts before speaking—but right now he didn't want to miss another opportunity to say what had been on his mind. "Ah... Egelina-Marie, there is a thing I must say."

Bakon's eyebrows went up. He hadn't heard this tone from Nikolas before.

Nikolas took hold of Eg's hands and smiled at her, looking up slightly. She was an inch taller than his humble five-foot-eight. "No more *Monsieur Klaus*, please. You must call me *Nikolas*. Will you do that for me?"

"Um," said Egelina-Marie, her cheeks reddening. "Um, sure. If you're sure?"

Bakon couldn't believe what was happening. He'd heard about when Nikolas had asked William to call him by his first name. Bakon had never imagined it would happen with him and Eg; after all, Jennifer was Nikolas' own daughter, and William his prospective son-in-law. Bakon had always doubted how Nikolas really felt deep down, until now.

Nikolas smiled warmly at Egelina-Marie. "Quite, yes? You've earned your place. Your influence is wholesome and good. I allowed the formalities to continue until I could extrapolate a likely trajectory, and I am content with what I have now projected. So, I am formally asking for a reduction in the state of formality. Yes?" He could tell by the look on her face that his initial simplicity had been lost.

Egelina-Marie choked up. It had taken a moment to figure out what Nikolas meant, and she could barely believe it. With a sweet smile, she managed to say, "Okay," and then kissed Nikolas on the cheek.

Nikolas turned to the surprised Bakon. "Same for you, Bakon. No more *Monsieur Klaus*. Yes? Good." Nikolas turned and started to head away. "I'll be back in a moment. We can't keep all the children waiting, now can we? So much to do!" His muscular body bounced along and he sang to himself.

Bakon gave Eg an affectionate shove. "Look at you, Sergeant. I think you've been attacked on the cheeks by sentiment. Are your eyes misting up?"

"You're no better. I can see it. That dark, rough exterior doesn't know how to handle one old man who truly has always thought of you as one of his own. And by the way, *don't* make me hurt you," she said, smiling, and poking back at him. "I *am* a trained professional."

"I'm a professional ruffian. I—" countered Bakon.

"No, you're not really—you just *pretend*," said Eg, grabbing him by the fur collar of his coat. "But you can always be *my* tough guy. Come here—"

Just as they started to lean toward each other, three sail-carts came sliding up the path to the house, each piloted by a yellow-hooded driver.

"Careful! Here comes a little girl with a slingshot. Need a helmet?" joked Egelina-Marie. She could see she'd teased Bakon enough, and gave him an innocent smile.

The sailing Yellow Hoods engaged their handbrakes and pulled down their sails. Turning their steering wheels gently, each brought their sail-cart to a complete stop, with a spray of snow. Tee, Elly, and Richy climbed out. The winter afternoon sun danced off their yellow hooded cloaks.

"Hey guys," said Tee, pulling back her hood and allowing her long, dark brown hair to pour out. "Are you ready to go? I can't believe we're officially doing it in Mineau this year!"

Thirty years ago, there was only the city of Mineau at the foot of the mountain. As Mineau grew into a trading hub, some freethinkers decided to establish a more secluded town up on the mountain's plateau. They'd kept to themselves and were careful, at least at first, about whom they would let feel comfortable enough to stay in town. They decided to use an old nickname of Mineau as the new town's name, not only because they liked the name, but also knowing the political headaches it would cause and how much more likely it would make the outside world just want to leave them alone. Thus, Minette was founded.

This was the first year the city of Mineau would

officially celebrate Solstice with Minette. Both town magistrates had decided it was a great opportunity to bring the towns together—something attempted every now and then, and in different ways. The Solstice celebration wasn't unique to Minette, but the *way* they did it was—the presents, and bringing everyone together to feast, sing, and dance outside.

"Woo!" said Elly, looking at the sleigh. "Are those sacks *all* full of presents? That's even more than last year." Her dark blond hair was almost the same length as Tee's.

"We started preparation a week earlier this year! Four weeks, we worked," said Nikolas as he returned, brass tube in hand. He jammed it into the sleigh in a secure spot.

Turning to Elly, Nikolas continued, "Egelina-Marie offered to help, which made us a small army! Each of us had our roles and we worked at our specialties. The Cochon brothers carved all the wood parts. Tee and her parents assembled the pieces. Egelina-Marie and I painted. When all the toys were dry, I went over each to make sure they were perfect." Nikolas looked back at all the dull-colored sacks and did some calculations in his head to make sure he had enough.

"You always worry you didn't make enough, Grandpapa," said Tee, interrupting his thoughts.

Nikolas was content that he had everything he needed. He looked around at the smiling faces and noticed the sail-carts had skied in. "You have made another improvement, Richy, yes? Mind if I have a look? I was wondering, at the back of my mind, how you were using the sail-carts in this snow." He twiddled his fingers in anticipation.

"Sure!" said Richy, with pride. Ever since Nikolas had built the sail-carts for them last fall, Richy had spent countless hours with his. He'd become the daredevil of the trio, and consequently found himself spending almost as much time repairing or tinkering with his sail-cart as actually using it. He didn't have to tell Nikolas there had been changes—it was obvious.

Richy flipped his sail-cart onto its side. "I removed the wheels and put these skids on. I got stuck a couple of times in the snow when they fell off, so I put in this cross-brace—Tee's idea. I also nailed this little box on the back, for tools. I had to put a buckle and strap on after I littered tools around the forest. I still owe my dad chores as payment to replace them."

Nikolas bent down and gently ran his hand over the snowy skids. "Now what inspired you to use this wood?"

Richy glanced over to Elly. "I tried some others—they didn't work so well, but then Elly found this type of tree in the forest that bends well. She said it's used for bows, so we used that for the skids. The problem is we can't go very far—the snow ends up stuck to the wood a lot. We have to keep scraping it off. Maybe I'm using the wrong wood."

Nikolas stroked his beard. "No, no... the wood is fine.

It is exactly the right wood to use. I know what you are missing. I must fetch something for you, yes?" He went into his large shed, still filled to the rafters. Few dared to enter for fear of being buried. It seemed to have a Klaus-shaped tunnel carved through. Soon he emerged, triumphant.

Klaus held a few bars of hardened yellow wax. "This is a special wax from a friend, an expert—very talented. Rub this on the skid bottoms until they are slick, and keep some with you."

Hearing Nikolas mention wax took Bakon back. When he and his brothers had first met Nikolas, he'd put wax dust on a makeshift tent to make it rain-resistant. He marveled at how Nikolas helped people.

"Wow, that's awesome," said Richy. He took a bar and started applying it to his sail-cart's skids. "Like this?"

"Keep going!" said Nikolas enthusiastically. He handed a stick each to Elly and Tee. They started copying Richy.

"Your parents must be proud of your innovations, yes?" asked Nikolas.

Richy paused. "Um, to be honest, they didn't really notice." He looked at the snow-covered ground. "Sometimes I feel they don't know what to make of me."

Nikolas put a reassuring hand on Richy's shoulder. "I am sure there is something distracting them. You keep doing this. You were born to do these things, so do them! I am sure whatever it is your parents are struggling with, they both want the best for you."

Bakon caught Richy's eye. "I still hear tales in the taverns of how some Yellow Hood flipped his sail-cart into that villain, Andre LeLoup, sending him flying. The maniac who, after Egelina-Marie took him down, comes back and nearly has his revenge—except *you* stop him. You're a *legend*, kid," he said, offering his handsome, roguish smile.

"Thanks, Bakon," Richy said, with half a smile.

"Anytime, kid," said Bakon, walking past him and messing his hair. "We misfits, we stick together."

Richy flashed a full smile, and got back to waxing his sail-cart's skids.

"I've got the horses!" said Bore excitedly, walking the four horses forward.

"And here's the rest of the gear for attaching them to the sleigh," said Squeals, dropping the gear into the snow. "Feels heavier than last year."

Bakon was about to give his brother his disapproving, disappointed face when he stopped himself. After a moment, he punched him in the shoulder instead. "Feel heavier, *now*?"

Squeals glared back at Bakon with a cheeky smile.

Nikolas thought about how this would likely be the last year when all this would be necessary. His secret invention, the horseless cart, would soon change everything. But first, he needed to give a copy of its plans to the Tub, to make sure his friends and allies had the advantage he suspected they needed.

The Tub was a secret society, led these days by a butcher, a baker, and a candle and stick maker. Founded upon noble principles, the Tub's influence grew, over time spreading to all of the kingdoms, but eventually coming into conflict with another such society, the Fare. After centuries of a cut-throat, cloak-and-dagger war, the Tub finally achieved the upper hand. They used that opportunity to bankrupt the Fare, and shackle its members with a crippling peace agreement that would see certain actions taken by any Fare-man as grounds for execution. In the decades since that agreement was put in place, the kingdoms had enjoyed relative peace.

Nikolas had been involved in the Tub for a long time. He'd never completely bought into their ways or principles, but he had his own reasons for supporting them. He'd always been on the outside, often thinking that their struggles weren't necessarily his. The recent events with LeLoup and Simon St. Malo had made him rethink that.

"Elly, what's poking out of your cloak pocket there?" asked Egelina-Marie. "Something is trying to escape."

"Oh," said Elly, securing the forearm-length metal rod. Its small handle was visible and had caught on the secret pocket's edge. Elly collapsed the handle back into the base, and placed the rod back into the pocket. "Just one of my shock-sticks. At least the other is behaving," she joked.

Elly had grown a bit quicker than Tee in recent months, making them now the same height. The two best friends had birthdays only a month apart and seemed to inch slightly ahead of the other every couple of months. While Tee was the daring one always jumping into adventure, Elly was the loyal friend who always jumped in after, knowing that together they'd get out of whatever it was. "Since we tangled with LeLoup, I think it's always best to be prepared. We've helped more than a dozen people since, by being prepared. Although, my shock-sticks seem to need more winding and don't give off as big a shock these days. We got these new ones—"

Elly caught herself, not wanting to reveal to everyone the secret treehouse at the top of the mountain, and how new equipment just seemed to appear, though it had been a while since any had. "—about two months ago. We stopped using our old ones since they aren't as effective... maybe because of the weather."

"Hmm," said Nikolas to himself, making a mental note.

After checking the horses were hitched correctly, Nikolas turned to everyone. "It's wonderful to have your help. Now let's go have a wonderful Solstice! I'm sure it'll be the best yet."

Tee, Elly, and Richy hopped into their sail-carts and pulled up the telescoping masts. Within moments, the wind filled their sails and they started heading off.

"Okay, we'll see you down there," yelled Tee as she started to pick up speed.

Bore and Squeals climbed into the sleigh with Nikolas.

Bakon pulled out some cross-country skis and eyed them uneasily. "See you guys down there in a couple of hours—I hope."

Squeals leaned over the edge of the sleigh. "Bakon, if you think you're about to humiliate yourself, find a larger tree this time. It wasn't very sporting of you to take out that little one last time. Mind you, it did do a number on you. Try not to damage the family name," he said, laughing.

Bakon took a swipe at his brother's head. "Get out of here."

"See you in Mineau!" yelled Nikolas. He gave the reigns a flick and followed the departing Yellow Hoods.

Egelina-Marie and Bakon watched as the convoy left. Gradually, everything fell silent.

"Are you sure this is a good idea? Do we even have enough daylight left?" said Bakon.

"We'll be fine. Are you as scared as you sound?" said Egelina-Marie, putting her skis on.

Bakon had skied before, just not very successfully, unlike his younger brothers. He would have never considered trying again after the tree fiasco three years ago, but Egelina-Marie had a way of talking him into things.

"Follow my lead, watch what I do, and try to glide," said Egelina-Marie. "And if you get lost or go missing, I'll find you."

"Promise?" asked Bakon, sarcastically.

"Can I get back to you on that?" replied Egelina-Marie with a wink.

CHAPTER THREE

A LETTER OF WARNING

Maxwell Watt slammed his notebook down on the side table, whipped off his glasses, and looked at the fire snapping and popping away in the fireplace. The fire seemed to mirror his frustration at being interrupted again.

"Keep your blooming trousers on!" he bellowed as he got up and stomped over to the front door. After a second to close his robe before facing the winter weather, he angrily opened the door. "What do you want?"

A man stood there, holding a letter. "Special delivery, sir."

"Oh, sorry," said Maxwell. "A lot of people have been caroling this evening. A man can't be left alone with his thoughts, it seems."

"Don't appreciate the singing, sir?" asked the man drily, still holding the letter.

Maxwell looked around, in case friends or neighbors were about to approach who might take offense. "Singing

I don't mind, but packs of wild people howling at each doorstep like out-of-key wolves baying at the moon? I *do* mind. How can a man change the world with such horrible distractions?"

The man stared blankly at Maxwell and gently offered the letter again.

Realizing it was late at night, and devilishly cold, Maxwell quickly found a silver coin to give to the man. The man smiled respectfully, gave Maxwell a tip of his hat, and left.

Maxwell hurried back to the warmth of the fire and his comfortable chair.

"Who was that, father?" asked a teenage male voice from upstairs.

"Just a messenger," said Maxwell, putting his spectacles back on. "Go back to sleep."

Hearing the thump, thump, thump of feet coming down the stairs, Maxwell put the letter in his lap and waited.

"Franklin Charles David, I told you to go back to bed," he said sternly, though not convincingly. Maxwell wasn't a strong parent—instead he thought of his son more like a special friend.

The messy, dark blond-haired fifteen-year-old plunked himself down on the ottoman and warmed his hands by the fire. "Actually, father, you told me to go back to *sleep*. I wasn't asleep yet. So given that your directive was invalid, I thought I'd come see what the bother was about."

Maxwell tried to hide his smile. Franklin was certainly his son, much to the disdain of his ex-wife.

Franklin turned, peeking over his shoulder at the letter in his father's lap. "Who's it from? Costs extra to have it delivered at night, on a Saturday so close to Solstice. Must be important."

"I haven't yet had a second to look. Shall we?" said Maxwell, waving his son in. He hated to think that he played favorites with his kids, but he did, and he knew it. Franklin Charles David was the eldest by five years, and had shown signs of scientific genius at an early age. His daughter, Emily, was a wonderful girl, but Maxwell just thought of her as a pleasant child. Emily seemed to be very much his ex-wife's child, and Franklin his.

Maxwell leaned forward and held up the envelope. "It's from my friend, Mister Nikolas Klaus." He paused. "Hmm, that's odd."

Franklin yawned. "You get letters from him all the time, father. Why's that odd?"

Maxwell hesitated before opening the letter. "It's just that Nikolas replies to my letters, but he doesn't initiate— at least, that's been the pattern since we started corresponding two years ago. I send him one, and then he responds, without fail. Now… this. It's out of pattern. Why do you think he'd do that?"

Franklin rubbed his tired face. "I don't know, father. Just open it." He hated it when his dad needlessly tried to solve a puzzle when the answer was right there.

"Come on! Let's have a guess," said Maxwell, insisting they try to figure it out.

"I'm only doing this to speed up to the part where we actually open the letter, okay?" said Franklin, tired and now annoyed. "Maybe he wrote to tell you he invented something to make your steam engine look archaic? That he was just patting you on the head like a child?"

Maxwell seemed a bit hurt and glanced at the letter, now half expecting it to say exactly that.

"Maybe he has a new recipe for cookies that he just had to share? I don't know. Just *open the letter*. The answer is right in front of you. Look at it."

Maxwell made strange lip movements as he thought about what could be in the letter. "He rushed this the entire way. That costs a small fortune, like you said. What's so important to warrant that, I wonder?"

"Maybe he's daft like you and figured out a simplified solution to an equation that no one cares about," Franklin said, stretching. "Okay, that's it. I'm not waiting anymore. I'm off to bed."

Franklin made his way toward the stairs. He heard his dad tear open the letter, and when he got to the first step his father said, "*Stop*. Franklin Charles David, come here, please."

Sighing heavily and a bit more annoyed at having to turn back, Franklin returned to the ottoman and glared at his dad. "What could your letter possibly have to do with me?" He then noticed his dad had turned a shade of gray. "What's wrong, father?"

With a slightly trembling hand, Maxwell removed his spectacles. "It seems that we've been betrayed. Mister Klaus was attacked by someone named Andre LeLoup, sent by Simon St. Malo."

Franklin tried to place where he'd heard the name *Simon St. Malo* before. He remembered enough to know St. Malo wasn't a good person.

Maxwell continued, "He was attacked for the steam engine plans. *My* steam engine plans. That means—"

Standing up, Franklin scratched his head and continued his father's thought. "That means that someone knows you two are corresponding, but doesn't know who is helping whom. Or, at least, they didn't. Maybe they do now."

Maxwell stood up and threw the letter into the fire. He wiped his sweaty forehead with his robe's sleeve. After a deep breath, he smoothed his already flat, thin, light brown hair with both hands.

"Did you read the whole letter?" asked Franklin, watching it curl up into ash in the fire. Evidently, there were several pages, and he hadn't seen his father leaf through more than two.

"I have to get rid of everything. They'll come for me next," said Maxwell as he started pacing.

"Did you finish reading it? It looked thick. Maybe he

knew who the traitor was?"

Maxwell nervously rubbed his cheeks with his hands. "I skimmed what I needed. I'm pretty sure I know what he was going to say. It's... it's obvious, really. I need to think."

Franklin glared at his father. "It's *not* obvious. You didn't know when you started reading it that there was a traitor! You have to stop doing *this* whenever you get scared. You always jump to conclusions! You really—"

"Franklin Charles David, please! I'm trying to *think*." Maxwell paced about the room, drumming his fingers on his pointy chin, and then said to himself, "Yes, I see it now. There's only one thing we can do. I need to send him in the morning." He sighed deeply. "Well, that's sorted then."

Franklin knew his father was a genius, as was he, but he'd seen his father in panic situations and knew how terribly his brain seemed to work at those times. His mother's announcement that she was leaving his father had been one such occasion. His father had been so distracted that he'd accidentally put the laundry on the fire, and put his sister outside instead of the cat.

Another time, when his father had an inventors' meeting coming up, he'd refused to listen to Franklin's advice about the amount of pressure a prototype steam engine could take. He nearly blew up the house.

With a scowl on his face, Franklin crossed his arms. "Send *me* in the morning? What are you on about? I'm not going anywhere."

Maxwell walked over to a writing desk in the corner of the room, sat down on the ribbed chair, and pulled out a piece of paper. With a distracted tone, he replied, "Yes, you are. You have to. They can't get their hands on it."

Franklin rubbed his face in frustration. "On *what*, father? On your never-going-to-be-finished steam engine? I haven't had the heart to say it, but it's never going to work. Let them have it. Maybe it can consume their fortune, as it has ours."

Putting his quill down, Maxwell turned and looked at his son. He could see that Franklin was right on the cliff of losing faith in him. He motioned his son closer.

Franklin hesitated, hating being treated like a child, but he could see something in his father's eyes that he hadn't seen in a while. Rolling his eyes and giving in, he dragged his feet to stand beside his seated dad.

Glancing about as if a spy could be hiding in the room, Maxwell whispered, "It *does* work. It's been working for the past month. I didn't want anyone to know, so I kept messing around, purposely blowing things up every now and then. Nikolas' last letter helped —I had it working within days."

Franklin folded his arms and curled his face in disbelief. "I don't believe it. It's working?"

"Yes," replied his father, nodding.

"For real?" said Franklin, putting his hands on his

hips.

"Yes," replied his father, smiling.

"Really?" asked Franklin. He was starting to feel that his father had been more devious than he'd thought possible.

Maxwell smiled a rarely seen devilish smile. "*Yes*, Franklin. This will change the world, but we can't let St. Malo get his hands on it. I'm sure the only reason he's still around is that he's in league with others, and they'd tear the world apart with my invention." He returned to the letter he'd started writing.

Franklin was stunned. "You got it working," he repeated several times, quietly. Finally, he came out of that loop and said, "You got it *working*... and I didn't even notice. You cheeky monkey."

His father looked at him quizzically. "Cheeky monkey? Is that any way to talk to your father?" he said, trying to sound firm.

Franklin chuckled. "My father? No. A sneak who has been making me think that he's only half the genius I hoped he was? A cheat who made me believe that my father was an old codger? That man is one cheeky monkey indeed."

Maxwell changed to a serious look, and his eyes locked on those of his son. "You'll need to take my plans to Mister Klaus himself. He's the only one I can trust with them."

Franklin blinked, surprised. "Me? By myself? Why

me? Wouldn't the journey take weeks?"

Maxwell stood up, maintaining his look at his son, who was only an inch or two shorter. "You're the only one I trust to carry my plans there."

Worried, Franklin thought about all the people his father knew, hoping to think of someone he could mention that would take the burden, but he couldn't think of one. "Why can't you take it, father? I can come with you. We could—"

Maxwell sighed and smoothed his thin hair again. He removed his spectacles in order to clean them on his shirt. "You don't understand, Franklin. They will be looking for me, whoever they are. They won't be looking for you, at least not yet. I will try to go north, maybe to Eldeshire where we spent the summer a couple of years ago, but I'm certain they'll catch me before then. I doubt I will evade their clutches for long."

"Father, we don't even know who they are—you said so yourself. Now you're imagining them as having—"

Ignoring his son, Maxwell continued, "The plans have to get to Nikolas. I need you to put them in his hands. He'll know how to keep them safe."

CHAPTER FOUR

TALE OF THE MOUNTAIN MAN

Many citizens of Minette enjoyed going down to the larger city of Mineau a couple of times per year. As far as cities in the kingdom of Freland went, Mineau was average size, but compared to Minette, it seemed enormous.

The main road from Minette to Mineau wound its way lazily down the mountain, over streams and small bridges, through forest and large, snowy clearings. In summer, the trip was one hour on horseback, but in winter it could take anywhere from one to eight hours, depending on the potentially brutal weather.

When Nikolas' sleigh arrived at Mineau two hours later, he found Bakon already there, sitting on the back of one of the sail-carts. Bakon was nursing a bruise over his left eye, and a fat lip. The Yellow Hoods were nowhere to be seen.

He glanced over to Egelina-Marie, who gestured that they shouldn't discuss Bakon's situation. Nikolas nodded, while the other two Cochon brothers chuckled to themselves.

He wondered what the Yellow Hoods were up to. In a brief couple of months Tee, Elly, and Richy had used the carts in ways he'd never imagined. Nikolas didn't like being unable to predict the outcome of his decisions—something that rarely happened. Lack of knowing how his inventions might be used in the world was one of the biggest reasons he seldom felt comfortable with sharing them.

He found himself questioning his intent to hand over the plans for his horseless cart to the Tub. The LeLoup incident had inspired him to finally solve the last of the design problems and build it, after wrestling with it for so long. He'd shown the first prototype to Tee and her mother, Jennifer—his daughter. Yet, no one knew just how far he'd been able to push things since. He'd figured the best thing to do in passing the innovation over to the Tub was to give them a design from a month ago and then see what happens.

The Yellow Hoods would typically make the trek down to Mineau with their parents, but now they were masters of their sail-carts. Tee had celebrated her thirteenth birthday mere days ago, and the three were behaving like teenagers, going off to who-knows-where in their sail-carts. Each set of parents had taken a different approach in dealing with this.

For Elly, her parents had witnessed the change

firsthand. From their front steps, they'd watched; standing facing backward on a rapidly moving sail-cart, Elly had thrown a shock-stick at one of LeLoup's horsemen, defeating him. They'd watched as she spun in the air, seated herself perfectly, and brought the sail-cart to a quick stop right in front of them.

Since then, Elly responded to every worry her parents tried to throw at her with her clear, convincing logic, all tied back to what they had witnessed. While they didn't like the idea of the sail-cart, they believed that if she and Tee stuck together, then they'd come out unscathed together. In the end, Elly's parents occasionally wondered about the odd cut and bruise, but if Elly seemed happy, they didn't worry.

As for Tee, almost as soon as she could walk, her parents knew they had trouble on their hands. She loved adventure and had a mind for getting things done, and William and Jennifer each blamed it on the other's heritage. William's father, Samuel Baker, was one of the three top leaders of the Tub, while Jennifer's father, Nikolas Klaus, was a renowned master inventor, also affiliated with the Tub.

Tee's parents weren't sure whether she hunted for danger, or if danger just seemed to find her. They were thankful for Tee's incredible natural luck, and her close, trusting friendship with Elly. Where that wasn't enough, they'd invented all sorts of devices and mechanisms to try to stop Tee from doing such things, say, as piloting her sail-cart off the edge of the cliff near their home.

Unfortunately, for Richy, his parents had withdrawn from the situation and more or less left him to do whatever he wanted. His parents were wrapped up in their own affairs, and Richy was kept in the dark on such matters. They'd often stop an emotionally charged conversation whenever he would walk into the room. They didn't notice him working on improving his sail-cart, or the amazing things he could do with it. Even when he wanted to tell them about it, they just smiled and said they'd look at it later, but later never came. Richy's parents thought they were protecting their son by keeping him far from their troubles, without realizing the effect it was having on him.

Tee, Elly, and Richy returned to the parked sail-carts with some Mineau friends who were eager to see the much-rumored contraptions. Some of the teenagers quietly marveled at the sleigh, too, not sure if it was okay to interrupt Nikolas while he chatted with adults who came to greet him. Everyone, regardless of age, seemed to be excited to meet the group from Minette.

"I better be off," said Nikolas, shaking many hands and climbing back into the sleigh with Squeals and Bore. Egelina-Marie and Bakon stepped onto the sleigh's back skids and held on for the ride.

With a clicking noise from his mouth and a flick of the reigns, Nikolas convinced the horses to head to the town's square. As they navigated the streets, kids poured out, drawn to the sleigh as if it were a magnet. Cheering and excitement grew until they reached the square. Some adults came out with their children, while others would come along shortly, not wanting to miss the highly anticipated festivities.

Tee laughed as the sleigh and the friends that had come out to see their sail-carts pulled away from view. "Do we still get that excited?"

A big-bearded, six-foot-eight man yelled, "There they are!"

Instinctively, the trio sprang apart, ready to take on the potential danger. They'd already pulled down their hoods and had their shock-sticks in hand.

"Oh, for crying out loud," said Richy, realizing who it was. "I think you scared me senseless!"

"Monsieur de Montagne!" yelled Elly to the huge man.

"Stop!" bellowed the mountain man as they ran toward him. His booming voice seemed like it could stop the falling snow mid-sky. "What have I told you?" he said gruffly, hands on his hips. "Do I *look* like a noble gentleman? Just *Pierre*."

Richy frowned. "You're wearing a nice fur coat, for starters. Where's the usual pile of poorly stitched-together furs?"

Elly gave Richy a quizzical look. "He's also combed

his hair," she said, pretending to be shocked.

Tee added, "Did he trim his beard? Where's the bird's nest gone? Those poor, poor birds."

"Careful—" said Elly, gesturing to her friends to step back. "He might have even... washed!"

Richy leaned in for a sniff as Pierre shook his head and looked at the sky. "Hmm. He doesn't smell like three-day-old dead bear now. It's weird," said Richy.

"I think he *wants* to be a nobleman," said Tee. "It must have been a rhetorical question."

Pierre's cheeks were red from embarrassment and the teasing. No one had ever treated him like this, and he wasn't sure what to make of it.

Richy nodded. "Yup—you're looking too respectable for us *not* to call you monsieur."

"We blame our upbringing. But I think we're done. You can now continue your fake-yelling at us," said Elly, with a cheeky smile.

"Right, thanks," said Pierre, pointing and nodding at Elly. "Don't call me monsieur! I'm not some... *fancy* man... on the inside."

"Pierre!" they yelled affectionately, charging the bear-like man. He picked up the lot of them in a huge hug and danced around.

Over the past couple of months, the Yellow Hoods had started to build a reputation for helping people, whether finding lost children in the forest, or getting things from one side of town to the other. The one rescue that was changing their lives was that of the mountain hermit, Pierre de Montagne. Pierre had spent practically every day since then teaching the Yellow Hoods everything he knew about mountains, forests, and tracking.

Elly skipped along, letting out some of her happy, excited energy. "So, is this really your first Solstice celebration?" she asked Pierre as they all walked along together.

"It is my first," he said pensively. He'd been raised by hermit parents. "I watched a couple of times from the forest—the celebrations here, and in Minette. Minette's were my favorite. Here, it's more of people just singing in the streets or walking around."

"Why didn't you join in?" asked Richy. "It's not like you need an invitation."

"Well—" started Pierre, stroking his beard. It felt odd, being so smooth. That morning, he'd traded for a brush, and had to ask the woman at the trading post how to use it properly. She'd been happy to help. "See, when you get old like me, sometimes you feel you can't change. You feel like a wheel stuck in the mud. It takes a good push to get you out."

"Were *we* your good push?" asked Tee.

Pierre chuckled and patted Tee on the head. "Yes, you were. You gave me new purpose in life. Anyway, I want to hear what you think of this Solstice stuff. Is it true that darkness runs away after the celebration?" asked Pierre. "Because that's what I hear."

"Did you hear those screaming kids? If I was darkness, I'd already be running the other way!" said Elly. Everyone laughed.

Several weeks earlier, Pierre de Montagne's lungs had been filling up with ice-cold lake water. He'd always feared that one day he'd end up as the hunted, instead of the hunter. The master of the forest felt like a fool—and a soon-to-be dead one.

The hermit lived in a small log cabin between Minette and Mineau, almost at the base of the mountain. His parents had been hermits, too, but had passed away when he was seventeen. Pierre was raised to dislike "towners," as his mother called townsfolk, and so whenever he went into town, he traded for what he needed and then left. Despite feeling lonely, and curious about the towners, he lacked the courage to do anything more than a bit of spying.

That morning, Pierre had walked out of his cabin, into the snow, and looked around. The winter landscape was the same as ever, but he wasn't—he felt old. While his hair had just touches of gray and white hidden in rich brown, his body ached more with each passing season. His endurance wasn't what it used to be. He wondered if this might be his last winter.

After getting dressed, he headed out. He was armed

with two homemade javelins; one he kept on his back, and the other ready in hand. Soon, he spotted a full-grown deer and began his hunt. Each time his prey moved, he followed. Each time it slowed or stopped, he would hide, wait, or proceed slowly. Hunger had taught him over the decades that patience, persistence, and alertness were critical.

Pierre saw the deer's ears perk up a moment before the noise. Just then, three yellow-hooded kids zoomed through on contraptions that appeared to be strange sailboats. Seconds later, the kids were gone, never having noticed hunter or prey.

The deer darted away, and Pierre cursed the towners. "I'll have to start all over again," he said, huffing and puffing.

He searched for the deer's trail for some time. "There we go," he said to himself. He paused as something else caught his eye. "What's this?" he said, walking over to inspect another set of tracks, mere feet away. He patted his big hairy beard with a mitt in wonder as he bent down to examine the other tracks.

"What is this?" he repeated. He took off his right mitt and moved his finger through the four-toed paw print in the snow. He laid the mitt beside it and was disturbed to see they were nearly the same size.

"What kind of cat is that large, yet with a print that shallow? It almost floats on the snow," he said, mystified. He studied another one of the paw prints.

"Diamond shaped... diamond shaped... I know that shape. *Why* do I know it?" He sat there in the snow and stared at the trail the prints made. A lost, painful memory surfaced. His eyes widened, and again he looked at the prints in earnest.

Picking up his mitt, he looked around, worried. He didn't want to say out loud what he was thinking—out of superstition—but in his mind he kept saying *dire lynx?* over and over.

Dire lynx were larger, far more aggressive versions of their small cousins. Sightings were rare enough that most people doubted their existence, believing them just a fiction created to scare children. Pierre knew better—one had fatally wounded his father.

"How long have we been tracking the same prey?" he muttered, deeply worried that he hadn't noticed it before. He started following the lynx's trail backward, curious about where the lynx had come from, and how long they had been hunting side-by-side.

At first, Pierre only intended to backtrack a little, but the further he went back, the more curious he became. Once the trail reached his own cabin, Pierre froze. "You... you weren't tracking the deer," he stammered, his heart racing. "It's me... I'm your prey."

He went into his cabin to get his flintlock pistol. He wondered for a moment if he should barricade himself inside, but he knew that if he did, then when he would eventually stepped out, the dire lynx would strike. Pierre steeled his nerves and headed back out.

He quickly returned to where the kids had zoomed through and scared off the deer, desperate to pick up the trail of where the lynx had gone. Every shadow made him jump and prepare to defend himself. Worse than feeling old, Pierre now felt vulnerable.

Then, he heard a sound that chilled his blood. He turned to see the giant, snow-white dire lynx standing on a fallen tree twenty feet away. The lynx's low, rumbling growl was foreboding. Its pale blue eyes fixed on Pierre. The predator was telling him that at the time of its choosing, it was going to kill him.

Pierre felt cold inside, and his hands and legs felt numb. Thirty years ago, he'd have dared to draw his pistol, or whip out a javelin and throw it, but he knew he was no longer fast enough. He couldn't believe he'd neglected having a weapon ready in his right hand, at all times, having put them away so he could walk and crouch better.

The last thing he wanted was to be left mortally wounded in the snow. Sorrow and regret at having lived a hermit's life crept into his thoughts. *So many things,* he thought, *so many things I should have changed.*

The dire lynx started to coil up. Its growl got louder. Just then, the loud voices of the kids returned from out of nowhere. With the lynx momentarily distracted, Pierre sprang up and ran for his life.

The Yellow Hoods were having fun carving up the late autumn snow on their skid-mounted sail-carts. They were just about to start the long sail back to the main road and return home when Richy noticed something.

"Hey, did you see that?" he asked, pointing to some trees.

Elly looked over her shoulder but saw nothing. "No," she yelled back, over the sounds of the flapping sails and the skids moving over the snow.

"I thought I saw a guy running—like he was scared. Maybe I'm wrong," said Richy.

Tee quickly studied Richy's face. "Turn around, guys. Richy, you saw something. Let's investigate. If it's nothing, there should still be enough sunlight for the sail home."

"You were right the last two times, Richy. Let's see if it's lucky number three," replied Elly, turning her steering wheel and managing her sail in the strong wind.

Over the years, Pierre had run across more than a dozen people lost in the forest. He'd helped many, but he'd always looked down on them as weak and ignorant. If they just had common sense, he'd told himself, they could've gotten out of the forest or the trap or whatever, on their own. Now he realized in his own desperate moment that common sense didn't come easy amidst fear and panic.

Just as the dire lynx was close enough to leap at him, it stopped. Still running, Pierre glanced over his shoulder, confused. He spotted three billowing sails coming his way.

Then his right foot touched the lake ice. His frantic, heavy gait betrayed him. In the blink of an eye, he was under the ice-cold water. The chill was penetrating. His limbs wanted to stop moving. He knew he should calm down, but he couldn't. He saw shadows, up above, fading away.

The frigid water bit at his skin, and his clothes resisted his attempts to remove them. He was getting tired of holding on. This was nature's true justice: the hunter, now the hunted. He would die a fool's death—nothing noble, nothing selfless, just a simple, stupid, avoidable death.

Elly chiseled away at the ice like a young woman possessed, having already dealt with the now-unconscious dire lynx. "Why have you stopped, Tee? He's going to *die!*"

Standing up, shock-stick in hand, Tee looked around. "I..." she started, unsure of what to say. When she'd faced down LeLoup months ago, it was the first time she'd felt the sweep of calm in a moment of crisis. An idea was bubbling its way up, getting clearer as it surfaced.

Tee sprang into action. "Richy! Help me get my sail-cart over there!" said Tee, pointing to a spot near the shore.

"Why?" said Elly. "Never mind—you're thinking of the mini-crossbows, right?"

"Right," said Tee, imagining how everything would need to play out. "They're the best chance we have of punching through the ice!"

"That's brilliant! It might kill him, but it's brilliant," said Richy.

"The brilliant part is if we can haul him up," said Tee, rolling some snow to put under the sail-cart so it'd be in the position she needed.

A minute later, they had the sail-cart propped up on the shore and everyone in position. Tee got on all fours and looked at the angle. Satisfied with the sail-cart's orientation, she stood up, backed away, and gave Richy the nod.

Richy, in the sail-cart's pilot seat, pulled the extra lever only present in Tee's sail-cart. Five mini-crossbow bolts shot out of the front of the sail-cart and pierced into the frozen surface of the lake in a thunderous crash of ice.

"Woohoo! They went through!" yelled Richy, punching the air. He then quickly raised the sail-cart's telescoping mast and sail, anticipating the next step in Tee's plan.

Elly ran to the smashed ice and started removing chunks. Tee pushed the sail-cart slowly onto the lake's frozen surface, hoping to avoid breaking through the ice. For her plan to work, they would need the full benefit of the wind.

"Come on! *Come on!*" yelled Tee, going red in the face. Then, the wind snapped the sail to its limits and the sail-cart started to creak forward.

"We're good, Tee!" said Richy.

Tee darted back to the black cables. She nervously grabbed at the first, but it was slack. She looked over to Elly, who checked the second—and it was taut.

"We've got something!" yelled Elly.

Finally, the top of Pierre's head broke the surface of the water. Tee and Elly, with the sail-cart's help, hauled him out of the water.

"Richy, he's up!" yelled Elly.

"We didn't kill him, did we?" asked Richy fearfully.

Tee discovered the mini-crossbow bolt lodged between Pierre's heavy coat and his javelin holder. The bolt tips were designed to grab, not just pierce. "Nope!"

"That's one lucky man," said Richy.

They tore off his coat, and Elly put her head on Pierre's chest. "He's not breathing."

"Are you sure?" said Tee. She took off a mitt and put her hand over his mouth. "I don't feel anything."

Elly and Tee worked together to pump water out of Pierre's lungs, but his eyes remained a blank stare.

"We did our best, Lala," said Richy to Tee. "He's gone."

Elly stopped and looked down at the lake.

Tee was shaking, and her eyes welled up with tears. "We've *got* to do something. He can't be dead. He can't! There has to be something else we can do. Come on— *think!*" yelled Tee, more to herself than to her friends.

"His body just doesn't remember it needs to breathe," said Richy, putting a hand on Tee's yellow-cloaked shoulder.

Tee snapped her fingers as she thought of how they'd taken down the dire lynx. "Shock-sticks!" she said, and grabbed the shock-sticks from her cloak's special pockets. She handed one to Elly, and then started winding up the other.

"Lala? What do you think you're doing?" said Richy, standing back. "You could kill him!"

"He's already dead, Richy!" replied Elly. "Let her try." Elly vigorously wound the other shock-stick and then handed it back to Tee.

Tee looked at Elly and Richy. Each nodded support as they backed up. Tee pressed the activation buttons and struck Pierre in the chest. Sparks flew, and Pierre convulsed wildly—and then, after a second, he coughed and blinked.

"It worked!" yelled Richy, punching and kicking wildly in the air with joy. "I can't believe it!"

Tee stared in disbelief at Pierre. "He's—he's breathing. We did it—"

Elly gave Tee a huge hug. "You saved him!"

CHAPTER FIVE

HOUNDING THE WATTS

The only sounds in the town home were of two leather boots still being broken in as they walked about the hardwood floor. Though the Hound had hired the best men available, he personally wanted to check everything.

Unlike his predecessor, Andre LeLoup, he wasn't going to fail Simon St. Malo. The man had power and influence and had granted the Hound the opportunity to move from unimportant henchman to someone whose name sent chills down spines of more and more people every day.

Simon St. Malo had been generous. The more he did for St. Malo, the more the twisted inventor did for him. The Hound was very much his namesake, a loyal dog who found what was needed and brought it home—no excuses. Every now and then, Simon would psychologically dig into the Hound to remind him of who worked for whom, but the relationship remained a productive one.

The Hound leaned against the open front door and stared into the crackling fire, trying to think like the man who lived there.

Before the Hound heard the voice of one his hired hands, he heard the crunching snow beneath the man's feet. It reminded him that before they left, they would need to brush the path between the doorway and the coach to erase any footprints.

"Sir," whispered the voice behind him, "we've secured Watt and his daughter."

"Excuse me?" said the Hound, peering over his shoulder with a glare that made the hired thug's blood turn cold.

The thug stammered, "By—by—by secured the daughter, I mean we've delivered her to her mother's house, as you asked, and all is fine."

"Did she wake?" asked the Hound, his gravelly voice needing little volume to be heard clearly.

"No, she didn't."

The Hound nodded approval, looking back at the enchanting fire. "And the mother?"

"She appreciates your assistance in dealing with her ex," replied the thug. "She's got everything she needs to make her side of the story work."

"When everyone wins, there's no mystery to be solved," the Hound said wistfully.

"There was, ah, an odd remark from the mother I

thought I should mention," said the thug.

The Hound stiffened and turned. He wasn't especially tall, nor large, but he was broad and muscular, and had an intensity about him that could wilt a tree. "*And?*"

The thug nervously fumbled with his hands. "She appreciated you taking care of Maxwell and her son, of whom she's not fond, it seems."

The Hound turned on his heel, back toward the fire. "So that's why everything didn't quite fit together. He has a *son*. Why didn't our little spy tell us that? Hmm." He rubbed his reddish-brown beard. "Maybe she thought he'd gone somewhere else? Maybe someone tipped Watt off that we were coming and he made up his own story to cover why his son wasn't here?"

"Why don't we ask Watt?" asked the thug, trying to get on the boss' good side. "He's still conscious, somewhat."

The Hound considered it, but decided to trust his gut. "He already blacked out twice at the sight of me, and I wouldn't believe anything he says anyway. He could send us on a wild fox hunt. St. Malo will decide what to do with him. By the time they get answers—*if* they can—it will be too late for us. We will have failed, and whatever Watt is up to could have succeeded."

The Hound stepped into the house. "I need to check things again, now that we know the son is missing. I'll see you in the coach shortly," he said, dismissing the thug. The Hound smiled secretly at the idea of riding around the kingdoms in expensive coaches, wearing fine clothes, eating exceptional food, and having impressive access to resources. Such luxuries facilitated his focus and dedication. Since LeLoup had died, his life had changed considerably.

Leading up to this evening, he'd taken time to gather information on Watt, before approaching the cleaning lady who spied for St. Malo. He'd then approached Watt's ex-wife and struck a deal, gaining her support to convince authorities there was nothing out of the ordinary about Mister Watt suddenly being out of town. This afternoon, he'd hired some thugs—indirectly—in order to set fires across town, to keep authorities distracted.

From the moment the Hound had turned the key in the front door and walked in, everything had proceeded like clockwork. Not a side table or shoe was out of place, and if they had missed anything, the cleaning lady was due at seven in the morning sharp, and would remove any final signs of him and his team having been there.

The Hound had generously paid the cleaning lady two-thirds of the promised money; she'd only expected half. She was to be paid the rest in a week, when everything calmed down. However, he was certain that St. Malo intended her to have the same fate he suspected was in store for the thugs he'd hired. He didn't like thinking about things like that—it bothered him and got in the way of getting a job done.

He went upstairs to double-check Maxwell's room, making sure that everything that should've been packed as part of a long trip had been taken. Then, he went through the daughter's bedroom one more time.

Finally, he entered the bedroom he'd thought was unused. The Hound checked under the bed, under the mattress, and all of the drawers. "Other than the lack of dust in some places, it looks like no one's been living here. Smart. The boy's probably traveling with a light pack," he mused. The Hound drummed his fingers on the fine chestnut dresser. "I was hoping for a hint of where you'd sent him, Watt."

He went back downstairs, sat on the ottoman, and warmed his hands by the fire. "What did you do with your notes and plans, Mister Watt? And where did you send your boy?" he asked himself.

The Hound looked around the room. He spotted the writing desk tucked in the corner and went over to it. After carefully going through everything, he went back to the ottoman, disappointed.

"What would I do with my life's work in this situation? Would I fear more for my son's life, burn all my stuff, and send him to a distant relative?" Staring into the fire a while, the Hound noticed something behind the logs. He got the poker and moved them around.

"You burned paper. That makes sense," he mused, and paused. "I'd burn a lot of things, but I don't think I'd burn my life's work. St. Malo made it clear how important this is to you. You wouldn't destroy everything." He stood up. "You gave it... to your *son*... to take to someone. Perhaps... *ah*." Satisfied with his deduction, the Hound slapped his knees and then stood.

With a final glance around, he turned and exited the town home. He carefully locked up, and then called over one of his thugs. "I need you to brush all around here—we want *no* sign of footprints. Do you understand?"

The thug nodded.

"Your money will be waiting for you at the tavern where we met earlier. Ask the bartender," said the Hound. He stepped into the coach and closed the door.

Inside the coach, Maxwell Watt, tied up and with a large man at each side, stared at the Hound.

"Watt, I know where you've sent your son," said the Hound, grinning menacingly.

CHAPTER SIX

MERRY SOLSTICE

It warmed Nikolas' heart to see the large crowd that had gathered for Mineau's first community Solstice celebration. He greeted and thanked every person who came forward with something to donate. Some apologized for the quality or number of gifts they were giving, and Nikolas reminded them no score was being kept, and that it was their act of generosity that was the important thing.

The line of children awaiting a gift started at the sleigh, then wound and snaked away so far that Nikolas couldn't see the end. There were Mineau guardsmen throughout, more as a reminder to everyone to behave well, than for any specific action. Nikolas loved seeing the children of the poor and rich alike, standing side-by-side, and eventually talking to one another. He'd seen remarkable friendships develop because of the Solstice lines.

Some people out for an evening walk stopped and stared, not sure what to make of everything. Some watched from a distance, often being approached by someone participating and thus being drawn into the event. If anyone had an issue with what was taking place, they kept it to themselves.

"I can't believe you guys made all this stuff," said Tee. The Yellow Hoods were responsible for taking gifts from the sleigh, one by one, and handing them to Pierre, who handed them to the line of Cochon brothers and guardsmen, and then on to Captain Gabriel Archambault of Minette and his Mineau counterpart's right-hand man, Deputy Captain Samuel Davis of Mineau, and finally to Nikolas, who handed each gift to a child.

It was Isabella, many years ago, who insisted Nikolas be the one to hand the gifts to the children, instead of being the one taking them out of the sleigh. The Magistrate of Minette had made a point of telling Nikolas, with Isabella at his side, that if Nikolas wasn't going to be the one to hand the gifts out, then there would be no community celebration. The Magistrate at the time felt it was very much Nikolas' creation. Nikolas was certain it was a bluff, but relented. From then on, he required everyone involved in the gift giving line to train together, so they could get through it quickly, without the children feeling they were having toys thrown at them.

The Magistrate of Mineau sat at the table closest to where the gifts were being handed out, but had been too suspicious at first to participate. He watched for twenty minutes as each present was placed into the hands of an appreciative child, on the stage he'd insisted be built for the purpose. Then, to the surprise of many, he got up and took the place just before Nikolas. He didn't feel right taking the spot he'd originally demanded, that of being the one to actually hand the presents to the children. He struggled to keep up, often forcing Deputy Captain Davis to toss gifts above or around him to Nikolas to maintain the flow. It made for a wonderful spectacle and drew cheers from the crowd.

After the last child, Tee looked down the line and saw there were still several gifts in people's hands. "Does that mean we actually have too many, for the first time ever?"

Bakon chuckled. "I thought that one year, but no. This is only the first wave. You guys weren't old enough before to help with the second wave—if you'd even realized there was one. Some people are so poor or embarrassed about something that they don't come out until everyone else is gone. They eventually do come out, hoping that Monsieur Klaus and the sleigh are still here. That's why we have the other sleigh full of gifts."

"What other sleigh?" asked Elly and Richy.

"The one that William and Jennifer brought," said Squeals. "You didn't know there was another sleigh, did you?" He and Bore chuckled.

"Yeah, Mister Nik is sneaky. Your mom and dad sneaky too," said Bore, in his dim-witted, deep voice. He was tapping his head and acting goofy.

"Grandpapa, why all the secrecy?" asked Tee as he approached, having caught wind of the conversation.

Nikolas removed the knit winter cap from his bald head and put it in his coat pocket. "That is because greed is a sad thing, and it does many things to the way people think. The second sleigh is smaller—don't think it is this size; it is not. It only has about two hundred more toys, maybe, but hopefully it is enough.

"And will they come? Every year they have, and so that is why we will sit here until dawn. Well, that is, except for right now," he said, looking at his pocket watch and picking up a lantern he had in the sleigh. "I have an appointment I must get to. Squeals, tell Jennifer and William to bring the other sleigh in now, yes?"

Squeals nodded and smiled. "No problem."

As Nikolas walked off, Squeals turned to the Yellow Hoods. "Go enjoy the town. You guys deserve it with all the good you've been doing lately."

Elly, Tee, and Richy exchanged uncertain looks. They loved the idea, but they each had a deep sense of duty.

"Are you sure, Squeals? I mean, we can wait with you guys," said Elly.

Bakon chimed in. "After these guys get back from bringing the other sleigh," he said, pointing to his brothers, "we're sending them off to enjoy the night, too. Egelina-Marie and I are sitting with... Nikolas... until morning, and then I'm having breakfast with her family."

"Did you just say *Nikolas*?" asked Tee. "It looked like it was painful to say."

"Almost as painful as saying you're having breakfast

with her family," added Richy.

Bakon shifted uncomfortably and smiled awkwardly. Part of him wanted to lash out, but that was the old him, impulsive and raw. Grudgingly he said, "He asked that Egelina-Marie and I call him that now. It's like trying to get a rock out of my mouth, every time. I guess it's… I don't know… it's weird."

"You'll get used to it. You can do anything," said Richy. He admired something about Bakon. Maybe it was that his reputation as a thug had been a disguise for work he was secretly doing for Captain Archambault back in Minette, or maybe it was because Richy couldn't imagine anyone being tougher.

Bakon gave Richy a wink. He then clapped his mitted hands. "Okay, enough. It's Solstice! Get out of here before I have to create a crisis for you Yellow Hoods!"

"Yeah, go have fun!" boomed Bore.

"Okay, okay," said Elly on behalf of the trio as they started to wander off.

Elly turned to Tee. "Isn't permitting someone to call him by his first name a big deal for your grandfather?"

Tee nodded as she thought about it. "It's a biggie. He's formal about things like that. I don't know if everyone from the eastern kingdoms are so formal, but he is, at least. I remember a story about how Grandpapa tortured my dad. Every time my dad wanted to talk him about proposing to my mom, Grandpapa just changed the subject."

"That's it? Just change the subject back. How hard can it be?" asked Richy.

"It took my dad months, and he needed the help of my Grandmama," answered Tee.

"Seriously?" said Richy. He pulled his coat in, as the winter night air was getting a bit nippy.

Elly gave a raised eyebrow to Richy. "Have you had a conversation with that man that he didn't want to have? His mind is an island unto itself."

Richy gave Elly a fake, surprised look. "*Unto.* Wow. Pulling out special words for the holiday, are we?"

Elly gave Richy a shove. "It's a word."

"Oh, I know it's a word. It's an *un*loved, *un*wanted word. A problem *un*to itself, if you ask me."

Rolling her eyes, Elly said, "That doesn't make sense."

"You know, last year," said Tee, changing the subject, "we were just three kids running around playing with our homemade yellow cloaks. *Now* look at us."

"Well, not all cloaks were created equal. You had yours from your grandfather, Elly made hers with her mom, and… I made mine," said Richy.

Elly smiled at Richy and said, "Well, yours was less of a cloak and more of an honest effort in trying to get a bed sheet to bend to your will."

Tee started laughing. She tried not to, but it was true.

Richy looked a bit hurt. "Hey! I lost blood putting

that thing together. I don't know how you girls do sewing."

"Oh, we know you lost lots of blood—it was all over that yellow cloak! Well, yellow and red, really," said Tee, laughing.

"Really gross," added Elly, shaking her head in mock disapproval. "I'm glad we have these ones now. I still wonder what they're made of."

Richy stopped and crossed his arms. "Really? You're so superior at sewing?"

"Well, like you said, you don't know how we girls do it. We're born with it. Born to make things, from babies, to buildings, to…"

"Got stuck looking for another 'B' word, eh?" said Tee, switching sides.

"Head plant," said Richy. "So *close*. You nearly finished me off, but just as you rounded the corner, the wheels fell off and you flipped your cart. Ha!"

Tee looked over to Richy. "Someone's been spending a bit *too* much time with his sail-cart."

Richy smiled uncomfortably, and a sudden chill doused the playful mood. Elly and Tee hadn't asked Richy what was going on at home, but it had been clear over the past couple of months that something was awry. Whatever it was, they hoped that if and when he was ready, he'd talk to one of them. They were surprised when he'd mentioned his family life to Nikolas earlier, in front of everyone. Clearly, it was worse than they'd thought.

For a few minutes, they walked in silence, occasionally waving to the kids they knew as they wandered the colored lantern-decorated streets of Mineau.

Richy sighed, letting go of the tension, and said, "They decorate differently here. Have you noticed the red, yellow, and green leaves together on every business? Not on a house, just on a business. I never saw that before."

After several seconds, Elly grumbled. "I wanted to make a killer snarky remark about how you wouldn't notice something obvious, but I drew a blank. A blank!"

"Oh my goodness—maybe you've lost your right to the throne!" said Tee, teasing her long-time best friend.

"Oh, no," said Richy, starting to laugh. "You're but a simple commoner now! Doomed to be snarked upon by your betters! Doomed to—"

"Watch it—I still have *plenty* of quick wit in my quiver, *Aldrich*," said Elly, squinting cheekily.

Richy and Tee stopped in their tracks and looked, mouths wide open, at Elly.

"Did you just declare a full and proper names war?" said Tee, scooping a handful of snow.

They had a sacred rule: Not one of them was fond of their proper name, and it was not to be used under any circumstances. Violation of this rule unleashed all manner of chaos.

"You're going down, El—" said Richy, interrupted by a snowball in the face from Elly.

"Snowball fight!" yelled nearby kids. They started to leave their parents' sides, in droves, in order to join in.

Within minutes, almost a hundred kids were laughing and throwing snowballs under the glow of the city's lanterns. The heavy snow that fell was perfect for compacting snowballs.

"Reminds me of when I was a kid," said one man to a beige-hooded figure beside him.

"I was never a kid like that. Might have been nice." The figure then walked away.

"What's her problem?" said the man to a guy beside him, who shrugged in response.

CHAPTER SEVEN

BAKON & EG'S BREAKFAST

Gabriel Archambault was Minette's captain of the guard. He'd already been proud of his daughter, Egelina-Marie, for following in his footsteps. He'd been in complete disbelief when he'd learned that not only was she an expert sharpshooter, but that she had also saved the life of Nikolas Klaus, a close family friend, on her first day on the job.

At the breakfast table, Gabriel tried to speak, but simply ended up glaring at Bakon. The men felt awkward. Conversation had done little more than start and stop. Everyone waited for Gabriel to say something, but instead he took another mouthful of sausage.

Egelina-Marie's mother, Victoria, had decided it was time for her daughter's boyfriend of a few months to meet them. It was an innocent idea, but she'd forgotten the local significance of Solstice breakfast. Where she grew up, Solstice night was the only thing that mattered. Here, the Solstice breakfast was about very close family. If boyfriends or girlfriends were invited, which was rare, it was a sign the family was expecting them—very shortly —to be joining the family. Egelina-Marie knew what her mother had simply intended in arranging the breakfast, yet she still wasn't completely comfortable.

"I'd like to say again—the sausages are amazing," said Bakon, trying to find something to say. "I particularly like the fried potatoes." The breakfast truly was excellent, and he savored every bite. He hadn't had homemade sausage, cooked beans, and pancakes in a long time. It reminded him of when Isabella Klaus used to cook for the family on special occasions.

Victoria smiled. She appreciated his comment this third time as much as she had the first. At this point, if they made it through breakfast with only minor injuries, she would declare it a success.

Bakon squirmed. He'd secretly been working for the captain for two years, as a covert hand of justice and for information gathering. Gabriel had always been more than happy to have the Cochon brothers rough up a stranger to get information, or drive an undesirable out of town. Gabriel had a soft spot for the brothers since the day Nikolas had taken them in—a day Gabriel remembered well.

"Bakon, what are your brothers doing this morning?" asked Victoria, trying to get things going again.

Bakon sighed in relief. He could answer that question without causing problems. "They're having Solstice breakfast with Jennifer and William Baker. It's the first time since Tee was born."

"I guess you wished you were there, then?" said Gabriel, sharply.

Egelina-Marie and Victoria shot angry looks at him.

"What?" he said, raising his hands in his defense. "He said it's been a long time. It probably brings back memories of good times. He probably *would* like to be there." Gabriel growled under his breath.

He had been happy for his daughter when he'd heard she had a boyfriend. He'd hoped it was someone up and coming, maybe even someone in the Magistrate's office. When he'd learned it was Bakon, he had misgivings. Whenever Egelina-Marie mentioned Bakon by name, he'd tried to pretend she was talking about someone else who happened to have the same unusual name. His wife had now made it impossible for him to continue fooling himself.

Bakon eyed a plate of food he wanted. "Eg, would you mind passing the—um—" He stopped, realizing how stupid he was about to sound.

"Eggs?" she said, chuckling.

"Yeah," replied Bakon.

"Isn't this nice, Gabriel?" said Victoria, trying to get conversation started again.

Gabriel knew what his wife was trying to do, and he knew that she was right, but this was their only daughter, their only child. He didn't want to let her go in any way.

"Don't you think you're a bit old for our daughter?" asked Gabriel, getting the question off his chest. "You're, what, twenty-six? She's just nineteen."

Victoria's face reddened with embarrassment and anger. Under the table, she kicked her husband in the shin. Wincing, Gabriel tried to glare back, but she had her finger pointing at him.

"I am not going to apologize for loving my daughter!" yelled Gabriel, pushing his chair away from the table and then standing.

Victoria bolted up and pointed for Gabriel to sit down. "I was *seventeen* when we got together!"

Gabriel started to yell back, "That's not the—"

With a flare of her eyelids, Victoria stopped her husband. Her voice was of a woman who was *not* going to have even the King of Freland ruin her breakfast. "You are behaving worse than my father ever did."

Bakon and Eg had been looking back and forth silently. All of them now looked at Gabriel, who glanced at each one in turn.

Victoria sat down, pulled her chair back to the table, and commanded to Bakon and Eg, "Eat."

They looked at each other and then their plates, and then back at Gabriel.

Gabriel frowned. "Don't cry," he said to Victoria as he noticed her eyes welling up.

His wife pierced him with her gaze. "I am *not* crying because I'm upset. If you'd learned *anything* by having two women in the house, you'd know that I'm *angry* and this is just how some women work!"

Gabriel sat back down at the table. He took a moment to compose his thoughts. "You know, your dad was a real jerk with me."

Wiping her nose and eyes with a napkin, Victoria chuckled, "The worst."

"And… I guess…" Gabriel straightened his mustache. He was terrible at apologies, especially the ones that mattered. "Bakon, did I ever tell you about this time when Victoria's father chased me down the streets of Mineau with a cleaver in his hand? It was part of the reason we moved up here to Minette."

Fifteen minutes later, Gabriel had finished telling a second embarrassing story from his youth. Everyone wiped away tears of laughter as he stood up and gave Bakon a hearty slap on the back.

Egelina-Marie started wiping the floor—she had spat out her tea from laughing so hard and unexpectedly. She'd barely managed to avoid spraying everyone at the table.

Gabriel put on his thick winter coat and turned to Bakon. "I have to get to work. No day off for the captain. But, do stay—you're welcome here."

"Thanks, but I have to get back to my brothers. After breakfast, there's a leak we need to fix," said Bakon, standing and excusing himself.

"Suit yourself," said Gabriel, smiling. Things had turned out better than he'd expected—a lot better. He knew he owed his wife a huge apology, and for that, he was going to need chocolate. He hoped that Victoria wouldn't see through his ruse of having to work.

After the men had left, Victoria turned to her daughter, who kept laughing as she remembered the bits and pieces of her dad's stories.

"You okay?" Victoria asked.

Egelina-Marie had a perplexed look as she thought about what had happened. "I'm not sure what the lesson was, mama, but I need to learn it," she said. She'd never seen her parents fight like *that* before, but figured they must have, in private.

Victoria gave her a hug and smiled. "There is nothing I wouldn't do for that man. As for the lesson, if your bear isn't listening, hurt his ego—and *nothing* wounds your father's more than being told he's just like my father. I thought his mustache was going to curl up at the ends when I said that!"

CHAPTER EIGHT

MEET THE MAUCHER

Nikolas removed his thick crimson coat and hung it up on the first of the café's coat hooks, as he'd done many times over the years. He looked at the red coat Isabella had made for him, remembering the last time they'd come to Deuxième Chance together. Isabella always thought the café's name, "second chance," applied as much to the two of them—having a life away from what seemed destined—as it did to the original owners.

From the outside there was nothing remarkable about the Deuxième Chance. It was no more easily noticeable nor any bigger or smaller than the average Mineau café, but it had been Isabella's favorite for some reason.

It had wide, honey-colored wooden floor planks, and white walls decorated with bits of town memorabilia and paintings of the founders and their family through the ages. It didn't feel like a formal establishment, but rather like you were visiting a close friend and were in their parlor.

"Good morning, Monsieur Klaus. Did you have a merry Solstice? You looked at home on that stage," said the current owner as he came out of the back to greet the day's first customer.

Nikolas made an uneasy face. "I don't like stages and whatnot, Jerome, but I do like making people happy, and bringing them together. I was honored to have Mineau invite me."

"You did a great job. May I offer you tea?" he asked. Jerome's father had taken the business over from Jerome's grandfather, and now Jerome owned it.

"Yes, please," replied Nikolas. "Oh—would you mind putting this behind the counter until I ask for it? It's important."

"No problem," said Jerome, accepting the brass tube from Nikolas.

Suddenly, it dawned on Nikolas that the café shouldn't be open. "Wait, Jerome—shouldn't you be closed, and having breakfast with family?"

Jerome lined up the glasses and mugs on the counter. "Oh, I did have family breakfast. There's only me and my aunt, and the sick man she's taking care of. But, I know my customers—they'll have had enough of their families and will want to go somewhere to have a nice drink, a tasty treat, and some peace and tranquility. Then, they'll return to face family some more. It is, honestly, one of my busiest days of the year." He looked at the clock on the wall. "They'll start arriving in an hour or two." He looked at it more closely. "I better wind it up—I suspect it's running a bit slow."

Nikolas appreciated Jerome's business savvy. "Good for you. Your grandfather would be proud."

Just then, with a burst of frigid air, a tall, regal-looking woman walked in and shut the door behind her. She leaned her silver cane against the wall and removed her white fur coat and hat. She looked around for someone to hand them to. Jerome swiftly came over to accept them.

"Thank you," she said mechanically, retrieving her cane.

"Nikolas," said the woman in a sharp, eastern kingdoms accent, "It's good to see you. It's been a couple of years since we last met. Was it in Marduchi?" She disliked speaking Frelish, but Nikolas always insisted that they speak the local language wherever they met—if possible.

Nikolas rose, held the woman's purple-gloved hand, and gave her a kiss on each cheek. "Anna, it is good to see you. I think it was in Parduchi, to the south of Marduchi."

Anna paused, not liking to be corrected, yet she didn't care for small talk, either. "Ah, yes. Olive and orange trees—I remember." She looked Nikolas over, up and down. "You're keeping well."

Nikolas smiled politely. "Thank you. And you, too. Please, have a seat," he said, gesturing to one of the tables.

Anna sat down and glanced around. "You always choose this place when you meet in Mineau. Why is that?"

Nikolas turned toward Jerome, who was behind the counter, and asked, "Jerome, a cup of Ernst Myers tea for the madame, please?"

Jerome stopped. "Um, did you say *Ernst Myers* tea?"

"Ah yes, of course. Well, *that* says it all," said Anna, smiling like a little girl surprised by a treat. Ernst Myers tea was a black blend so prized and rare that it was said some royal families had gone to war over the tea.

Jerome appeared nervous. "But, I don't think I have—"

Nikolas stood up, walked over to Jerome, motioned for him to relax, and then leaned over the counter to whisper. "It's in your office, inside a tin. The tin has been used as a bookend since you were a boy."

Jerome's eyes widened. "How do you know about *that*? My father said it was only for one person—"

Nikolas nodded toward Anna's direction. No longer whispering, he said, "*She* is the one person. Anna Kundle Maucher, also called—"

Awestruck, Jerome interrupted. "The candle and sticks maker—one of the three leaders of the Tub! Wow… I'm honored to have you in my café, Madame Maucher!" Jerome's father had told him tales of the Tub and the Fare. His grandfather was convinced Monsieur Klaus was involved, but never knew for certain.

Anna was annoyed. She hated that people outside the eastern kingdoms didn't know how to address her. "*Frau Kundle Maucher*, peasant," she muttered under her breath. Offering a thin smile, Anna said, "Please remember to make sure the water is absolutely boiling before steeping the tea," she said. "And, if you have any fresh biscuits, they would be... appreciated."

Nikolas gave Jerome a light tap on the arm. "Thank you, Jerome."

Jerome happily went off to fetch the tea.

Anna waited until Nikolas was seated. She didn't like small towns like Mineau—they were too simple, too unrefined for her tastes. She couldn't understand why Nikolas would live in such a place, forgetting that he actually lived in the smaller, more remote town up the mountain.

"You received my letter, but I have to say, I was quite surprised to get *yours*," she began.

Nikolas looked at his coat hanging by the entrance. "Had I read your letter when I received it, there would have been no follow-up letter, yes? But I didn't read it until after all the trouble with LeLoup. Things were different then. I decided it would be best if you came—I have something I want to share, but in person. Also, it was Solstice."

"Yes, well, I saw all that last night," said Anna with annoyed disinterest. "Frankly, I think it's wrong in some ways—but now's not the time to discuss philosophical differences."

A bit irritated, Nikolas ignored Anna's criticism. "You're right—it isn't the time. I wanted you to come in person because I've invented something I believe will be very important to the—"

Anna interrupted, clearly not listening. "The St. Malo business—I was surprised he hired Andre LeLoup to come for you. I was more surprised to hear what happened, to be honest. It's nice to know your protégés are coming along, even though it's against the Tub's rules —as you well know. We keep the secrets so that other generations do not have to bear their burden. We do wonder, though, whether you are teaching them anything secret? We assume not, but… it's almost like you're trying not to try?"

Nikolas didn't respond for a few seconds. He'd forgotten Anna's habit of getting under someone's skin, even an ally's. "Let's be clear," said Nikolas firmly, "They have done this themselves. Yes, I provided my granddaughter with the first yellow cloak, but I have not built anything or taught them anything other than simple science."

"You made those sailing land ships—didn't you?" said Anna, pointedly.

Nikolas chose his words carefully. "Those are *toys*. My granddaughter and her friends know *nothing*." Nikolas knew he was bending the truth, but figured it was close enough; Anna wouldn't be able to tell he was lying.

Anna's eyes narrowed and her lips tightened. "What are you talking about? I heard about some version of my Kundle sticks that you made for them—*against* our rules."

"Actually," said Nikolas, leaning back, arms crossed, "I had nothing to do with that."

Anna glared. "Are you telling me that you had nothing to do with the treehouse, the pulley system, any of it?" She leaned in. "We are not blind, and yes, we do have our spies, everywhere."

Nikolas took a deep breath. He held it as he played through in his mind the different ways this conversation could go. Part of him wanted to ask Anna why her spies didn't warn him of LeLoup—that Simon St. Malo had someone hunting for him. He slowly exhaled as he tried preparing his words, but he didn't get time to speak.

"It's Christophe," said Anna, revealing her suspicions. "We all thought him dead, but I'm thinking that *he* is how you are getting around the rules. He isn't dead, is he? You and he—"

Nikolas sat forward and stroked his beard. "I wish that were true, but Christophe *is* dead. The Kundle sticks in question have little design to them. While they are useful, they are not the type of weapon you designed, once upon a time." Nikolas bit his lip, for he'd long believed that Anna hadn't actually invented them, but had stolen the design from someone else. She had never invented anything since, and had never improved on them. "If you came here just for an argument of principle, you shouldn't have come."

Anna tapped the table with her index finger as she said, "I need you to tell me who it is. You *must* know. You've probably taken their Kundle sticks apart and figured that out. You wouldn't allow your granddaughter near them otherwise."

She was dead right about that, and given that he'd never taken one apart, he knew it would reveal he *did* know something. Instead, Nikolas decided to take a path he rarely took and let his frustration with her show itself. His face started to go red. He was about to speak again when Jerome came back.

Jerome gently put down a silver tea tray holding two teapots and two fine porcelain cups, among other items. "Here is your tea. I warmed the biscuits. I hope you like them," he said, reaching to pour the tea.

Anna glared at Jerome, stopping him. "I'm more than capable of pouring my own tea, thank you," she said sharply. She gestured at Jerome for him to leave.

Nikolas gave Jerome a painful smile, but nodded that he would also appreciate Jerome leaving. Nikolas then turned to Anna, trying to figure out what to say. He'd arranged this meeting primarily to discuss his horseless cart and give her the plans, but now he didn't feel like doing that. He wasn't even going to ask if she'd brought a supply of her special waxes.

Suddenly, the door whipped open and a tanned, bald,

mustached man entered. He had a desperate look on his face. Before he could say anything, Anna stood up and banged her cane against the floor—and two four-inch spikes sprung from the silver cane's round, golden head and started crackling with electricity. Anna was ready to fight.

The weary man put up his hands upon seeing the weapon. "Please—I need help! My daughter is lost in the forest! She's only eleven, and the snow is getting worse! Please, help!" The man wore a coat that looked like it had been sewn together from others. He looked poor, but honest. His facial features, tanned skin, and accent made it likely he was from a southern kingdom.

As quickly as Anna had moved toward the man, she moved back. Once seated, she deftly twisted the silver head of her cane. The spikes disappeared as quickly as they had emerged.

"Come in—close the door," said Nikolas to the man, his hands up to demonstrate he intended no harm. "My friend here… she overreacted."

"What was that?" said the man.

"It's not important. Your daughter is," said Nikolas. He got up, welcomed the man in, and gestured to an available chair.

Nikolas turned to the owner. "Jerome—" he started. Nikolas could see Jerome was still surprised at what he'd seen. It was clear to Jerome that this was truly Anna Kundle Maucher, and this was indeed a meeting of the

Tub—right here, in his café—and he was unsure that was a good thing. Nikolas gave a friendly smile, and continued, "Tea and food for the man, please?"

Jerome nodded and disappeared.

The man was uncomfortable sitting, and kept glancing around the room. "Please—there isn't much time. We must find my daughter!" he said, looking back and forth between Anna and Nikolas.

"We will. But first, we need to know what happened, so that we can get the right people to help," said Nikolas calmly.

The man took a breath and nodded. This made sense to him. "We were attacked by red-hooded bandits, just outside the eastern archway entrance to the town."

Anna frowned and looked at Nikolas. "*Red* hoods? Do you know anything about this, Nikolas?"

"No," replied Nikolas sharply.

The man continued, "They attacked the cart we were riding on. One of them knocked out the driver with a staff to the head... another had a sword, I think. He jumped on me and roughed me up. The third one had a bow—I remember because an arrow shot past my head. The bowman told Mouni—my daughter, Mounira—to run into the forest, and then they all chased after her as if they were going to hunt her.

"Please, it happened only five minutes away. I tried some doors, but no one opened. This was the only place I found open. Please help her! I'm sure you don't want refugees from Augusto, but please have mercy."

"Refugees?" repeated Nikolas, trying to put the pieces together. He glanced at Anna, who wasn't surprised by the man's statement. She knew that the southern kingdom of Augusto had broken out into civil war months ago, but had no plans on sharing that knowledge with Nikolas.

"We like southerners just fine," said Jerome.

Nikolas finished building a plan in his mind. "Jerome, Anna—take care of this man. I'm going to fetch Pierre de Montagne and the Yellow Hoods."

"Who?" asked Anna as Nikolas left, but he didn't look back. She then turned and looked at the man.

"Thank you. My name is Alman Benida. Please—help find my daughter," said the man.

Anna smiled coldly. "We will." She turned to Jerome. "Please go find something useful to do."

"But this is my café," said Jerome defensively. He couldn't believe she would ask such a thing.

Looking right through Jerome, Anna said, "Lock the door, then. On behalf of the Tub, I need half an hour with this man."

Alman looked at Anna in disbelief, and wondered, *Did she just say the Tub? What did I just walk into?*

After Jerome left, Anna turned back to Alman. "While

we wait for Nikolas' people to return with your daughter, I need you to tell me everything you remember about what happened in the south, and your trek here. Everything."

CHAPTER NINE
SPIRITS OF THE RED FOREST

The expansive Red Forest bordered Mineau's eastern and southern edges. In winter, the forest's red pine trees refused to submit to winter's will, while in the spring most of its deciduous trees would sprout red leaves—save for the odd golden oak. The golden oak was the heartiest of the deciduous trees in the forest, losing leaves last, and growing them first. They were rare enough that many considered a golden oak leaf to be a good luck charm.

Everywhere Mounira looked was red and white, with brown tree-trunks that all looked the same. The snow was halfway to her knees, and higher in some places. While the frigid morning wind was gentle, it was still able to pierce the warm bundle her father had put around her.

She'd seen snow for the first time only weeks ago, as she and her father had made their way north. Her father wanted to get as far from the war as possible. Along the way, she'd listened to advice from locals, practiced the local languages, and asked everyone about this strange thing called "snow."

They'd been traveling north for months. Having fled with nothing, her father always seemed to find a way to earn money no matter where they went. Sometimes, he found a merchant who needed something from another merchant, and sometimes he figured out what people needed. In one village, Mounira watched her father shine shoes—and many of his customers were far from nice. He refused to let her help, other than fetching rags or water. When she would ask if they could stay somewhere, he would refuse, insisting they needed to go north until it felt right.

Mounira thought about how, at this time of year, her mother would typically tend to the winter flowers—a parade of color, all in sections and rows, ensuring each color and flower could be seen with its brethren and stand out, while also harmoniously blending into a greater whole.

Snow fell from a high branch, landing on Mounira's head and bringing her back to the present. She pulled off her furry hat with her left hand, shook it, and then awkwardly put it back on. The bandits had chased her until she was deep into the forest, and then they'd disappeared. She was exhausted and had no sense of direction or time. She'd started to cry when she saw the wind blow snow and erase her tracks, but she quickly turned it into anger. She understood anger—anger and pain.

Mounira pulled the blanket that was tied around her a little tighter. Under the blanket, she wore a thick set of coats, badly sewn together. She felt the cold in her bones, and it hurt. At the insistence of her father, her hand was covered in three warm socks. How silly she felt now for having argued about it. She was thankful he'd done the same with her feet. Her boots, though heavy, didn't keep out the cold the way she'd hoped.

"This way," the forest seemed to whisper.

Mounira looked around, trying to see where the voice came from. "Am I imagining it?" she asked herself. She turned to where she thought the voice had come from. "Maybe the legends of helpful forest spirits are true? Maybe Mama was right and Baba was wrong!"

"Come on. Quickly. Just a bit further," said a different voice. The wind made it hard to hear, but Mounira was certain that this time it was a voice, not her imagination.

Tripping on a hidden tree root, she fell, landing on her left arm and packing the snow in front into a perfect form of her body. Snow covered her face, and she wiggled desperately.

"Come on. Get up already," said the same voice, clear this time, and notably male.

"Why doesn't she just get up? Come on," said another male voice, hidden in the trees.

Mounira struggled to turn or otherwise get free.

"She's going to suffocate. Where's the fun in that?" said a female voice.

Mounira fought furiously until the blanket tied around her loosened and she managed to flip herself over. She stared up at the dark, gray, snowy sky and took a couple of breaths to calm herself down. The sweat on her short, dark brown hair sticking out the back of her hat quickly froze.

"Oh, I get it," said the first male voice.

"What, Hans?" inquired the second male voice.

"Yes, Hans, do tell," said the female voice playfully.

Mounira sat up, looked around, and tried to locate the voices among the trees, some of which seemed to move. *Could they really be fairies?* she wondered.

"No matter what she does, she can't ever do it... right! Ha ha," said Hans.

"She's a lefty," said the second male voice. "Do you think she lost her whole right arm, or just part of it?"

"Well, we haven't played with a lefty. Is it still sporting?" asked the female voice.

The wind calmed just enough that Mounira was certain she heard the faint crunching of snow. "They aren't spirits," she said to herself, annoyed at having entertained such a childish idea. "These are cruel, twisted monsters."

She unconsciously moved the stump below her right shoulder, confirming for herself that what they said was true, but wishing it wasn't.

"Who are you?" she yelled, her anger evident. "I can hear you! I know you're people!"

"We aren't *people*. Are we, Saul?" asked Hans, from somewhere in the trees now.

Mounira noticed snow falling from a red pine tree thirty yards away.

Saul's voice came from another tree. "I think we might be. What do you think Gretel?"

"Oh, no. We're the spirits of the forest. Spirits who work for the Ginger Lady, remember?" she replied.

Feet aching from the cold, Mounira moved toward the voices. "I'm lost. Help me!" she urged.

"You're not lost—you're exactly where *we* wanted you to be," said Gretel cheerily.

"Help you?" asked Hans, sounding like it was an absurd request. "Hmm. Shall we, Gretel?"

"Well, if we don't, she won't get to where she needs to go. This way," said Gretel, with a sweet voice. Twenty yards away, a red-hooded figure briefly stepped out from behind a pine tree.

"How do they move around?" Mounira wondered out loud. She wasn't sure if she'd heard some machine-like clanking a moment ago. She shook her head—that didn't make any sense.

"Come *on*," said Gretel, annoyed. "We'll bring you to Mother's."

Mounira could swear she heard the male voices chuckling. She was so tired and cold she couldn't remember any more if the bandits had also worn red. She staggered forward, hoping these weren't the same people. Maybe these red-hooded voices would soon take pity on her.

Several minutes passed, with only a voice promising that she was *almost* there, as she dragged herself through the snow. She cleared her mind and focused on moving toward the voices.

Finally, exhausted, Mounira stopped and dropped to her knees. "I'm *not* going any further until you tell me where I'm going!" she yelled out. The anger that fueled her was fading.

For a while, there was nothing.

"Okay, then, but you're ruining the fun," said Hans. "If you look up to your left, up that ridge, you'll see trees in a line. That's the shortcut to Mother's house."

"Follow the breadcrumbs," said Gretel. "That's what we used to do."

"What breadcrumbs?" asked Saul jokingly.

"Oh, did they get eaten by the birds? Those flying rats always eat them. Horrible things," said Hans.

"You're such a cat person," said Saul.

Hans, Saul, and Gretel laughed.

Mounira, her teeth chattering and body numb, forced herself up to the ridge.

CHAPTER TEN

THE ROAD FROM AUGUSTO

Mounira fell to her knees in the snow again. She was now at the ridge, and able to see through the trees. She was hungry, thirsty, and, above all, exhausted.

"Only a little more," she told herself. She stuck her arm out to lean against a leafless tree. "I'll rest for a minute… just a minute." Her thoughts carried her back to the day after her eleventh birthday a couple of months ago.

It had been a great celebration with her parents, siblings, uncles, aunts, cousins, and grandparents. Twenty-eight of them had gone to the annual parade in the capital city, where the soldiers and royalty would march among selected schoolchildren and merchants. Every fifth year, all the royals came out, and Mounira and her cousins were excited to see them.

The kingdom of Augusto was humble in size compared to neighboring kingdoms, yet it was the second most prosperous. Citizens benefited from generations of monarchs who placed the people first. Augusto was also well-regarded by its neighbors for having the best mediators and consulars. Its capital and southernmost city, Catalina, had a strategically-positioned port, considered by many as easy to defend, and ideal for trade.

The weather was beautiful and warm that September day. Mounira wore the new white dress she'd received the day before. Everyone remarked how beautiful she was, and each time she smiled and curtsied politely. She couldn't imagine a better birthday.

Mounira's family had made a point to arrive at the parade early, so that the children could line up at the rope that sectioned off parade participants from spectators. The smallest of the children were up on the shoulders of uncles and aunts. Everyone danced to the street music.

As the official walking band arrived, the crowd went wild. Mounira waved her homemade flag. The band was followed by schoolchildren and merchants, and then the first of the royal family. The royals threw flower petals from baskets held by beaming volunteers.

"The princesses are so beautiful! Look at their dresses!" yelled Mounira to her cousins, who were yelling the same thing back. No one could hear a word over the crowd's roars.

Then time slowed down for Mounira, and all she could hear was her heart beating: *dub-dub, dub-dub, dub-dub.*

The king and queen, who'd been walking toward Mounira to shake hands with the crowd, fell down. The princes and princesses started running, and some of them fell down, too. Soldiers started pointing at people with their rifles, and made people fall down, while other soldiers pointed their rifles at those soldiers, and made them fall down. Bursts of red mist appeared in the air. None of it made sense to Mounira.

Mounira wondered if it might be some kind of game. Maybe everyone knew about it and was playing along, and she'd missed it somehow? She hadn't been paying attention on the walk to the parade. Had her parents tried to tell her? It was getting hard to think. Her heartbeat was so loud that she was getting dizzy.

Standing there, right arm frozen in the air in the middle of waving her flag, she turned to see some of her cousins lying down, others running. Some seemed to have strange cherry stains on them. So many people were either running or lying down; hardly anyone was just standing anymore. Mounira felt left out and confused.

She turned the other way to see her father, ten yards away, looking upset and confused. She wondered if he'd been left out, too. When he saw her, his look changed— and he charged toward her. At that point, time resumed normal speed. Mounira could barely react before her father snatched her up and ran for all he was worth.

"Baba, why is everyone screaming? Why are their guns firing? Is this a game? It's scary. Baba, what's happening?" she repeated. Her running father offered no response.

They were halfway up the hill to their house when a soldier appeared in the middle of the cobblestone street. The green outfit and black sash around his waist were now a symbol of fear. Mounira's father slowed for a moment before deciding to proceed—there was no way to know whether the soldier was friend or foe.

As they approached, the soldier raised his rifle. Alman stopped, closed his eyes briefly, and the soldier fired. Realizing the target was behind him, Alman resumed running. Glancing over his shoulder, he spotted several other soldiers in green and black ready to return fire.

Mounira felt a quick tingle, which erupted into intense pain. She felt her body weaken and she started to slide off her father. She could see his face melt from fear to anguish as he guided her to the ground.

Her father's tears fell on her face like cold droplets of ice. She wanted to reach up to wipe them, but saw only her left arm go up briefly, before coming down. She felt heavy.

"Baba, it hurts..." she whispered with all her might.

"Mouni!" he yelled. She tried to understand why he was so upset, but passed out.

She awoke in the back of a horse-drawn wagon. She saw her father walking beside it, and then she fell asleep again. Mounira couldn't remember how many times she'd briefly awoken, or how many times she'd tried to say she felt cold or hot. Time didn't matter.

In the darkness of sleep, only one thing kept her company—the pain, the horrible pain. It haunted her dreams and waking moments. She was scared, but didn't have the strength to call for her dad. There was nowhere to run from the pain.

In a dream, when it seemed like the pain was going to consume her, it started to rain. The rain was icy, familiar. The rain gave her strength. Mounira glared at the huge pain monster through the dreamy rain. Summoning all her strength, she yelled, "You will *not* beat me! I will show you! I am stronger than you can imagine!"

"What did she say?" said Gretel to Hans and Saul.

"I'm stronger than you can imagine," repeated Mounira to herself, looking around blearily. For a moment, she was confused. Her pain had awakened her, pulling her back to the reality of the snow and the leafless tree. Perhaps the pain wasn't always her enemy—it didn't want to die, either. Mounira stood, shaking her head to wake up. Her pants were wet and freezing.

"I have to keep going," Mounira said to herself.

CHAPTER ELEVEN

DRIVEN BY THE SEASIDE

"What's in the shiny tube?" asked the scowling, thin-haired, unshaven man. Franklin had only just stepped into the tavern of the seaside town. To date, Franklin's journey had been filled with thrilling and scary moments, but overall he felt he'd done well.

With his best steely-eyed gaze, Franklin looked to the man seated at the bar. "Inside are the fingers of everyone who's tried to nick it," he answered sharply, yet his stomach twisted with fear.

The scowling man squinted, sized Franklin up, and then started to laugh. "I like that, boy. I like that a lot," he said jovially to his bar mates. "I'm going to use that next time. What's in the bag, Grimmy? Oh, it's the fingers of... no wait, the noses of everyone... no, I think fingers are best."

Franklin sighed. He'd managed to get safely to the southernmost tip of the island kingdom of Inglea, to this seaside town of Chestishire. Now, a new challenge stood ahead. It was one thing to ask if he could ride on the back of a cart to speed his journey, but it was going to take something else to get him across the waters to the shores of Freland. He'd heard tales about boys on ships finding themselves sold to service in foreign lands—and worse.

One of Franklin's hands held the straps to his travel bag and the brass tube. Both were slung over his shoulder. His free hand started shaking, broadcasting his feelings. He looked at it and made a fist. Spotting a suitable empty table, he sat down. He knew better than to stand on display. His clothes already stood out, but he hoped not by much.

Franklin pulled out his last bag of coins and held it under the table's surface. He ran his right hand through the remaining coins. "Thirty-six," he whispered. He hoped it would be enough to hire a boat and get the rest of the way to Nikolas Klaus, but he was doubtful.

He'd been hard on his dad about many things, especially money. They constantly seemed to be going from boom to bust and back again. Franklin believed his father saw money as a simple thing, not worth managing carefully. Now, he had newfound respect—the task was harder than he'd anticipated. Like his father, Franklin had no financial schooling, no financial role model, and no idea about what things should really cost. He knew, logically, that given he was only a third of the way through his journey, he should probably have used up at most a third of his money—but just a quarter of it remained. He owed his father an apology.

"I can see by your scowl that you're not used to places like this," said the waitress as she sauntered up. She had a mess of curly reddish hair and large, friendly green eyes. Her freckles were a match for her flowery dress. Franklin was slightly intimidated by her larger frame and booming voice. She held a wooden serving tray under her arm, and Franklin imagined she could use it as a weapon, if necessary.

Giving Franklin the once over, she put on a skeptical face. "Are you supposed to be in here? How old are you?"

Franklin narrowed his eyes, doing his best to look intimidating. "I'm old enough to have enough money for whatever I want." He realized how awkward that had sounded.

"Well, a young man with words like that will soon find himself with bruises instead of money," she replied. She gave a practiced smile. "Relax a bit. What is it you want?"

Franklin looked around, trying to think of something. He'd briefly forgotten that in a tavern, he would be expected to order something. Though he felt guilty for using up money when there might be a cheaper alternative, he was hungry, and already here. "Do you have a sandwich? Anything that isn't going to make me sick?" he said, feeling the grime on the table.

The waitress rolled her eyes. "We'll find something,"

she said, and headed off.

Franklin took a deep breath and then got out his notebook and writing materials. He uncorked his precious ink bottle and jotted down a few ideas and observations he'd been holding in mind. His thoughts then returned to the challenge that lay ahead.

He analyzed each person in the tavern. He couldn't see anyone who looked like a sea captain. He checked his notebook to see if he'd previously written down thoughts on hiring a boat and finding a captain—nothing useful.

When the waitress plunked the plate of food down hard in front of him, he didn't flinch, much to her surprise. He looked up with a smug smile. "Thought I'd jump?" he asked.

The waitress paused to consider her answer, and decided to cut him a break. Franklin was evidently away from home, and, judging by his worn clothes, for more than a couple of days. She could detect the nervousness under his bravado.

"Yes, I did," she admitted. "You can't be more than fifteen. What's your story?" She sat down opposite him, tilted her head, and waited for his answer.

Franklin was uncomfortable around women. Having the waitress sit and stare at him felt personal. His stomach tightened. He could feel the part of his brain that dealt with words already getting mixed up. Under the table, he clenched his fist. "Are you... *allowed* to sit down with customers?"

The waitress smiled mischievously. "Oh no, of *course* not. I'm sure in a moment the owner will come over—to throw you out. He's the giant bald guy back there, the one with so much hair growing out his ears he could comb it over the top of his head."

"What?" yelped Franklin. He straightened and nervously glanced around. His naturally pale face went white, while his cheeks went red. "But I—ah—"

The waitress laughed. "*Relax.* Listen, I'm not sure what you're doing here, but you stick out like a sore thumb. Why are you here? Maybe I can help get you on your way." She had a soft spot for dumb boys.

Franklin wasn't sure whether to trust her, but he did need help. He decided to let his guard down. "I need to get across the sea... to Freland."

"Oh, is that all? Go to the docks, then. Why are you in the middle of town?" she said.

"This is the middle of town?" He was certain he'd walked to the southernmost edge. He felt like an idiot, and hated that feeling.

"I'll admit this is a small place, but go to the docks. Did you think a boat captain was just going to walk into the bar? Reminds me of an old joke..." she laughed again, got up, and left.

Franklin was annoyed with himself. "How did I miss that?" he said to himself.

After a couple of minutes, the waitress returned. Since she'd left him sitting there, he'd done nothing but mentally beat himself up. She'd set fire to the internal doubt that had always existed within.

"You haven't touched your food. You okay?" she asked.

He looked at his food. He didn't want her to see the defeat in his eyes.

The waitress now felt bad. "Oh, come now. I was just teasing. You *are* at the tavern closest to the docks. The docks are only half a mile down the road. Provincial rules don't permit taverns any closer. Something about how if someone can be clear-headed enough to walk all the way to the docks from here, and then drown, then it's the fault of the patron, not the establishment."

Franklin glared back in anger. She'd made a fool of him. She was nothing but a mere peasant with the nerve to play a trick on a young man of noble blood—never mind one that would change the world someday. While he enjoyed playing tricks, he couldn't take them. His father had spoken to him about it, and he had tried to be a good sport, but it didn't work. He had a deep-seated fear that he wasn't actually smart—that, somehow, he was just fooling everyone. Sometimes he wondered if people just assumed he was smart because his father was a genius. At other times, the mental limits of those around him frustrated him.

The waitress sat down again. "You don't like having your leg pulled. Sorry, love," she said, half-apologetically. "Wasn't intending to upset—just trying to have a little fun. Relax! You're all wound up so tight. If you don't relax, you're going to attract a wee bit more attention than just being a lost boy from a well-to-do family."

Her assessment surprised Franklin, but he wouldn't show it.

"Look," she continued, "you've probably already learned that the world is different than you expected, but I can tell that you've seen *nothing* of its rougher side. You'll need to realize the world is unlike your privileged home town. It's rougher, but also full of amazing things." She smiled at Franklin with a motherly look—and that rubbed Franklin the wrong way.

She doesn't have insight, he thought to himself. *She's just dishing out generic advice—things she heard others parroting.* "Thanks," he said coldly, folding his arms. "Your insights are... astounding." His sarcasm was biting.

Insulted, the waitress stood up. "Fine. Eat up, *pay* up, and be on your way." She turned and walked away. "Arrogant little jerk," she muttered.

Franklin finished his lunch and stepped out of the tavern. He was determined to show that waitress—and all those like her—that he wasn't some lost boy. He was going to get across to Freland and find Nikolas Klaus, no matter what.

CHAPTER TWELVE

GINGERLY LOST

Mounira stumbled clumsily in the snow.

"Just a couple more steps," urged Gretel. "You can do it."

Mounira stepped out from the tree line, spotting a large clearing surrounded by more red pines. In the midst of the clearing were the remains of a burned down old house. She looked around, confused, tears in her eyes.

"You've arrived," said Hans triumphantly. "Welcome to Mother's house!"

Mounira looked around wildly. "I don't understand—there's no house here! Just—"

Gretel was annoyed. "*This* is Mother's house. She still owns it. We used to come here and she'd tell us about the children she used to have here, long ago, before the bad men came to steal them away. That's when she burned it down. She didn't want anyone to know about our other house, the one where we still live."

Saul continued, "We thought you'd like it. You can stay here if you like."

"I bet she's going to complain it has no walls," said

Hans.

"And no roof," said Gretel, giggling.

Hans laughed. "Some people are so picky." The trio went on with their banter.

Mounira looked at the ground, shaking with rage at having been tricked. Her body was numb, except for the pain from the stump. The pain reminded her that she wasn't asleep, that she wasn't going to awaken shortly from the nightmare, that this was real.

Then it dawned on Mounira that she was likely going to die in the middle of this snowy, red forest, and her rage collapsed into fear. Her lip started to tremble, and tears rolled down. "*Why* are you doing this?" she said, her voice breaking. "Show yourselves! Look in my eyes and tell me!"

At the edge of the clearing, three red-hooded figures stepped into view. They wore matching red cloaks.

The red figure on the left leaned against a tree. "We thought we should have some fun. We tracked you for a while, and thought you'd be fun. I have to say, you have been, Lefty," said Hans.

The figure on the right turned around. "I'm getting cold. I think it's time we go," said Saul, bored.

"Just before we go," said Gretel, the middle figure and shorter than the other two, "let me leave her a *present*."

"Breadcrumbs?" asked Saul.

"Oh, better than that. She'd freeze to death before she could follow," said Gretel.

"What are you doing, now?" asked Hans, curious.

Gretel held her hands apart so Mounira could see. "Here is some flint and steel. Seen them before? I don't know if you southerners have such things, so let me explain. You just need to hold the flint—this part here—in *one* hand, and then strike down with the steel part—this piece here—in *another* hand… like this." Gretel made sparks appear. "Make sure the sparks land on some *dry* leaves. Then, *voilà*, you have a nice warm fire."

"Oh, that's vicious, Gretel! She only has one arm!" said Hans, bursting into laughter. "And dry leaves? Ha!"

Gretel chuckled. "I'm going to leave these here for you." Gretel dropped the flint and steel in the snow. "Come on, boys. Mother's probably wondering where we are."

Saul looked at Mounira, nearly frozen. She was just a kid, while they were twenty years old. They'd never led someone into the forest to die before. At first, he'd thought maybe Hans was right, that it would be fun. But looking at Hans and Gretel's faces, and looking at Mounira, he felt strange inside—unsettled.

A moment later, the trio had vanished.

Mounira screamed as she ran to where Gretel had dropped the items, falling twice. She couldn't feel her feet to balance herself properly. She frantically hunted for the flint and steel with her numb hand. Her tears nearly froze her eyelashes shut.

"I'm stronger than you imagine," she said to herself, borrowing a phrase from her mother's favorite book. "I am a *titan*. I will take the fear you have given me and make it the sword from which I will have victory." Her teeth chattered furiously.

She felt around in the snow with her ever-more-numb hand. Despair crept in. "Where is it?!" she yelled. Snow blew around as she frantically searched.

"Mama, help—*please*. Don't let me die here," she said. Then, her hand hit something solid.

CHAPTER THIRTEEN
GROOMING THE HOUND

The corridor was silent as the Hound stopped to look at a particular painting he hadn't noticed before. He looked at the oil lamps; he'd never seen them all lit before. Studying the painting, he quickly recognized one of the three men as a younger Simon St. Malo, perhaps age twenty. A shorter, dark-bearded man, likely in his thirties, stood with his back to Simon. An older, clean-shaven man stood behind them, slightly elevated, arms behind his back. There was both a sense of camaraderie, and tension among the figures.

The Hound looked for a nameplate at the bottom of the frame but was surprised there wasn't one. He glanced at the other paintings in the corridor, all of which had nameplates. Just as he was about to leave, a glint of gold from the top of the painting caught his eye.

After checking that no one was coming, the Hound carefully lifted the painting off and leaned it against the wall. He read the top nameplate and then wondered aloud, "Why are you called *Faces of the new Fare*? What's a *Fare*?" He studied the painting for another minute, but found no better clue.

After carefully placing the painting back on the wall, he continued his walk to the gold-trimmed double doors that sealed off Simon St. Malo's study. The Hound's boots picked up the same rhythm he'd had since the first time he'd walked down this corridor, months before.

Standing at the huge doors, his stomach tightened, as it always did. He knocked on the door. An old, bald, sickly-looking man opened it. Cleeves was wearing his usual dark green and brown outfit with frills, which seemed more and more out of place compared to how those around Simon had been dressing recently.

"Greetings, Cleeves," said the Hound. He'd never had a conversation with the old man, but always did his best to show him respect. He still had no idea how the man might fit into the grand scheme of things.

Cleeves looked him up and down, as he always did. It was remarkable to Cleeves how different the Hound looked and behaved now, compared with his unsightly first appearance. He liked the Hound better than he had LeLoup, but he kept that opinion to himself.

"Would you care for tea and biscuits today, Mister Hound?" asked Cleeves drily.

"Yes, thank you, I would appreciate that," replied the Hound.

Cleeves gave a look that showed he didn't care for the

over-the-top manners. He moved out of the way to let the Hound enter. "Mister—", he started to announce.

"I am aware he's here, Cleeves, thank you," snapped Simon, shaking his head. He was halfway up a ladder attached to one of the many thirty-foot-high floor-to-ceiling bookcases. "Do you think me deaf? Really, Cleeves, sometimes I wonder why I keep you."

"Tea, sir?" asked Cleeves to Simon, ignoring the attack.

"Of course, tea. What a silly question. Have I ever said no?" asked Simon. He returned to hunting for a particular book. "Come in, Hound. Don't leave the door open like that. You might let a stray animal or commoner in here if you aren't careful."

The Hound stepped in and tried to imagine how a commoner could get through the guards and checkpoints that led up to the study's entrance, let alone the mini-castle that surrounded. Simon's patron was as paranoid about security as Simon was.

Looking at the ceiling, the Hound noticed skylights had been added, and the enormous chandelier removed.

"You noticed the natural light," said Simon, climbing down the ladder with two books under his left arm. He wore a beige shirt and maroon pants, which the Hound was surprised to see. Simon's salt-and-pepper hair was short and brushed, and he remained as clean-shaven as ever.

Simon offered a half-smile. "If you're wondering

about the modern clothing and my lack of scholarly robes, you can thank Richelle Pieman and her minions. They believe—and they aren't wrong—that we need to project a more modern presence on all fronts. After seeing everyone else adopt it, I decided to give it a try."

The Hound, unsure what to say, offered, "It looks… comfortable."

Simon looked down at his pants and black boots. For a moment, Simon sounded like a regular, down-to-earth guy. "Remarkably, it is. Lighter too. I hated pantaloons, which is why, as much as possible, I wore the robes. These are, honestly, an improvement. I don't like agreeing with Richelle, but on this front, I think she's right." Realizing he had said something that might make him seem weak, Simon corrected himself sharply, "I know she's right. It's obvious, and once I was brought into the discussion, I whole-heartedly agreed. However, I think everyone can agree that fashion is not on the same level of importance as my work."

The Hound nodded, not because he agreed, but because he feared the consequences of not doing so. St. Malo had been good to him since the beginning, but he'd heard stories about what happened to people who got on St. Malo's bad side—supposedly an easy thing to do.

"Come," said Simon, walking through a labyrinth of recently rearranged eight-foot-high bookcases that divided up the otherwise enormous room. The Hound was sure St. Malo enjoyed being one of the few who knew the way through.

A moment later, they emerged to a newly set-up area. There were two dark wooden worktables covered with neatly stacked papers and brass tubes. Nearby stood a pair of comfortable chairs with crimson and blue cushions, and side tables. The fireplace was about twenty feet back, near an ornate door the Hound hadn't noticed before.

Simon turned up one of the freestanding oil lamps near the seating area and motioned for the Hound to sit. As soon as they were seated, Cleeves arrived with the teacart, poured the tea, and then disappeared again.

Tea in hand, Simon looked at the Hound, and waited. The Hound was familiar with Simon's deliberately awkward pauses, which he used to create tension. It no longer bothered the Hound as much.

"How are you, Hound?" asked Simon, seeming genuine.

The Hound was taken aback. This was the first time Simon hadn't addressed him as "dog" or else hurled some other similar insult to remind him of his place in Simon's hierarchy.

"I'm... well," replied a suspicious Hound, picking up his own cup of tea.

Simon took a slow sip of tea, cradling his cup. "I'm glad. Your recent successes have not gone unnoticed. Someone of importance wants to speak with you. You should feel honored."

"Thank you. If I may ask, who is it?"

Simon's grin was both sinister and joyful. "Have you ever heard of Lord Marcus Pieman? Perhaps you've heard of the society known as the Fare?" Simon's grin widened.

The Hound thought back to the painting. When he'd read the golden nameplate, he hadn't recognized it, but now that Simon said it, he knew the name. There were stories and rumors about a group called the Fare, a group who had nearly taken control of every kingdom this side of the eastern mountains long ago. "The new Fare painting," said the Hound.

Simon nodded. "Let me guess—you have heard of it as the enemy of the Tub, as something that faded away a long, long time ago. All of which is true, save the faded away part. Lord Marcus Pieman rebuilt it. That painting you saw was commissioned shortly after I joined."

"Why does the leader of the Fare want to talk to me?" asked the Hound nervously.

Simon put his cup gently down on the saucer sitting on the side table. He then leaned forward. "There is *one* thing you must understand," he whispered, sharply and crisply, "whatever Marcus is going to talk to you about, you work for *me*, now and always. You are an extension of *me*. What you do, what you hear—all of it needs to get back to *me*, regardless of what you are told. Understand?"

The Hound looked at his patron and nodded briefly.

Simon smiled and leaned back. "Then, by all means,

have the chat with Marcus. I'm sure he'll be talking to you about fitting into our little secret society. Oh, and in case it isn't obvious, mention it to *anyone*—"

The Hound politely waved off Simon's concern.

"Good." Just as Simon reached for his cup of tea, he stopped himself. "Oh—I have something to show you! Come," said Simon joyfully. His ability to shift moods quickly was dizzying.

Simon led the Hound to the ornate door by the fireplace. The door was twelve feet high and its mesmerizing carvings made it seem like it was a door within a door within a door. It opened to a bright room that had a large desk at the far end, a seating area by yet another fireplace, and a single workbench. Something was on the workbench.

Simon walked over to the workbench and picked up two oversized, metallic, gear-covered gloves. The gloves were directly connected to two control boxes with dials, which in turn were connected to a large, strange-looking rectangular metal box. The metal box was smooth at the edges and sealed.

"What is all of this?" asked the Hound.

"*These*," said Simon proudly, "are my *shock-gloves*— superior in every way to that toy you first brought. I took apart the shocking stick, and I'll confess it was well made —for a toy. But it inspired me, and I came up with these.

"You wear the gloves, attach the control boxes to your forearms, and wear the battery unit on your back. It's heavy, but the power is immense. My initial experiments were exceptionally positive. I will admit the battery is based on one of Marcus' designs. I am an electromechanical genius, while Lord Pieman understands chemistry like few others."

"I don't see any cranks," said the Hound, looking the invention over with fascination.

"They don't have any," said Simon, almost insulted. "One cannot crank enough to produce the necessary power. That's why I built a wagon, to allow for one to charge these anywhere. Unlike the sticks, which can only be used once per charge, *these* allow more uses, depending on how high you set the dials, right here on the control boxes." Simon pointed out the dials.

The Hound picked up and examined one of the strange metal gloves. He was amazed. "You made *these*, from that stick? Wow." The gloves looked intimidating, and he liked that—a lot. "These are thick," he remarked.

Simon grinned. "Ah, yes. I wanted to ensure they wouldn't electrocute the wearer, if used in bad weather. And—"

"Electro...?"

"*Electrocute* means to shock," Simon snapped, annoyed at having been interrupted. "I don't want the wearer of the gloves to get shocked if a little water gets on them." Simon resisted his urge to kick the Hound out and not waste any more time with him.

"Oh, that's smart," said the Hound, apologetically.

"The shocking stick seemed to have that principle, but I improved on it, significantly. Still, *don't* let the wires get cut, or the tank punctured. That could result in... let's say... *significant* unpleasantness."

"What? What are wires? What's—" said the Hound, confused. He cringed at having made a second ignorant comment.

Simon grumbled under his breath before sporting a fake smile and continuing. "*Wires* are these flexible rope-like things, here. They are what allow the energy from the tank to flow through to the control boxes, which then controls how much goes to the gloves."

"Oh, got it," said the Hound, nodding. "This is amazing."

Simon relaxed, feeling the Hound was genuinely in awe of his genius. "Now, I need you to field test them. I need to know how they perform in real situations. Also, given how you've added some muscle in recent months, you should be able to handle the weight for several hours at a time."

The Hound was surprised by his patron's remarks. Simon didn't seem to miss the details of anything.

"Cleeves has replacement clothes for you, in the newer style. I had your new long-coat made larger to accommodate all of this."

"Great," said the Hound eagerly. "I'll give these a try."

There was a knock at the door. It was Cleeves.

"Send him in," said Simon, anticipating why Cleeves had disturbed them. "It should be Marcus. I'll leave the two of you alone. Remember what we discussed."

Simon stopped just before leaving and turned to the Hound again. "Oh—I presume you came all the way back here to make sure that Maxwell Watt was properly handed over and secured."

"Yes," replied the Hound.

"And he is secured, then?" asked Simon.

The Hound put his arms behind his back, unconsciously standing at attention. "Yes. I saw to it myself. I made sure he is comfortable and his door properly locked. I checked the guard rotation. I also tested the door to his room, and the one at the base of the tower."

Simon thought through his mental checklist. "Excellent," he said, turning to go. "I do so love a reliable pet."

"Shall I bring your tea in here?" asked Cleeves, who stood dutifully by the door.

"Um," said the Hound, looking about. "I have no idea what to do, Cleeves."

"That's quite alright," said a warm, charming voice. "You must be the Hound." A white-haired man stepped into view. His clean-shaven face was evidently that of the man from the painting in the corridor, but older. He wore an eyepatch over his left eye.

The man turned to Cleeves. "Arthur, would you be so kind as to bring us some fresh tea, and whatever fresh bits you can scrounge up?"

Arthur Cleeves bowed and smiled. "For you, Lord Pieman, anything."

The man then turned to the Hound. "My name is Marcus Pieman. Please, call me Marcus. We have much to discuss and, unfortunately, very little time. I have a mission for you already."

CHAPTER FOURTEEN

MAKINGS OF A HOOD

The strong winter wind propelled the sail-carts through the Red Forest. Pierre held on tightly to the ropes tied to the sail-carts as they pulled him along on his skis.

It was well past noon and they'd been searching for hours. They had found the beginning of a trail near a burned-down old building, but just beyond the protective circle of trees it had disappeared. They only had an idea of the direction someone had taken—and they hoped it was Mounira.

"Okay—let's split up and do a final look around. We won't have enough light to get back if we go any further," said Pierre, letting go of the ropes. He grabbed the poles off his back and skied around. The Yellow Hoods split off in different directions to have a look around.

Ten minutes later, just as Pierre was about to call everyone in, Richy yelled, "Wait, I think I saw something!" He pulled down the telescoping mast and sail and hopped out of his sail-cart.

Elly, Tee, and Pierre quickly made their way to Richy.

Richy dashed through the knee-high snow to a little stone alcove under a great golden oak tree. It was nearly perfectly hidden under the tree's enormous, powerful roots. A last, desperate flicker of something had caught Richy's eagle eyes.

"That's the biggest golden oak I've ever seen," said Pierre, marveling at it as he skied over.

"How did you see that, Richy? It took me a few seconds looking straight at it to see the hiding spot underneath," said Tee, climbing out of her sail-cart.

Richy was too focused on getting to the alcove to hear her.

Pierre planted his poles and removed his skis. "How did she manage to find this?" he said to himself. "This has to be hundreds of yards from the burned building. Unbelievable."

"I hope it's her," said Elly.

Pierre nodded, realizing he was jumping to conclusions.

Richy climbed into the small alcove and saw a kid, all curled up. He took his mitts off and placed his hand over the remains of a fire. "It's still warm!"

"Give me some room," said Pierre. Richy climbed out and Pierre got his upper body into it. "This is a small space indeed." He pulled off his mitts, rubbed his hands together to warm them up a bit, and then placed them on the girl's neck.

"I can feel her soul moving in there, but slowly," he said as he felt the slow thump, thump, thump of her blood pumping. "Tee, get the fresh blankets ready for bundling her up. Elly, get the sheep bladders. Richy, get the sled ready… I still can't believe she found this special place," said Pierre.

"Blankets are ready!" said Elly, from behind him.

"The water bladders are still very warm," said Tee.

"That grandfather of yours is amazing, coming up with a way to keep them warm this long. I was certain you were going to tell me they were ice cold," said Pierre, while trying to figure out how to pick up the girl. "I think this is the right girl. She's got that southerner's skin color and looks young enough."

Elly let out a sigh of relief.

"What's *special* about here, by the way?" asked Richy.

"There are a handful of places like these in these forests. Legends have it that people, long ago, planted the first golden oaks on huge rocks like this so that in a blizzard, they would be able to find shelter under them— just like this girl did. There's always some dry brush in its nooks and crannies. I can't imagine how she found it," said Pierre as he slowly removed Mounira from the alcove, trying to keep the once-tied blanket around her. Slipping for a moment, Pierre corrected his balance, but the blanket fell open.

"Where's her right arm?!" Richy shrieked.

"Wow—she doesn't have one," said Elly, astonished.

"Look at her feet," said Tee, pointing at Mounira's red and blackened skin.

Pierre examined her feet. "She burned them... but how? Why would it have been so bad? Surely she would have felt the pain and done something," said Pierre as he motioned for Tee and Elly to lay the blankets on the stretcher.

They quickly and quietly made sure Mounira was bundled up and tied properly to the sled, which they attached to one of the sail-carts.

Tee climbed into the alcove and looked at the smoldering remains of a fire. "I found some flint. There's got to be some steel around here." Tee carefully searched through the leaves and twigs in the far corner. "Found it!"

Elly walked over. "So, wait... she made a fire with one arm, and her feet?"

"We've got to go," said Pierre. "The sheep bladders aren't going to keep her warm forever. We have to get moving."

"A fire with her feet and one arm," said Richy, trying to imagine how Mounira had created the fire as he climbed into his sail-cart.

"That would have deserved a *La la*," said Elly, thinking of Tee's trademark victory sound that she'd seemed to have outgrown.

"You got that right," said Tee, pulling up her mast and setting sail. "Mounira's got some Yellow Hood in her."

CHAPTER FIFTEEN
DIFFICULT DECISIONS

Nikolas had returned to the café after having got the search party together. He'd had to bang on the door to be let in, and wasn't sure why Jerome had a strange look of relief when he saw Nikolas again.

He knew the best thing he could do at this point was make preparations for when the search party returned with Mounira. He quickly convinced Anna and Alman to come with him to his town home, a couple of blocks away.

Nikolas had had the town home built nearly twenty years ago. It was a beautiful, simple two-story place where Isabella and Nikolas would stay in Mineau now and then, as a mini vacation away from the kids. Isabella loved the shopping and bistros in Mineau, and he loved the bookstores and random merchants who would come by. He occasionally made the second home available to the Tub for whatever needs they had.

Finally, there was a knock at the door, and Nikolas

answered it. Alman sprang up to see Pierre standing there, carrying a huge bundle in his hands.

"We need to get her into some dry clothes, and get hot water for the sheep bladders!" said Pierre. "I don't know how she's doing, but I know it's not good."

"I'll take care of boiling some water," said Anna.

Nikolas led the way to the bedrooms upstairs.

Alman waited for the Yellow Hoods to step in and remove their boots and coats before approaching. "I want to thank you, from the bottom of my heart. You have—"

"Thank you, but go," Elly interrupted. "We know where you need to be." Tee and Richy nodded in agreement.

Alman smiled with tears in his eyes. "I don't know how to repay you all," he said, and then he ran upstairs.

"I'll see if there's anything left for us to help with," said Tee, following. A couple of minutes later, she came back down. "We should head home. Grandpapa said he'll let us know when we can visit her. "

Pierre came down the stairs behind her. "I'm heading out, too. I'll make sure you get back to Minette safely," he said. "You three made me proud. And, Richy, you have a keen eye and a trustworthy gut. That's two lives you've saved, now."

Richy smiled awkwardly.

Pierre gave each of the Yellow Hoods a rub on the head, and then headed out the door. "Come on! Nothing we can do in here except get in the way."

"Do you think she'll be okay?" asked Richy to Anna. She was heading for the stairs with a hot kettle.

"She will be fine," said Anna, with fake empathy. She looked at Tee. "Nikolas learned a lot about medicine from your other grandfather. The girl is in good hands."

Tee was surprised. "I didn't know Granddad knew medicine?"

"Sam Baker may be a small man, but he is very knowledgeable. Now, off you go," said Anna, ushering them out.

After the Yellow Hoods were on their way, Anna went upstairs. "Here's the hot water you needed," she said, handing the kettle carefully to Nikolas. "I'll be on my way. I wasn't planning on staying the entire day."

"Understood," said Nikolas. "Thank you for your assistance."

Alman leapt off the bed where Mounira lay wrapped in fresh blankets. "Yes, thank you," he said, shaking Anna's hand, surprised at the strength and firmness of her grip.

Anna looked at the girl. "Your daughter looks like a fighter. She'll make it," said Anna flatly. "Good luck." With that, she left.

Once the sheep bladders were refilled and placed between layers of blankets, Alman made himself comfortable beside his daughter. There was just enough room for two.

Nikolas thought back to how many scares he and Isabella had had with one or another of their children, of how many times they had lain with one of them, waiting and hoping for them to get better. Sometimes, Isabella would bring him paper, a quill, and ink—so he could sketch ideas while he lay there—but not once did he use them. He understood what Alman was going through. "I'll be downstairs," Nikolas said, and then left the room.

Alman kissed his daughter on the head, and fell asleep.

Hours later, Mounira awoke, confused and groggy. "Where am I?" she asked, waking her father. "Why can't I move?"

Alman smiled and stretched. "It's okay, Mouni. You're safe. You were very cold. Anciano de Montagne and the Yellow Hoods found you. Anciano Klaus bundled you up and made sure your soul could warm up properly," he said, stroking her cheek.

"Baba, I feel so hot," she said, yawning and looking around. "Can you take some blankets off?"

"Let me go and ask Anciano Klaus, okay? I'll be right back."

Mounira lazily looked around the simple bedroom. Oil lamps in the corners gave the room a warm glow. Sunlight peeked through the closed curtains, telling Mounira it might be late morning.

Alman returned with a smile. "He says it's okay to

unwrap you. We should also change the bandages on your feet, anyway," he said, helping her out of the blankets.

"My feet are fine," replied Mounira.

Alman's face paled, and inside the terrible weight he carried got heavier. "Mouni, I must tell you… you burned your feet."

Mounira shook her head. "No, they're fine. They feel fine. Maybe they caught a little fire," she said, annoyed. "You don't trust me. Look, I'll show you." She unwrapped her bandaged feet, and only then realized how bad they looked.

Confused again, she looked to her father. The feisty girl who was just telling her father off now needed him. "But… but they don't hurt, Baba. *Why* don't they hurt?"

He cuddled her and rocked her gently. "You'll be okay. You are tough inside, and you will be fine. Your feet need time to heal, that's all. Okay?" he said, kissing the top of her head and smoothing her short hair.

Nikolas walked in with fresh bandages and placed them on the bed. "Let's have a look at your feet, yes?" He bent down to examine them. "Can you feel this?" Nikolas touched the bottom of her foot.

"Yes," said Mounira.

"Alright," said Nikolas. He then pulled out a butter knife and poked her right foot a bit sharply. Mounira had no reaction.

"Nothing?" said Nikolas.

"I felt a pushing, but that's all," she replied.

"Interesting. You feel soft things only, yes?" asked Nikolas.

Mounira had to think about it. "I think so," she said, uncertain. "I just don't really think about how things feel, except for maybe my stump, because sometimes I can't block it out."

"I understand," said Nikolas, standing and giving her a compassionate smile. "Well, we will put more cream on, and bandage your feet up, and you will rest. Maybe in a day or two you can meet my granddaughter, her friends, and the mountain man Pierre who found you. Would you like this?"

Mounira nodded, and yawned again.

"Anciano Klaus, if I may have a word?" asked Alman, getting up. "Mouni—"

His daughter smiled. "I'll be fine, Baba. I'm tired anyway. You go have your chat. I'll be fine." She felt good about this place, and these people. As Alman and Nikolas left the room, Mounira closed her eyes. She recalled bits of conversation between the Yellow Hoods and Pierre. She remembered being lifted up and bundled warmly. She slowly recalled, in reverse, events that had brought her here.

Downstairs, Nikolas refilled the kettle and placed it on the kitchen stove. He set out some warm cookies on a plate, and gestured for Alman to have a seat.

"When did you make these?" asked Alman.

Nikolas chuckled, thinking of how many times he'd been asked that question over the years, particularly by Tee. "Magic elves made them for Solstice," he joked.

Alman chuckled. "That might work on your granddaughter, but I'm a bit wiser," said Alman.

"Oh, no. My Tee saw through answers like that at a remarkable age. Your daughter strikes me as the same— smart, and quick, yes?" Nikolas recognized the confusion on Alman's face. "Sorry, is my speaking... awkward? Sometimes this still happens to me. Here we are, two men speaking in languages they do not think in, yes?"

Alman nodded and took a bite from a cookie. "This is good. Thank the elves."

Nikolas appreciated the compliment. "All joking aside, I haven't slept yet. While you were lying down, I scribbled down ideas about some things, and then I needed a distraction—so, I made the cookies," said Nikolas.

"Ah," replied Alman. He briefly paused. "Anciano Klaus, I cannot thank you enough for your kindness and generosity, yet—I need to ask you something more." His face became serious. "May I impose a great burden upon you? There is no one else I have met... with whom I felt I could ask such a thing."

Nikolas leaned forward to study the man and contemplate what had been asked. Black rings under

Alman's eyes and slightly sunken cheeks suggested that Alman had neither slept well nor eaten well in weeks, if not months. Nikolas could see the heavy burden in the man's eyes, and he'd noticed earlier that his voice carried guilt with each mention of Mounira.

"My friend," Nikolas replied, "if I can shoulder this burden for you, allow me to do so."

Alman's eyes welled up. "Can you... take care of my Mouni—my Mounira, while I go back to see what has happened to the rest of our family?"

"Of course—I understand. I can, yes," Nikolas replied, thinking back to the harsh reality of his own adolescence, and the family he'd lost.

Alman then recounted to Nikolas the fateful day he'd grabbed Mounira and departed Catalina, and how he'd kept bringing them further and further north, without any real plan.

Nikolas sighed heavily, taking it all in. He resettled himself in his seat. "That is horrible. No one should have to go through that," he said. "I hate to ask... but I noticed you did not mention what happened to her arm. Might I hear about that?"

Tears flooded out of Alman, and the man sobbed for several minutes. Uncertain what to do, Nikolas imagined what advice Isabella might have given him. Nikolas could read people, but he wasn't the best at figuring out how to help them cope emotionally. He tried patting Alman's hand, but the gesture felt foreign, so instead he went to fetch a set of handkerchiefs, and then made some tea.

Alman took a few deep breaths to regain his composure. "She was shot in the arm as we fled. I bandaged it… but it had become infected as we traveled. Mouni had a fever; her skin felt like it was on fire. She couldn't stay awake any longer than just to drink some broth. I didn't know what to do, other than try to keep her cool and give her water and broth."

After blowing his nose, wiping his eyes, and drinking some tea, Alman continued the story. "One day, an old soldier stopped the horse and cart we were riding in. He asked questions, and realized something wasn't right. He insisted on seeing Mounira. When I showed him, he made the driver take us into the nearby town. I thought he was going to put us in jail, or have us shot.

"Once in town, the soldier ran into a tavern, cleared it out, and told us to get Mounira inside. It was then that he looked at me and told me the *only* way to save her was to remove the arm."

Nikolas stroked his short beard. "I can't imagine," he said sympathetically.

Alman's lip trembled. His hands shook. He stared at the ground, silently, and then continued. "I didn't want to. I… I almost wanted her to *die* so that I wouldn't have to make the decision, but the old soldier wouldn't let us leave. He had his pistol pointed at me. He kept saying, 'If you don't do this, you will regret it the rest of your life.

I've seen grown men in her condition, and they don't last much longer. Remove the arm, or you'll lose her. *Remove it.'*

"The old soldier said he would have done it, if his hands didn't shake so much, but I'm not sure I believed him. So... I did it. It was horrible. Mouni's fever was so high that she didn't know what I was doing, but she screamed. The old soldier and the driver had to hold her down... I—"

"Enough," said Nikolas, slapping the table and startling Alman. "I understand better now. *You* must understand your decision was the *only* one. You chose correctly. You need to accept that, yes? She lives—because of *you*."

Nikolas took a sip of tea, settled himself down, and continued. "She's a strong little girl. She has survival genius, from what Pierre said." Nikolas tapped the side of his head with a finger. "I can't imagine what she'll be like in ten years. All of that would have been lost, if it wasn't for you. Do not carry this guilt any longer."

"I believe the spirit of my mother guided me," said Mounira, standing at the bottom of the stairs, a short distance away.

Her father turned to look at her. "Mouni? What are you doing there?" He looked at her feet in shock and horror. "You shouldn't be on your feet! You need to rest!"

Mounira shook her head and walked forward, slowly. "I cannot rest. My mind is filled with rage toward those

Red Hoods. I want to find them and make them pay. I want them to *never* hurt anyone again!" said Mounira with fire in her eyes.

Nikolas motioned to Mounira to come over. "I promise you that we will stop those Red Hoods. But the best thing you can do against them right now is to heal, and show that you overcame their evil, yes?"

Mounira thought about what Nikolas said, and the soft way he said it. She nodded her agreement, and then turned to her father. "You did the right thing, Baba. Listen to Anciano Klaus. I am good, see?" she said, holding up her one arm and wiggling her fingers. "I'm tough. I'm your *ladrillita*, remember?"

Nikolas chuckled. "The little brick."

"Right," said Mounira, and then did a double take. "Wait—you speak our language?"

"A little," replied Nikolas. "Enough, as Isabella would say, to get myself into trouble."

Mounira looked into her father's eyes. "Go. Find our family. Then, come back here and get me. I will be okay with these good people. You must go, Baba."

Alman hugged his daughter and rocked her back and forth.

"Baba, I love you. We need to know what happened to our family. I'd started to believe you never wanted to know what happened to Pedro, Farouk, and everyone else."

Her father pulled back, and stroked his daughter's face. "Mouni, I want to know—more than anything," he said, tears rolling down his cheeks. He had a spark in his voice that Nikolas hadn't heard before.

Mounira smiled lovingly at her dad. "*Go*. I will be fine. These are good people. If anything, you should feel sorry for them, having to deal with me!"

Her father laughed and gave her another big hug. "Oh, I do."

Alman stood and offered his hand to Nikolas. "Thank you. I know you will treat her as you would your own granddaughter."

"You're going *now*?" said Nikolas, surprised at the abruptness.

"The sooner I leave, the sooner I return, yes?"

Nikolas stood and shook Alman's hand. "Yes, yes, of course. Let me give you some supplies. You have a long road to go, yes? Mounira is now my family."

CHAPTER SIXTEEN

A Family, a Fare

Marcus splashed water on his face. He smiled—things were going well. Forty years of planning and careful execution were paying off. He'd achieved what he'd only dreamed of back when he took over the remaining pieces of the Fare, long ago.

The Fare had been broken and scattered at the hands of the Tub, though they hadn't made it seem that way. When Marcus had taken over, he'd found the peace agreement riddled with holes, and he took full advantage. Bit by bit, he rebuilt the Fare, his way, replacing its dark ideas with his vision of a truly *greater* good.

The primary differences between the Fare that Marcus had built, and the Tub, were that he understood human nature, and he was willing to do *whatever* was necessary to bring about his vision. The Tub, on the other hand, seemed to be happy to let society rot.

Only now were the Fare truly violating any part of the agreement—yet, now, the Tub was no longer in much of a position to enforce the agreement and oppose the Fare.

Marcus reached for a towel and slowly dried his face. He'd removed any unnecessary servants from his presence long ago, after several assassination attempts and uncovering many spies.

The stubbly face in the mirror, with its full head of white hair, had the wrinkles of wisdom befitting a man of his advanced age. Yet, youthful purpose and energy remained. Only his left eye showed any signs of the battles, its dull gray standing in contrast to the other's deep brown.

He put the towel in the discard basket and stepped into his dressing area. He moved carefully to a velvet-covered shelf with soft cushions. Each cushion held a technological marvel.

"What will Nikolas think of this, when he sees it?" he said to himself, picking up one of the monocular goggles. Its strap was the finest leather, and the lens and mechanism around it—pure genius.

"Three years of work and, I'd dare say, I've caught up to my dear Abe. I'd forgotten the enjoyment of creating a thing of substance."

Abeland was Marcus' elder son, and though he'd been off leading the Fare's efforts in the southern kingdoms, he never seemed too far away. Abeland was good at keeping in touch; he'd send regular letters, and find ways to visit when he could. Abe's energy and focus had eliminated any possibility of his having a family, a sacrifice that weighed on Marcus' mind. Marcus' wife had said Abe was a sharper, more driven version of his father. Marcus wondered what she would have thought of Richelle, their granddaughter.

Marcus got dressed in a beige cotton shirt with a high collar, a brown vest, and flat-front pants. "I'm finally getting used to looking like this," he said to himself.

He looked around for his collection of special metals, which he kept in small bottles. "Now, where is that strip of magnesium?" He wasn't used to being in this mansion, but it had been necessary to move here, in order to be at the center of what they had going on across kingdoms.

After looking through the shelves and four dressers in the dressing area between his bathroom and master bedroom, he finally found his collection in a bottom drawer.

"Ah, here we go," he said, pulling out a particular vial. It was too thin to fit a pinky finger, but was about as long as one. He picked up the monocular goggle and went to his desk in the open office area, which adjoined the bedroom. He placed both items down carefully, and then pulled out a small toolbox from a side drawer. Using two pairs of tweezers from his toolbox, he positioned his good eye over the working area, carefully broke off a piece of the metal, and then slotted it into a tiny chamber in the monocular goggle. He then took a small glass bottle of vinegar from another drawer and placed a couple of drops on the metal, and then sealed the chamber.

He felt it heat up slightly, and then he flicked a tiny switch on the outside of the eyepiece until the once dull-gray glass rim started to emit a golden glow.

"Now, let's see if the improvements work." He strapped the device over his damaged eye. After adjusting the lens, the world had real depth again. He looked out the window, at one of the prison towers. "Wonderful! So clear this time—just like having spectacles on."

With a flick of a finger, an additional lens fell into place in front of the eyepiece. Closing his good eye, his left could now see everything magnified several times. "Excellent. I see you, DeBoeuf, by the window of your tower. Don't worry—we'll have a chat soon. Sorry to keep you waiting, but I've been busy."

He flipped the extra lens back up, opened the sliding doors to his planning room, and entered. The high, white walls were covered in maps and lists. An enormous table was centered in the twenty-by-twenty, dark-hardwood-floored room. Miniature horses, cannons, and soldiers stood positioned strategically on the table's surface. Nearby, a side table was set up with a checkered board and some wooden gaming pieces, some of which had been knocked over.

Marcus picked up one piece and looked at it. "I'm sorry, old friend, but the time has come to take you out of play. I hope you won't be too annoyed at me but, ultimately, this was your plan, at least originally."

There was a sudden knock at the planning room's door to the main corridor.

"Come in, Richelle," said Marcus.

Richelle entered and looked at her grandfather, puzzled. "How did you know it was me, Opa? There's no pattern—no rhyme or reason why you should expect me. I changed my boots to be extra quiet."

"Sometimes, my dear, I guess," said Marcus, smiling at his twenty-nine-year-old granddaughter.

Richelle was born, strong and vibrant, to Marcus' younger son, the Duke Lennart, and his wife, Duchess Catherine, in the eastern kingdom of Brunne. The Duke's family had an idyllic life: gentle winters, warm summers, a good people to govern, and a great relationship with the royal family.

At one year old, Richelle had fallen ill and started having frequent, horrible coughing fits. She would spring fevers all of a sudden, and then—mysteriously—within days the fevers would vanish, only to return within weeks. As each month wore on, her condition worsened, and she weakened.

When the letter arrived informing Marcus of Richelle's situation, he couldn't accept the prognosis of the king of Brunne's best doctors; they had concluded his granddaughter wouldn't last more than three months. He immediately ordered his servants to leave his estate for the day, and locked himself in his study. Marcus' wife,

Richelle, had died only a month earlier, and he could not bear the thought of losing her namesake, too. There must be something he could do.

Duke Lennart angrily dragged the servant who had awoken him in the middle of the night to the manor's entranceway. He didn't believe for a minute the servant's claim that his father was standing in the entranceway. He looked forward to beating sense into the servant after proving the servant to be a liar. To Lennart's astonishment, there was his father, Lord Marcus Pieman, looking like a man possessed, and soaked to the bone.

"Father?"

Marcus had traveled for three weeks, non-stop, across the eastern kingdoms. He'd hired fresh horses where available, and hired coaches and drivers to travel through the night when he needed to sleep.

Marcus's eyes burned into his son's soul. "Tell me she hasn't passed yet."

It took Lennart a second to figure out what his father was talking about. "Richelle's alive, but she isn't well, not well at all."

For the next several days, Marcus was near Richelle when she had the energy to play, and held her when she couldn't sleep. He grilled the doctors for every piece of information, every idea they had. He knew in his bones they were wrong, but couldn't blame them for their conclusions. They were well trained, yet limited by what was currently possible. Marcus—a master inventor and a specialist at pulling other people's inventions into something new and more marvelous—always thought *beyond* the realm of the currently possible.

Whenever Richelle had a coughing fit, Marcus would pat and rub her back, and make shushing noises until she would coo happily or fall asleep.

Marcus himself barely slept. Often, with Richelle asleep on his shoulder, he would work through ideas and potential inventions. His design sheets had areas circled with the names of other inventors he was certain could create the piece he needed. His alchemical ideas included formulas, plant names, notes about what was missing, and whom he needed to ask. Marcus wasn't sure if the right path would be machine or medicine—yet he was determined to go down both paths, as far as he could, to help his granddaughter. All he needed was time, which, every couple of hours, he quietly asked Fate to give him.

One morning, Lennart found Marcus packed and ready to leave, with Richelle asleep over his shoulder.

"You're leaving us, then?" said Lennart, reaching out hesitantly to take his daughter.

Marcus moved slightly away from his son. "I can't leave her to die, son. I need to take her with me. I will make her well again."

Lennart looked at his father and nodded agreement. Marcus found his son's reaction odd—he seemed already prepared to part with his daughter.

"Good luck, father," said Lennart.

A month later bore the first bit of promise for little Richelle. Marcus was able to acquire the ingredients for a medicinal concoction that reduced Richelle's fever and coughing. He cried with joy the first time she slept peacefully for a few hours. The effectiveness of the medicine eventually wore off, and Marcus continued down a long road of making her well.

Seven months after they'd left, Marcus received a letter stating that Catherine had delivered a son. The letter also made one particular point crystal clear: he and Catherine didn't want Richelle returning while there was any possibility she could infect another child. As the months and years went by, Marcus found it harder and harder to hide his contempt for his son and daughter-in-law from Richelle.

Marcus brought her to meet the best inventors, chemists, and doctors throughout the kingdoms, each providing him with advice or remedies or machines to try. Richelle learned not to fear them, but instead came to understand how the fringe of knowledge was a strange and philosophical place.

Sometimes Marcus would wake up, realizing that he'd fallen asleep at a workbench, only to find Richelle trying to put a concoction or machine together herself. Every time she sprang a fever and became frail again, nothing in the world could distract him from taking care of her. Often it fell to his elder son, Abeland, to make sure that Marcus ate and took basic care of himself, as well as to make sure that his father's other plans unfolded as they needed to.

One morning, when Richelle was six, Marcus awoke to find her playing in the courtyard with her uncle Abeland. She stopped running around the hedges and smiled at her grandfather. There was loudness to her voice that he'd never heard. "Good morning, Opa!" she exclaimed. Richelle had finally beaten the condition that had once seemed certain to be her doom.

That evening, Marcus talked with Abeland about his duty to bring Richelle back to her family. She had no memory of them, other than the stories she'd been told, and only knew their faces from the few paintings Marcus had around. Lennart and Catherine's letters were always addressed to Marcus, and never Richelle. The couple now had three sons, and evidently had moved on with their lives without Richelle.

A royal messenger interrupted the discussion.

"There has been an uprising, Lord Pieman," said the messenger. "This letter has been sent, without rest, by way of the late king of Brunne."

"*Late king?*" said Marcus, astonished. He snatched the letter and opened it quickly.

Meanwhile, Abeland paid the man and dismissed him. Turning back, Abeland could see his father's face had paled.

"Father, what is it?" asked Abe, already guessing at the letter's content.

Marcus' voice cracked and his hand trembled. "They were… killed. This letter is from the royal messenger who witnessed the burning of their home, and the mob storming it. All of Brunne has fallen into chaos."

"Lennart…? Catherine…? The boys…?" asked Abe in disbelief. "All of them?" His father nodded mournfully at the mention of each.

Abe leaned back in his chair, and stared at the marble floor in shock. "I was there only last month. I'd gotten into an argument with Lennart about permission to let Richelle visit, or at least tell her that she had three—"

Just then, Richelle emerged from the shadows, her face a complex mix of sorrow and anger. "They didn't want me back, did they? I'm better but they have always been sick—sick in their heads. I'm so glad you saved me from them, Opa, and that you play with me, Uncle Abe. I'm happy they're dead. They were mean and evil—" she said, climbing onto her grandfather's lap, "—and I don't ever want to talk about them again."

Stepping into the room, Richelle noticed the new eyepiece Marcus was wearing.

"I like the black with gold trim of your new eye… *thing*. It's different from Uncle Abe's. What does he call it —a monocle?" said Richelle, trying to get a closer look.

"A monocle is a single-lensed spectacle. This is much more," said Marcus, looking down from his six-foot-one-inch height to Richelle's five-foot-seven.

Richelle touched the device a couple of times, carefully, remembering the first time, years ago, that she'd seen Abeland wearing one over his right eye. "Monogle, maybe?"

Marcus smiled. His granddaughter had a thing for names and style. "Whatever it is, I based this one off an old design of Abe's.

"By the way, you always manage to make clothes that bring out those beautiful, hazel eyes. The red hood is new, isn't it?"

Richelle smiled in appreciation. Under the red cloak she had pushed over her shoulders, she wore a black jacket with white strips on the arms. Her black pants flared at the feet. Marcus had seen the prototypes, and the torture-tests she put her designs through. Richelle made sure her outfits wouldn't restrict her fighting ability, and she tested the reaction that people had to her styles. She also insisted on hidden pockets for small items, just in case. Her designs were continuing to evolve, and he was proud to see it.

Raising an eyebrow, she said, "For the past year, I've been sending these red cloaks to my agents throughout the kingdoms. I'm building an Order of the Red Hoods. It's developing nicely. Some of them aren't even aware that they ultimately work for me. The goals should be obvious enough."

Marcus frowned, feigning surprise. "And so they are. For the past... *year*, you say?"

"Yes," said Richelle with a sneaky smile.

"And I had no idea?" he replied. He'd certainly known, but had figured she would tell him when she was ready.

"Do you object?" she asked, a bit sharply.

Marcus shook his head. "No. I think it's a good idea. Even Herr Klaus has built a little team... the Yellow Hoods, I think? It's important to be able to show the Tub that we have a united set of agents across the kingdoms."

"*My* agents—" Richelle corrected, with a biting smile, "who are at *your* disposal, my liege. Just like Uncle Abe has *his* agents." Every couple of months, Richelle's ambition grew. Her ability to plan where and how armies should attack was remarkable, and her skill in royal courts was equally impressive.

Marcus grimaced uncomfortably. "I assume this ties into your psychological war, the design of these new clothes?" asked Marcus, gesturing to how he was dressed. "As well as the vocabulary changes you insisted on?"

Richelle beamed. "Absolutely. For people to accept a different philosophy, they must—"

"—see, feel, and touch the new way things will be," interrupted Marcus, having repeated that mantra to her since she was little. "You've been listening."

Richelle winked. "Oh, a messenger delivered this. It's for you." She handed him a letter. "I'll see you at breakfast."

"Thanks," said Marcus, raising a finger and making Richelle pause. "One more thing. I think I'll take lunch with Madame DeBoeuf. She's been up in that tower for weeks, and I've been a horrible host. Would you mind having everything set up in the north garden, out of the view of those southern towers?"

Richelle nodded obediently. Thinking through the setup in her mind, she asked, "Do you want an overt guard contingent, so such a nice leader of the Tub can see a show of strength around the gardens, or would you like them hidden so she feels things are more... friendly?"

Marcus rubbed his forehead, trying to remember. "Have we been allowing her to walk the grounds? I've forgotten."

She winced slightly at the question. Richelle knew he had a million things on his mind, but hated any sign that he was human, had limits, or might be old. "No, we haven't. You wanted her kept up there. However, you'd ordered that we send up the guards she likes best, to have company worth talking to. We also provided her with books, and what she needed for cooking," reminded Richelle.

"Ah yes, I remember," said Marcus, stroking his chin. "Let's have the guards visible. I'll apologize, telling her that I'll do my best as things progress to see if our pretend benefactor can be more lenient, and then, slowly, we'll make it seem like she's earning our trust. Also, starting tomorrow, she may walk the grounds with the captain of the guard and a couple of soldiers. The flowers are beautiful this time of year. She loves that sort of thing."

"Of course," said Richelle, grinning. They were approaching their goals. Soon, she hoped, she'd be able to follow through with her own plans. "Hmm. You know— it would be a lot easier if we just got rid of all these people. Instead, we treat them as honored houseguests. They *are* prisoners, you realize?"

Marcus frowned, disappointed. "You sound like Abe used to. It would be *easier*, yes, in the sense that we wouldn't have to worry about things like dining arrangements, or letting them get some fresh air. In terms of everything else, it would be far more complicated. I'm surprised at you, Richelle. I would have thought you could see that by now."

"Is that all?" asked Richelle, dismissively.

"Yes, thank you," said Marcus, wandering over to the window and looking down the four stories at the majestic grounds below. "I do so love the early spring flowers—so filled with hope, opportunity, and color."

Marcus opened the sealed letter and started to read the update from the Hound.

A minute later, Marcus called out, "Richelle!" He was rubbing his stubbly chin again in thought.

Richelle ran back up and looked at her grandfather quizzically. "Yes?"

The gentler grandfather figure she'd been talking to minutes ago had been replaced with the brilliant strategist. His brown eye sparkled and his presence now filled the room.

Marcus smiled devilishly, holding the letter tightly. "It seems we have an unexpected opportunity. The Hound has been offered a deal—by another leader of the Tub." He flicked the letter on the back of his right hand, making a snapping sound. "Apparently, the Hound is one to take initiative. He followed up on some rumors and met up with the Tub leader at an inn called The Pointy Stick."

Richelle shook her head. "Who names an inn that?" She wasn't interested in the possibility of any deal, but was very keen to know they were on the heels of a second leader of the Tub.

Marcus laughed. "Well, The Pointy Stick may be our new favorite spot in Freland. The Hound needs to know what I think about the opportunity. I'll come up with something on the way. I think that, merely by having discussed such a prospect, the Tub must be a lot weaker than we'd thought. This accelerates things."

"With whom is the proposed deal?" asked Richelle, intensely curious.

Marcus grinned, folding the letter and putting it in his breast pocket. "Prepare a coach. It seems I'm heading all the way to Minette immediately after my exercises and a quick breakfast."

Richelle didn't like that he wouldn't share the

information, but she knew why. She would do the same, in his shoes. "Fine, but I'm coming with you," she said firmly. "It could be a trap."

Marcus thought for a moment. He'd wanted to have her here, to lead, but she had a point. She was one of his best warriors, and she had agents in the area—which could prove useful. Even though he didn't completely trust her motivations, it was a sound idea.

"Fine. On our way, we can discuss how we want to handle this," said Marcus, tapping his breast pocket.

Turning to go but then turning back, Richelle asked, "Should I inform Simon?"

Marcus winced and held on to the battlefield table, in thought. He looked about the room, in silence. "Blast, you have a good point. We have too many games in play. We must simplify."

Richelle giggled. "Why do things related to Simon always get complicated? Mister Stimple makes things so difficult."

Marcus rolled his eyes and sighed. Simon *had* always been one to make things needlessly difficult. "You know, he's gone by the last name of St. Malo for more than a decade now," he reminded Richelle for the millionth time.

She scoffed. "You can call a rose a rock, but it doesn't make it so."

"No, but it would reduce its value," quipped Marcus.

Laughing, Richelle proposed an idea. "I'll prepare a

letter on your behalf that will, *accidentally*, go by slow messenger to Simon. He should get it when you are already in Minette."

Marcus smiled. "Excellent. Now, I must pack."

CHAPTER SEVENTEEN

INITIATION

It was late March by the time the Yellow Hoods decided to bring Mounira up to see the treehouse. Tee, Elly, and Richy hadn't been up themselves since early December, having focused instead on helping Mounira deal with her recovery, and helping locals in need. This was the first time they'd taken Mounira out on their sail-carts on anything seeming like official Yellow Hoods business.

"So, how does this work, exactly?" asked Mounira, pointing at the wooden handlebar, pulley, and rope system that would lead up the mountain to the treehouse.

Richy stepped forward, his bright blue eyes shining in the late morning sun. "Well, this is the mechanism for going up the mountain. You hold on to the wooden bar with both hands, and then kick this lever here at the bottom of the tree. The weights start to come down, and you're pulled up. In summer, you can kind of run and jump up the mountain—it's a lot of fun. It's almost like flying. Coming down the mountain, you glide about ten feet above the ground."

"Oh, neat," said Mounira. She eyed the bar. "*Both*

hands?" she said, looking back to Richy.

"Um," he said, embarrassed.

"Don't worry. You'll be fine," said Elly, hiding a smile.

Mounira had been spending a lot of time at Tee's house, with Tee one-on-one, and with Tee's parents. More than once, Tee had dropped by Elly's house with Mounira and found Elly to be in a foul mood. Today, though, things seemed to be different.

Tee pointed to the weights. "The coolest part is that after you've gone up, or come down, the system resets itself. It takes about a minute or two."

"Huh," said Mounira, looking at the well-hidden metal foot pedal. "So the pedal releases... *oh*, I see it. Clever. Did you guys make this?"

Richy scratched his head. "Actually, we don't know who made it. We thought maybe Tee's grandfather did, but too many things didn't add up. The only thing we know is that somebody's supporting us in being the Yellow Hoods. They made these cloaks, and our shock-sticks, too."

"Interesting," said Mounira, shaking her head in disbelief. "So, you blindly trust these things from someone you don't know, who is spying on you? Huh. I wouldn't."

Everyone was silent. Tee, Elly, and Richy hadn't really thought about it in quite a while. They'd discovered everything before they'd encountered LeLoup, and they'd taken it for granted that everything was innocent and well-meaning. They were kids who'd discovered treasure. Now, though, Mounira had a point.

Mounira had a habit of asking a ton of sharp questions. The others weren't sure if it was a cultural difference, or something else, but it was hard to take sometimes. Maybe, they thought, she was just trying to fit in too hard, or maybe she felt a bit insecure because she was a couple of years younger than them.

"Well, ah, moving on," said Richy, "we discovered—well, Tee discovered—the up-the-mountain and down-the-mountain network of pulleys and ropes a while ago. There are five going up, and four going down."

"What does that mean?" asked Mounira. "*Five* going up?"

Elly sighed and raised her hand, volunteering for the taxing job of answering yet another question. "Each one takes you up part-way. See that area up there? It's a plateau. This part takes you up to that flat part of the mountain, and then stops. The next one is only a couple of yards away from where this one drops you off. There's also one a couple of yards the other way, for coming back down."

Mounira nodded, having imagined a mental model of how this likely worked. "So, it's probably done like that so you wouldn't slide all the way back down if something went wrong—or else slide all the way down the mountain too fast...?"

"Um," said Richy, scratching his head and smiling, "I

hadn't thought about that. It makes sense, though."

"One more question," said Mounira, tapping her chin as she gazed up the mountain.

"Go ahead," said Tee, trying not to sound tired of the non-stop questions.

Mounira crouched down and placed her hand on the remaining inches of snow. "Have you tried wearing skis to go up the mountain, while holding the wooden bar?"

Richy was ready to answer just about any question—except that one. His mouth agape, he stopped and looked to Elly and Tee. They were all impressed with the idea.

Elly answered. "Actually, no. Had we thought about that, we could've tried going up weeks ago. Honestly, we've only tried to let it drag us up through the snow, but that has... problems, so we waited for the snow to mostly melt. With skis though, I think we really *could* ride on top of the snow. I don't know why we didn't think of that."

Richy chuckled. "I think it's too much fun being dragged up and nearly falling off. But, if we had another LeLoup situation, I'd be all for using some skis."

"You know," said Tee, "that makes me think of using a board with wheels on it, in summertime."

"I was thinking the same," said Mounira. "The weights would be able to pull you faster, like a current pushing you in a stream."

"Huh," said Tee, looking at Mounira differently. "Your dad isn't an inventor, is he?"

"No," said Mounira. "Nobody in my family is."

Tee folded her arms. "Did you learn about science from anyone, or from books?"

"No," answered Mounira, shrugging her shoulders. "It's just—I don't know… hanging around you guys, I'm seeing things I never noticed before."

"Oh," said Tee. She remembered her granddad, Sam Baker, telling her once that, while there were geniuses like Nikolas, there were plenty of other kinds, too. Tee wasn't sure Mounira was a genius, but she had definitely underestimated her young friend.

"I wonder… if you made the wheels—" started Mounira.

Richy snapped his fingers and completed her thought, "—shallow enough, then you could have wheels and skis on the same board?"

"Yes!" said Mounira.

"Hmm," said Richy, bending down to look at the sail-carts for a moment. "It wouldn't work for the sail-carts, though. The wheels and skis would need to be on opposite sides; otherwise, uneven terrain could cause the sail-cart to get stuck."

"I've got some paper and a quill," said Elly, removing her backpack. "But I don't have any ink."

Mounira jumped up, excited. "I have some ashes! In my pack!" She grabbed at the leather satchel she had on her belt.

"You have *what*?" asked Elly. Richy and Tee were curious, too.

"Ashes," said Mounira. "Where I come from, we use ash for lots of different things. Sometimes, for writing. We just need to melt some of the snow for water, and mix it carefully."

"Cool," said Richy, picking up some snow. "I'll make water."

"Great!" said Elly, reaching into her backpack.

"Wait!" yelled Tee, her hands outstretched, and getting everyone's attention.

"Is this a *La la* moment—because I'm not seeing it," said Richy wryly, teasing Tee.

Tee gave him a friendly glare. "No. Don't you think this would make more sense to do at the *top* of the mountain, at our three-floor *treehouse*, where we have a *table*? Not here in the snow?"

Elly, Richy, and Mounira each wore their own version of a boy-do-I-feel-silly expression.

"I don't hear any yeses!" said Tee, stepping forward, playing up her role. "You know, times like this remind me of when I was young—"

Elly immediately threw her hands up. "Stop! I surrender. I give in. Please!" she joked. "Please—stop impersonating my mother!" Elly fell to her knees and then dramatically flopped over in the snow. "*Can't. Take. It.* Losing my will to live! Mommy?"

For minutes, everyone roared in laughter. It was rare that Elly did anything that silly, and only with people she completely trusted.

After a few more minutes of joking around, Richy grabbed the wooden bar and headed up first. He dashed and jumped his way up to the plateau.

Mounira was to go next. She grabbed the handlebar with her one hand and looked nervously at Tee and Elly. She wasn't quite sure how—or if—this was going to work, but she was determined to have no special treatment.

"Are you sure we shouldn't tie you to it, or something?" asked Elly, innocently.

"I'll be fine," said Mounira, uncertain. "I can do anything you can do."

Tee wasn't convinced, but wasn't going to play a big-sister card to overrule Mounira. "Okay, well, worst case, you'll come barreling back down as a huge, angry snowball. We'll *probably* be able to stop you from rolling all the way down the mountain," she said.

"Yeah, *probably*," added Elly. "Ready?" Elly asked Mounira, and then immediately kicked the foot pedal.

"*Aaahhh!*" yelled Mounira as she held on for all she was worth, running up at first, and then snowplowing and spinning the rest of the way up to the plateau.

"Huh! And here I thought you'd accepted her," said

Tee, giggling.

"No," said Elly, smiling evilly. "But I'm not jealous anymore."

CHAPTER EIGHTEEN

A GINGER OFFER

"Mother, we have returned," said Hans while opening the old wooden door, nearly taking it off its hinges. The once-majestic two-story home had long ago fallen into horrible disrepair.

Saul sighed and dropped his head. His shoulder-length, light brown hair briefly covered his face. "I bet the wood's rotted through. *Everything* is." Coming home always drained him.

They only seemed to notice what the house was really like whenever they returned to it. The smell of ginger lingered from years gone by, back from when Mother used to bake regularly. They'd learned in their teens how she used to lace all the goodies with *the Ginger*, a special mix of herbs to make children docile, passive, and even forgetful. Mother had told them she'd never used it on them.

Gretel took their red hooded cloaks and hung them up. She removed thin strips of leather from her hair and shook loose her mid-back-length platinum blond hair. She tucked the thin strips into a small pouch on her belt.

She looked at the fine cloaks that they had been given just months before. A long time ago, they'd had nice things. It was comforting to have something nice again. They wore those cloaks every time they left the house, like a uniform.

"What was the name of that man who gave us the red cloaks?" Gretel asked Hans.

Hans was standing in the kitchen, his light brown eyes scanning the mostly empty cupboards for something —anything—to eat. "The one who hired us to clean out that shop? I can't remember."

"Yeah, that one," she replied.

"Thomas something, I think. Why?" he asked, turning to her.

"I was just thinking about the cloaks. He said they would help him remember us, and that we could trust other people with the same ones. Something still bothers me about that. I don't feel like we got the whole story," said Gretel.

"You worry too much," said Saul, hiding his own concern.

"I'm sure we'll find out, some day," said Hans, "but until that happens, I don't care. That cloak stopped a knife from going into my gut last week. I'm thankful to have it."

Gretel smiled in agreement. The cloaks were not only nice-looking, but they had useful hidden pockets, and they'd discovered by accident the fabric was tough enough to stop a knife. Gretel wondered if it could stop an arrow, or maybe even a bullet.

She found herself looking at the moldy ceiling, and getting angry. She detested the house, but her brothers wouldn't leave, and she felt she couldn't just leave on her own. More than the house, she hated the nightmares that always seemed to take place somewhere in the house— nightmares that never made sense. She loathed Mother with a fury she kept tightly locked away, deep inside. She pushed those feelings so far down that sometimes she forgot about them.

Years ago, the house had been filled with a never-ending stream of children. While they weren't always happy, at times there was happiness. They would play outside, or on the main floor, and then Mother would put them to bed, upstairs, locking them in, safe and sound.

Slowly over the years, Mother's mind had decayed. It was her forceful insistence that stopped them from fixing things such as the leaking roof, eventually forcing them to seal off the mold-ridden upper floor.

"Why were you gone so long?" screeched a nasty old woman coming out of one of the ground-floor bedrooms. Her hair was wispy white, and her clothes, like those of Hans, Saul, and Gretel, were dirty and falling apart. She wore a beige shawl over her shoulders that was more brown-orange than beige. She held a gnarled cane, as she had for decades.

The old woman plopped herself into a broken rocking

chair that barely moved, although she moved her body back and forth as if it did. "Tell me! Why were you gone so long?"

Hans, his back to her, answered. "We ran into some people, Mother. We decided to have some fun. We weren't long. And anyway, you always say that."

"Don't talk to me like that!" the old woman barked. Her eyes darted around the room, as if she were seeing imaginary children running around. She pulled her shawl tightly around herself. "Tell them to close the door," she muttered. "They're always leaving the door open."

Hans closed the cupboards, giving up on the idea that there was anything to eat, and turned to Mother. Looking at Mother terrified him. He was willing to pounce on three or four travelers to rob them, or simply for fun, but Mother always made his gaze bend to the floor—made him like a scared, little boy.

Saul sat on the floor, arms wrapped around his legs, leaning against a wall. His stomach always turned when he took in that permanent smell of ginger and mold.

"Saul?" said Hans.

He looked up and realized that Hans was trying to get him to answer Mother. "Huh? Oh, yes. Those people just needed some help with their wares. They had too many nice things, and we helped them by taking some," said Saul flatly. He hadn't enjoyed it. He hadn't enjoyed much of anything in a long time.

Gretel wanted to say something witty to lighten the

mood and poke fun at Saul, but she just looked past Mother's chair and out the window. The snowless ground would have flowers soon, and she liked flowers.

"Show me what you got," the old lady commanded. She rose to her feet, cane in hand.

Gretel looked at Hans nervously. He picked up the bag he'd left just outside the door and showed it to Mother.

Mother had a look, and started shaking her head. "Garbage... garbage... oh, this might fetch us something," she said. Items she thought were of no value were tossed onto the floor. "At least you didn't completely waste my time," she said, grilling Hans with her eyes.

Mother's eyes narrowed and she raised her cane. "Are you holding out on me, boy?"

Hans shook his head nervously and stared at the ground.

"Fine. I'm going back to bed. Keep quiet," said Mother as she left the room.

When Mother's door closed, Hans and Gretel sighed in relief. Saul shook his head.

"You two are getting greedy. That was a huge risk," said Saul.

Hans pointed at the bedroom door and said, "She's going to be the death of us. If we share more with her, she'll do what she's been doing—using it up, and having no food for us."

"We almost have enough saved for the three of us to leave," said Gretel.

A knock at the door surprised everyone. They stood, frozen, looking at the door.

"Are we expecting anyone?" said Hans, moving for his rapier he'd left on the kitchen table.

Saul gave an idiotic look to his brother. "Do we ever have anyone come here? Who could find this place?" He went over to Mother's bedroom door and knocked. "Mother, there's someone here. Do you want us to open the door?"

The bedroom door whipped open and the bent-over old lady glared at Saul. "No—you'll just screw it up." She hobbled over to the door, muttering under her breath. Looking at the old, rotting front door, Mother suddenly felt anxious. She thought of the last time that there had been an unexpected knock, many years ago. She turned to Gretel. "*You* open it!"

Gretel got up off the chair at the kitchen table and opened the door.

Before them was a broad man with a reddish-brown beard. He was dressed in a beige and brown leather coat that went down to his boots. The serious look on his face made it evident he wasn't there by accident.

"I'm here to see the Ginger Lady," he said gruffly.

The old woman stumbled forward clumsily. "I'm she.

Who sent you?" she asked desperately.

The man stepped in, and quickly scanned the home. "My name is the Hound. I've been sent by the Fare. They request you pay an old debt you owe."

"Hmm," said the old lady, licking her dry lips. She'd always been richly rewarded whenever someone connected to the Fare had asked something of her, and she did owe them. A decade ago, she'd been too greedy in stealing children, and would've been caught, if it weren't for the Fare's help. As a condition, she'd been forced to give up the children—and she had, except for Hans, Saul and Gretel, whom she'd hidden.

Mother stood there, shuffling back and forth. She didn't want to appear desperate, but she was. She'd been more disoriented and confused lately, and wanted to enjoy life like the old days at least once more before her time came. "What are the terms?"

The Hound noticed the three red hooded cloaks by the door and remembered what Marcus had written in his letter. He wondered if the trio knew they had been marked as part of the Order of the Red Hoods. He almost asked, but then remembered he needed to keep things simple and to the point, as Marcus had instructed.

The Hound examined the trio again. He figured they were about twenty years old. While he could see Hans and Gretel as twins, Saul seemed to be the odd one out. He stopped himself before asking anything else and got back to the script.

"They said you may have children again, once you've successfully acquired someone they want and have handed them over to me," said the Hound. The reaction on the old woman's face told him such a reward was clearly of value to her. He tried not to imagine what it meant.

"Mother?" said Hans. "You can't have children again, you're too—"

Mother repelled Hans with a glare that ripped the man's mental wounds open. He wilted before her.

"Those terms are acceptable. Now who do they want?" asked Mother, licking her lips again.

CHAPTER NINETEEN

WATT TO COME

It was a beautiful, early April morning. Nikolas, Tee, and Mounira walked up the mountain road, back toward Nikolas' house, carrying the bags they'd filled at the market. Going into town to pick up fresh goods had become a daily ritual.

Tee's family had made Mounira feel like a long-lost cousin. Wherever she accompanied them, the family would introduce her as a close family friend. So far, the only people Mounira had met whom she didn't care much for were the Cochon brothers. She was afraid of them, and despite assurances from Nikolas and others that she needn't be, she remained unconvinced.

"Look—a letter," said Mounira, pointing to an envelope tacked to Nikolas' front door.

"Oh. I wasn't expecting anything," he said, walking up the steps to free it. "I wonder if Maxwell is still stuck on how to properly vent the unneeded heat…"

"Is Maxwell the steam engine inventor?" asked Tee.

Nikolas nodded. He was about to put the letter in his pocket when he noticed something about the handwriting on the envelope. "Tee, Mounira, come here. What do you see when you look at this?"

Mounira put down the bag she was carrying and took the letter. She looked at it for a moment, and then shrugged. "I just see the directions where the letter was to be sent, and also that it was sent by an *M. Watt*, from another place."

Nikolas smiled. "Well, you should already know that there is something more to it than that. You've been with us for a while. Tee's had a couple of years of practice at this. Tee, what do *you* see?" he said, opening the door and taking in the first of the bags.

Tee put her bags down, and Mounira handed her the letter. When Nikolas came back out, Tee was about to answer, but then Nikolas noisily cleared his throat and nodded in Mounira's direction before vanishing into the house with more bags.

Tee held the letter so she and Mounira could both see it. "See the ink, here?" said Tee, pointing to the upper left corner.

"It's messy," replied Mounira, annoyed. She felt like she was being talked down to, though suspected it might just be her imagination—Tee had never talked down to her.

"The man who sent this is an inventor. My Grandpapa tells me he is a very good one. He does things on *purpose*. If you look at how he wrote his name and address, what does it tell you?" asked Tee.

Mounira thought about it. She accepted that Tee was genuinely trying to teach her. "He—" she started, hesitating. "He... wrote it, and it smudged, which means... he didn't let it dry. He wouldn't usually do that, right?"

Tee smiled. "Exactly. Plus, I'm sure Grandpapa sees that this was also delivered by a short man, with a heavy wink in his right eye, and one arm—" said Tee sarcastically. She'd stiffened upon realizing what she'd said, and looked at Mounira uncomfortably.

"What?" asked Mounira, puzzled.

"I said—" replied Tee, her face scrunched in angst. She couldn't repeat it.

"*One-armed?*" said Mounira, pretending to be horrified.

Tee nodded. "I'm sorry! I—"

"Oh my—how *could* you? You said it, didn't you?" said Mounira, starting to laugh.

"One-armed," said Tee in a squeaky voice. "I'm sorry."

Mounira gave her a frank look. "So what! Should I make a weird face if I say *two-armed*?"

It dawned on Tee that Mounira was not sensitive in the slightest. Tee had forgotten her common sense and had instead reacted like her Aunt Gwen, an expert in bad reactions and being hypersensitive.

"I look like an idiot, don't I?" said Tee.

Mounira laughed. "You said it—not me. I would never be so rude to say that, *but*... I won't *disagree* with you." She put her chin up high. Tee burst into laughter.

Nikolas returned, reclaimed the letter, and asked the girls to bring everything else to the kitchen. He sat himself down atop the steps leading to the front door, opened the letter, and then carefully read it.

"Hello? Grandpapa?" repeated Tee. Nikolas had been preoccupied with the letter.

"Oh, sorry," he said, standing up. "Tee, I need you to take this letter to your parents." He placed the letter back in the envelope and handed it to Tee. "It should have arrived three months ago. It's curious that it arrived at all."

Tee was surprised. "Do I need to take it *now*? What's so important?"

"Yes, now, please," he said, giving her a quick kiss on the forehead. "The letter tells me that my dear friend Maxwell Watt had sent his son to me with—if I understand his coded language—his finished plans for the steam engine. His son should've been here by now. He isn't. Your father is good at getting the word out to the right people. We'll need everyone looking for young Watt."

CHAPTER TWENTY
OF SPICE AND SUBSTANCE

"Captain Archambault, sir, do you have a moment?" asked the guardsman running up the downtown street in Minette. The sergeant, in his late twenties, was scrawny and out of uniform. Elsewhere, the man probably wouldn't have been permitted to serve, but Captain Archambault didn't care who applied. Rather, what mattered was whether an applicant could complete the training, and be useful.

Captain Archambault dismissed the other guardsmen around him and turned to the one approaching. "Sergeant... *Bertrand*." Gabriel had made a point of knowing each name and face that reported to him, after having been fooled, months ago, by LeLoup.

Sergeant Bertrand stopped in front of the captain, smiled, and nodded. "Yes, sir. Do you have a moment?"

"I do, if you walk with me," Gabriel said. "I haven't eaten lunch yet... Let me see what time it is." He looked up at the position of the sun. "*Two* o'clock."

The sergeant pulled out his pocket watch and flipped its silver cover open. "Sir, yes—almost two. That's impressive."

"Oh, it's a survival skill," grumbled the captain, walking toward his favorite restaurant. "Broken too many watches in my time. It's been good, though. I've come to learn the patterns of people at different times of day. I know the sounds birds make at different times of day in spring versus the fall. Telling time by what's happening around you is a lost art—almost."

The sergeant pushed back his long, dark bangs. "Oh, by the way, congratulations on your daughter's promotion, sir."

Gabriel stopped and glared at the sergeant. "I'll have you know I had nothing to do with that," he said. "The Magistrate decided, on the advice of a committee. No congratulations should be offered to me. She has done extraordinary work since she started. Whatever sentiment and compliment you care to pay, you should pay to Sergeant Archambault directly."

"But I thought—"

"That I'm her father? *Not* when I'm on duty—and, as you know, I'm on duty a lot." Gabriel started walking again, annoyed. He looked back at the sergeant, who didn't know what to say. Gabriel thought perhaps he'd been too hard on him. "Come on, Bertrand, keep up."

"Yes, sir," said the sergeant, hurrying.

Gabriel continued, "We're halfway to Guido's and

once I'm there, the only thing that will have my attention is their special of the day. Hmm… funny thing about Guido's… it's owned by a woman named Teresa. Never had a husband or anyone in her life named Guido," he mused. "Well, I'm sure you didn't come to hear me talk about this, or breaking watches. What do you want?"

"Well, sir, I was enjoying my couple of days off in Mineau when Captain Charlebois found me this morning and asked that I deliver a message to you immediately, in person."

Gabriel slowed, looking seriously at the sergeant. Gabriel hadn't spoken with his Mineau counterpart since Solstice, four months ago. They rarely spoke more than once a year, and it was never by sending a guardsman with a message. Gabriel wiggled his thick, gray mustache. "What did Matthieu say, Bertrand?"

"Sir, Captain Charlebois said you should come down, with Monsieur de Montagne, right away." He looked nervously at the captain. "Something to do with… cooking, I think. Sorry, I ran all the way from where I had the cart let me off. Oh, I—ah—had to commandeer a horse and cart."

"That's fine. Part of our job," said Gabriel. He put his hand over his scrunched up face as he tried to imagine what Matthieu could've been referring to. As it hit him, his eyes widened and his face paled. Gabriel grabbed Bertrand by the shoulder and pulled him in close.

"When you say *cooking*, might you mean an herb or

spice?" said Gabriel. He hoped he was wrong.

"Yes!" said Bertrand, snapping his fingers. "*Ginger!* Something about ginger. Sir."

Gabriel straightened himself, and smoothed his mustache. "That will be all, sergeant. Thank you."

Bertrand was confused by the sudden change in his captain's tone and body language, but nodded and left.

Gabriel, having lost his appetite, turned away from Guido's and headed back to his office. When he spotted the Yellow Hoods across the street, he paused. The three were with the new girl, Mounira, whom he'd met twice. They were acting like typical teenagers, laughing and goofing around.

When Richy met Gabriel's gaze and offered a smiling nod, Gabriel's blood chilled. He forced himself to wave back. He thought of Matthieu's message, and how what it meant tied back to Richy, some ten years ago. Gabriel was certain the boy still didn't know.

He entered the administration building. The attendant, who served only to stop people from coming to see the captain without an appointment, looked up. He had been doodling at his desk. "Take the rest of the day off," Gabriel told him. He then entered his office, and locked the door.

After carefully moving aside the bookcase where he kept his most important files, Gabriel reached into a hole in the wall and pulled out one of the notebooks he kept hidden. He carefully moved the bookcase back, situating it precisely where it had been before. Satisfied, he sat down at his desk with the old notebook.

Blowing the dust off, he slowly moved his fingers over its title: *Regarding the Ginger Lady and abducted children — Lt. G. Archambault*. The captain felt proud of certain cases in his career, especially those that had made him a better investigator and a superior guardsman.

Then, there was this one.

CHAPTER TWENTY-ONE

THE ABBOT OF COSTELLO

The boat came to a stop, and Franklin Charles David Watt looked around nervously. The foggy dock of the small town of Herve was before him.

"Off you go, lad. You didn't pay for a tour, just a trip across," said the captain of the two-crew sailboat. "We're heading further down the coast. If you changed your mind and want to come, it'll cost extra."

"No, I'm fine," said Franklin, his voice breaking with fear. Stomach in a knot, he stepped onto the dock. He'd never been to another kingdom. While the primary language in Freland was the same as in Inglea, he feared everything would feel alien. He stood and watched the departing sailboat quietly get swallowed up by the thick morning fog. He shivered under his ratty fur cloak.

It had taken him weeks to find someone willing to bring him across, but by then he didn't have enough money. He'd tried gambling, thinking his superior intellect would help at cards, but instead he lost most of his remaining money. Under a fake name, he started working at the docks. Despite being robbed twice, he finally saved enough for the crossing.

By afternoon, he felt more settled, having rented a room from a kindly, grandmother-like innkeeper. She had generously fixed him up with some warm soup, and had drawn him a rough map of the town and the path to Minette.

Franklin figured he probably still had two weeks of travel ahead, and by coach—which would be expensive. He only had two days' worth of money.

Walking around the town, Franklin got a lot of stares. His clothes were worn, torn, dirty, and out of place. When he tried talking with locals, many of them waved him away, or else flipped him a coin, thinking he was a beggar.

Franklin was frustrated. Even with *his* level of genius, things were unbelievably hard. He was scared that he was going to fail his father and prove, as his mother often said, that he wasn't as smart or as capable as he liked to believe.

He was also worried about his father, and wondered whether he had made it to Eldeshire, as planned. At one point, the weight of everything was too much, and Franklin leaned against a brick wall and slumped to the ground in despair.

"Oh, that's just perfect," he said to himself, feeling his bum was wet. "Not a puddle anywhere—except where I decide to sit. Just perfect." He hung his head in defeat.

"Hello there, young sir," said a short, plump, long-mustached man in puffy sleeves and bright stockings. He wore a black coat that went to his knees, making him look rather like a clown of distinction.

Franklin looked up at the man and rolled his eyes. "Do you live in a museum? I haven't seen anyone dressed like that, outside of paintings."

"Excuse me?" snapped the man, twirling his long, thin mustache. Franklin quickly remembered where he was, and his situation.

"Yes, sorry," he said, jumping up and quickly brushing himself off.

The man nodded repeatedly. He twirled his mustache and then said, "I am the Abbot of the nearby monastery, at Costello. We wear such attire when we leave the monastery—our tradition for more than a hundred years. Now, my rude young man, does your name happen to be *Watt*?"

"Pardon?" said Franklin, trying to understand the man's accent. It was clear the man wasn't speaking his native language.

The abbot frowned and looked around to make sure no one was listening. "I said *Watt*."

"Pardon? I don't understand your question." Franklin looked around as well, trying to understand who in the world could possibly be interested in them. He was certain that looking around, all paranoid, at people walking the streets was a suspicious thing to do.

Rubbing his double chins, the abbot said, annoyed, "No—I said *Watt*. Is your name Franklin *Watt*?"

"Well, not exactly," said Franklin. It was a point of pride for Franklin that his name was not simply Franklin, but rather Franklin Charles David Watt. He carried the names of his grandfathers, both of whom had been men of distinction back home.

"Not exactly, what?" said the abbot, at a loss as to what Franklin meant.

Apologetically, Franklin said, "No, it *is* Watt. It's just —"

"Stop it! Is your first or middle name *Franklin*, or isn't it?" growled the man, fists clenched. "This is absolutely ridiculous," he muttered.

"Yes," said Franklin, nodding.

"And is your family name *Watt*?" asked the abbot.

"Yes," said Franklin, nodding again.

"Good," said the man, relieved. He sighed and unconsciously rubbed his belly. "Well, then, I've been looking for you. If we can skip further nonsense, I'd like you to—please—come with me."

"Who sent you?" asked Franklin. It suddenly dawned on him that the men who were after the steam engine plans may have discovered that he, and not his father, had them.

"Pardon?" said the abbot, not expecting the question.

Franklin then spotted some armed guardsmen coming toward them and got a bad feeling. He started running.

He made it back to the inn, ran up the stairs, and fetched his belongings. He rifled through his backpack and pulled out a bulky, metal armband. It had a thin rope attached that led into his backpack, and a bolt tip sticking out the other end. He yanked up his right sleeve and strapped on the armband. Just then, the door burst open.

"We need you to come with us," ordered one of the three guardsmen.

"Sorry, gentlemen," said Franklin, stepping toward the open window. "I'm… oh, forget it," he said, unable to think up anything witty. Sweat beaded down his forehead as he thought about what he was about to attempt.

Pointing his right arm out the window, Franklin slapped the armband's one button. A mini-crossbow bolt shot across toward a higher, neighboring building and the attached cable whistled as it came out of his backpack. With a satisfying *thunk*, the bolt embedded itself. Franklin hit the armband's button again. Immediately, the cable started to retract, pulling him out the window and toward the anchored bolt.

"What the devil was that?" said one of the guardsmen.

"Trouble—that's what."

CHAPTER TWENTY-TWO
CLUTCHES OF THE GINGER LADY

Ten years ago, Gabriel Archambault had been asked to work, temporarily, with his Mineau counterpart, Lieutenant Matthieu Charlebois. The magistrates of both cities had wanted their future captains to start building a strong working relationship. While Gabriel and Matthieu had met before, they'd never worked together. Each was to spend three months in the other's town, as a partner. Unfortunately, their first collaboration resulted in the initiative being cut short, as neither wanted to be reminded of the experience—or each other—for a while.

Every morning, even before the roosters would crow, Gabriel would awake and get himself ready. He'd kiss his sleeping wife and his nine-year-old daughter, and then hitch a ride to Mineau with one of the merchants heading down for the day. In the evening, he'd hitch another ride back, and enjoy the summer sunset.

By the time Gabriel would arrive in Mineau each morning, Matthieu would already be at the Deuxième

Chance café, where fresh coffee and pastries were waiting for Gabriel.

The fourth morning, after they'd chatted a bit, Gabriel proposed an idea.

"Matthieu, I'd like to get to know your town better. Over the past days, we've been glued together. Do you mind if I walk around town alone today?" He sipped his coffee and smiled. No one made coffee like the owners of Deuxième Chance.

Matthieu stroked his goatee. "Actually, I was going to say that I've got to spend most of the day dealing with paperwork. So, yes, I think that's a splendid idea."

A while later, Gabriel walked the busy streets of Mineau. He'd visited Mineau before, as a tourist, but this time he was on duty.

He noticed one nervous-looking man leaving and entering several stores suspiciously. Gabriel monitored him, up until the man found what he'd been looking for —his lost cat. He spotted a boy bumping into people deliberately, and caught him in the act of pickpocketing.

After a peaceful lunch with a couple of guardsmen, he took a walk on the eastern edge of town. The archways that defined the official entrance and exit matched those of Minette, though Mineau's were older, and larger.

While at the town's edge, he noticed a panic-stricken woman. After watching her pace back and forth, he deduced that something so profound had happened that her mind must've been caught in a loop. He straightened his uniform and approached.

"Mademoiselle, my name is Lieutenant Archambault. I work with Lieutenant Charlebois. I notice you seem distressed. May I offer some assistance?"

The woman pulled her black shawl around tightly. Her bonnet-covered head looked in all directions, until she finally made eye contact. Gabriel's big, warm eyes and his large, dark brown mustache gave her something to focus on. Her face was pale and tear-streaked.

"I—I—I—" she stammered.

Gabriel took the woman's hand and held it between his. She looked at their hands, and back into his eyes. His sympathetic look helped the woman calm down enough to catch her breath.

"Mademoiselle, let us start slowly. Did you *lose* something?"

She nodded.

"Did you lose it in the Red Forest, behind you?" he asked, motioning slightly with his head.

She nodded again.

Before he could ask the next question, she blurted out, "My *son!* I can't find my son! He—he was with me, and then there were voices in the forest, and they chased him away. Now I can't find him! I think somebody took him!"

At first, Gabriel thought this was a case of a boy lost in the forest, but after getting the woman to sit down and tell the complete story, he was convinced that it was something more.

Spotting a guardsman walking by, Lieutenant Archambault called him over. "Could you, please, help this poor woman look for her son for the next hour?" asked Gabriel. "If you can't find him by then, come and get me."

Late that afternoon, when Gabriel walked into Matthieu's office, neither was happy.

"Lieutenant Archambault," said Lieutenant Charlebois, irritated, "I appreciate you helping our citizens, but in Mineau, we do not take a guard off patrol duty to help a woman whose child has run to play in the forest. This happens frequently, and the child almost always returns home within an hour or two."

"Oh," said Gabriel, sitting down in Lieutenant Charlebois' office. It was several times the size of his own office back in Minette. Everything seemed bigger in Mineau. "So, the guardsman found the child, then?"

Lieutenant Charlebois was taken aback. "Ah—well… no," he replied, a little defensively.

Gabriel nodded to himself. "I was with the first woman for an hour, and only then asked your guardsman to spend an hour with her. Children get lost in Minette, too. It's rare that it's longer than twenty minutes. After that first woman, I ran into *three* other families—each claiming a child had been taken from them—*today*—one way or another."

Flattening his mustache and leaning forward,

Lieutenant Archambault looked his counterpart in the eyes. "I think we have a real problem. I don't know about Mineau, but I've never had that many children go missing in so short a period, with none of them being found by now. By the way, you'll have a couple more guardsmen come say that I re-assigned them."

"Where did these events happen?" asked Matthieu, his brow now showing real concern.

"All on the eastern edge of town, near the Red Forest. I knew Mineau was big, but hadn't realized there are three archways to the east. A child was taken at each."

"Wait a moment—" said Matthieu, leaning back. "Are you telling me that we have someone stealing *children*?"

"Yes. That is exactly what I'm saying," said Gabriel, with a grave expression.

The lieutenants then spent their next two days searching the Red Forest together. They had a dozen men with them, and yet found nothing. Worse, two more children had gone missing in the meanwhile.

On the third day, the pair decided that just the two of them would head to the Red Forest, hoping that, without the distraction of ordering around less-experienced guardsmen, they might be able to find something on their own.

As they headed out, Gabriel noticed a gruff-looking man covered in furs exiting a nearby trading shop. The man's hair and beard looked wild and unkempt.

Gabriel had an idea, and ran up to the man. "Excuse

me! I'm Lieutenant Gabriel Archambault, of Minette. This is Lieutenant Matthieu Charlebois, of Mineau. Might you be a tracker?"

The rough-looking mountain man looked at each of them in turn, each wearing a slightly different uniform. He was naturally suspicious, as he liked neither people nor authority. Yet, when he looked into Gabriel's eyes, he could see the pain and exhaustion. For the first time in a long time, he decided he would be civil.

"I know how to track things," said the man, backing up slightly and folding his arms. "My name is Pierre de Montagne. What's the matter?"

"Woohoo! I can't believe that worked," yelled Franklin as he finished scrambling onto the rooftop. Franklin waved to the guards who remained floors down, and a building over. They stared at Franklin in disbelief, through the open window of the rented room.

"That was a *lot* faster than I thought it'd be," Franklin said to himself as he detached the black cable from his armband. "I've got to thank Mister Klaus again for sending me the design for my birthday. I should've made another bolt, though, because *that* one isn't coming out."

Franklin removed the armband and put it back into his backpack. Before heading down the rooftop stairs, he sneaked a peek to see if the guards were still at the window. They weren't.

The thrill of using the armband morphed into panic.

"Okay, Franklin—they're going to come up here. All you have to do is run around a city you don't know well, lose those guys, then circle back to get the plans... assuming they haven't found them."

After descending to street level, he spotted the guards exiting the building across the street. He turned to face a street vendor selling smoked fish, and the guards ran right past him and up the stairs he'd just come down. Franklin glanced around and caught sight of the abbot, two blocks away, talking with a couple of guards.

"Quite a few people are looking for me. Can't imagine that's a good thing. The big question is," he said to himself, "do I try to get the plans now, or not?" Franklin pondered what to do. "They *could* have a guard up there waiting for me."

When Franklin had first taken the room, he'd deliberately secured the brass tube holding the steam engine plans to the bed's frame, positioned such that one couldn't see the tube just by glancing under the bed.

"Excuse me, aren't you—" said a man dressed similar to the abbot.

"Geez!" said Franklin, tearing off down the street.

"He's over here!" yelled the man, running after Franklin.

Franklin ran down every alleyway he could but eventually found himself at a dead end.

"Boy, you are making this harder than it needs to be," said a tall, thin man with an eyepatch and dark robes. He had three guardsmen with him. "You're coming with us —now!"

All of a sudden, there was a flash of red as a cloaked figure tumbled from a floor above. The figure sprang off one wall, hit a guard, landed, and sprang again. Within ten seconds, Franklin's four assailants were on the ground. The red-hooded figure stood with its back to Franklin.

"Who are you?" asked Franklin. "That was… *amazing.*"

The figure turned and pulled the hood down. Her long, braided, platinum blond hair seemed to sparkle. "You need to come with me," she said.

"Um, sure. My name's Franklin," he said, looking into her light brown eyes. She looked about twenty. Her face was quite striking.

"I've come to get you, Mister Watt." The woman peered left and right out the entrance to the dead-end alley, then turned to him. "Come," she said, offering a hand. "We have to get going. By the way, if you think that was good, you should see me with a bow."

Franklin stepped over the moaning men and took the woman's outstretched hand.

"What's your name?" he asked.

"Gretel."

Gabriel knocked on the open door of Captain Charlebois' office. Both captains wore the same grave look.

"It's good to see you, Captain Archambault," said Matthieu, with heaviness in his voice. He slowly got out of his chair and walked around the desk to shake hands with his Minette counterpart. "And, Monsieur de Montagne, also a pleasure," said Matthieu, shaking Pierre's hand.

"I wish it were for better reasons," said Pierre.

"As do I," said Matthieu. "I am, however, pleased that Captain Archambault could get hold of you so quickly. I thought that would present a challenge."

Pierre shook his head. "My life's changed recently, and for the better. I'm in the city more often these days."

Matthieu motioned to the two chairs in front of his desk. "Please, sit," he said, circling back around to his own chair.

Gabriel noticed Matthieu's desk was covered with old notes from the Ginger Lady case.

After making themselves comfortable, Gabriel spoke first. "It's been ten years, Matthieu. What makes you think the Ginger Lady has returned?"

Captain Charlebois sighed. "I wanted to tell myself it was just one child that had gone missing. That happens all the time, right?"

Gabriel leaned forward, elbows on his knees and hands clasped together. "I assume, like in Minette, this doesn't happen much anymore. People are wiser, and have taught their children better."

Matthieu sighed again. "Yes, exactly. I haven't had a claim of a lost child—at least not one missing for more than a couple of hours—in some years." He took a sip of his lukewarm tea. "When the first report came in, I immediately thought back to that horrible house."

Gabriel shuddered. "All those children, dazed and confused. The horrible smell of ginger and filth... overwhelming. I remember," he said.

Captain Charlebois leaned back. "It bothered me, there being no one in charge there, and how that three-year-old boy was the only one who could tell us anything about the Ginger Lady. I was certain she must have a second house somewhere in the forest, and that somebody warned her we were coming. It felt staged."

"I thought so, too," said Gabriel. "But we couldn't find anything... and then I returned to my duties in Minette."

"Actually, I have a confession to make," said Matthieu, now leaning forward, his head slightly hung. "I lied when I told you that we wrapped up the investigation, that day that I sent you home to Minette. I continued searching for that other house for almost two years. It cost me my marriage, and almost my job."

Gabriel looked at Matthieu and understood. What they'd seen that day in that house had deeply disturbed them both.

Matthieu looked up with a half-smile. "That brave

little boy... he was something! He looked like the people from over the eastern mountains. What was his name?"

"Richy," said Gabriel.

"Whatever happened to him?" said Matthieu. "I didn't want to ask, before."

Pierre looked in surprise at Gabriel. "Wait—*Richy* from the Yellow Hoods?"

Gabriel nodded and leaned back in his chair, folding his arms on his chest. "Matthieu and I knew we'd have to surrender all of the children to the Magistrate of Mineau, but we just couldn't let that happen to our brave little soldier."

"I'd forgotten we'd called him that!" said Matthieu. "Our brave little soldier, indeed."

Gabriel smiled sadly. "Pierre, after you left, we managed to get Richy to talk. That brave little three-year-old told us everything that happened, from his perspective. His speech was still slurred from the Ginger, and his memory full of holes, but you could see he was standing up for all the other kids, even if they were older. He got frustrated at his limited vocabulary. He was remarkable.

"We agreed we couldn't turn him over to have an unknown fate. So, Matthieu and I arranged things so that I could sneak back to Minette with the boy. The Magistrate never knew he existed. We didn't include him in the report—he was a ghost.

"I wasn't sure what I was going to do with the boy as

I arrived in Minette—and then I ran into Jennifer Klaus. She said she could see a story in my eyes, and asked me to tell her everything. And I did."

Standing to stretch his legs, Gabriel briefly paced the room before continuing. "The couple Jennifer found had just moved to Minette, or else had stopped for a visit—I can't remember, exactly. Jennifer convinced them to adopt Richy. She told them his name was Aldrich, but they always called him Richy. They couldn't say the name right; imagine Jennifer's frustration! Ha—they almost didn't want to adopt him because of the name Jennifer had given him. The couple was curious at first about his slightly different look, yet became captivated by his deep blue, almond-shaped eyes, and finally agreed to give Richy a home."

Pierre couldn't believe it. "I've been working with Richy these past months, and I never thought for a moment he was the same boy. Does he know?"

Gabriel stood behind his chair and leaned on it. "No, but I couldn't handle it anymore, seeing you with him, and seeing him around and helping people as a Yellow Hood. I was proud of him, but I feared what would happen if he learned the truth in the *wrong* way. So, I approached his parents a couple of months ago, before his thirteenth birthday. They listened, yet ignored my advice. Something big was going on between them, preoccupying them. Anyway, I can hardly look at the boy these days. I tend to talk to the girls and glance over him."

There was a heavy pause.

"So," said Gabriel, straightening up, "enough about the past and other distractions. Matthieu—you suspect the Ginger Lady is back. Were there any clues this time? Anything?"

Matthieu looked up from his notes and smiled. "There was a witness to one of the kidnappings. Apparently, there were three kidnappers, and they were wearing red hooded cloaks."

CHAPTER TWENTY-THREE

ESCAPING THE GINGER

"Watt's your name again?" said Hans, mocking Franklin. Hans replaced the gag over Franklin's mouth and shoved him, again, into the dank, dark closet where they'd been keeping him prisoner. "You really should've eaten breakfast. You're looking weak. Mother's going to notice you're not eating, and she'll be angry. Trust me—she doesn't like her children thin."

Hans shut the closet door and leaned against it. He'd taken responsibility for hauling Franklin out for meals and to relieve himself, and for getting him back in the closet. Hans didn't trust Gretel or Saul to get the job done, given what was at stake. Those two had been acting weird lately, and he didn't like it.

Saul looked at Hans leaning against the closet door. He could see that Hans enjoyed the cruelty. He wondered why he didn't enjoy it anymore. Maybe it was because things had become more and more violent. They'd gone from tricking people, to bullying them, to hurting them, to nearly killing them. It weighed on him.

Saul returned to the main room and looked at Mother. She pretended to enjoy herself, with the four children running around her, but she kept getting confused and frustrated. She tried to hum a tune to calm herself, which reminded Saul of when he was little. The tune was familiar, but quickly changed from being soothing to making his skin crawl.

Mother was angrily mixing another batch of her concoction, to slip into bread and cookies. "They'll have some Ginger, soon," she kept saying to herself, "and then they'll be quiet."

"You know, Mother—" started Saul.

Just then, to his surprise, Gretel grabbed him by the arm and took him outside.

"I know that voice, Saul," she said. "*Don't.*"

Saul pulled his arm free. "What are you talking about? You don't know what I was going to say." He seemed to be looking everywhere except at Gretel.

"You were going to tell Mother that she wasn't supposed to have us snatch those kids until *after* the Hound retrieves the Watt kid. Right?"

Saul glared at her. He'd been trying not to say anything for days, but couldn't hold it. He was afraid Mother might kill those kids, but worse, he was afraid of crossing the Hound. As soon as Gretel had returned with Franklin, Mother had sent them out to get her one child. Not satisfied, she wanted just one more. Then, the "final" one… and, then, another "final" fourth.

"You know, when I see her making that stuff, her *Ginger*, I panic inside. This is *wrong*. We shouldn't be doing this. We should… we should take those kids back."

Gretel rubbed Saul's upper arms. "Hey—you're just feeling a bit down. Sure, Mother's been a pain lately, but things are about to get better—I know it. I'm sure we'll be having fun soon, and we'll forget about this. Okay? Mother might be going crazy, but she's still… Mother," said Gretel softly.

Saul nodded, but just before Gretel was going to leave, asked, "Gretel, can you remember anything from when we were little? Anything specific before age five, or even seven? I keep trying, but I can't."

Gretel bowed her head. She didn't look at him as she answered, sadly, "Not now, Saul. I don't like to remember things."

Just then, Hans came out, shoving Franklin around again. Spotting Gretel and Saul, he said, "Hey, know *Watt* happened? Says he has to go to the bathroom… again! Apparently, Mother's gruel doesn't agree with him. Says he doesn't like the taste of ginger! Nonsense. But we can't have him making that house smell any worse. Ugh."

Gretel and Saul went inside to help with the children, and Gretel convinced Mother that the children didn't need another dose of Ginger.

Franklin wasn't sure how many days he'd been prisoner, but after feeling woozy the first two days, he started being careful with what he ate or drank. He felt low on energy now, but more clear-headed.

"Allow a boy some privacy, will you?" asked Franklin, pretending to sound groggy, and playing down his age. He kept his hands tightly together, to hide the fact that he'd unknotted his ropes.

When Hans removed the ropes around Franklin's feet, Franklin kicked him in the groin.

"Ugh!" yelled Hans as he doubled over in pain.

"Oh, goodness, it worked!" yelled Franklin, hopping around joyfully. "What to do? Right—run!"

Franklin dashed ten yards before briefly stopping. He looked back at the old, decrepit house and thought about the children inside. Leaving them didn't feel right. "I'll get help, and come back for them—that's the only thing that makes sense," he said, convincing himself. He started running again, with every ounce of remaining energy.

When the front door opened, Gretel and Saul saw Hans still hunched over. They could guess what had happened.

Saul grabbed his cloak and staff, and Gretel her cloak, bow, and quiver.

CHAPTER TWENTY-FOUR
THE CANOPY TRAIL

"That's a good find, Richy," said Pierre, looking at the patch of soft earth where Richy thought he could make out a recent footprint. "What jumps out at you?"

Richy pointed to the heel. "It looks heavy—here, and here. Maybe they were carrying something heavy, like a kid?"

"Maybe," said Pierre. "You have an amazing eye, Richy. Amazing." He looked back to the two captains and the guardsmen tending to the horses and sail-carts. "Captains! We found a possible footprint."

"Let me guess—a lone print again, isn't it?" said Matthieu, shaking his head. "Either these kidnappers are a hundred feet tall, with tiny feet, or you aren't able to track them."

Captain Charlebois didn't like the idea of calling in some kids to help, but Captain Archambault had convinced him to include them. Matthieu questioned the wisdom of having Richy involved, given his past. He was uncomfortable talking to Richy—he only nodded to him, or talked indirectly to him by way of Pierre.

"One thing is clear, Captains," said Pierre, looking around. "Someone trained these people. They know how to avoid leaving tracks. If this is the same Ginger Lady, maybe someone trained her kids."

Over the past three hours, Pierre and the Yellow Hoods had discovered only subtle clues that they might be going in the right direction. It felt like one guess followed by another.

Tee looked around at the thickly clustered trees. It had been a challenge to pilot the sail-carts through other than single file. She looked up at the thick forest canopy. "You know, Elly," she said, "something feels funny. We *know* they were around here. How would we get around, without people seeing *our* footprints?"

"You *think* they were around here," corrected Matthieu, visibly frustrated.

Elly walked around in silent thought for a moment. "Well… we might use our sail-carts, but it's spring, and they'd either leave tracks in the mud, or get stuck if we weren't careful."

Richy felt the soft ground. "We might make the tires thicker, or of softer stuff—but there would still be some clear trace."

"Right," said Tee, trying to imagine what they were missing.

"Hmm—what if they traveled on the ground as if it was snow—you know, like a lynx?" suggested Richy, looking at Elly. "Hey Pierre, is there a way to walk on the ground with snowshoe-type things that don't leave tracks? Like a lynx would on snow, but better."

Pierre stiffened at the word *lynx*, briefly flashing back to his narrowly escaped fate and the debt he owed the Yellow Hoods. "Not that I've seen, no. Mind you, someone like Monsieur Klaus might come up with something like that. They would be great shoes, if he could."

Matthieu looked at Gabriel. "Really? Impossible machines? *That's* what they're contemplating?"

Gabriel motioned for Matthieu to calm down. "Wait—you'll see. If you know Monsieur Klaus, the Yellow Hoods are sometimes like mini versions. They *will* see something that we don't."

Matthieu grumbled. "I have more faith in my five guardsmen. Yes, Richy found a footprint—*one* footprint. Everything else *we've* found, and, sadly, that isn't much. I think we should send these kids home—with their strange sailing land ships, or whatever you call them."

Tee wiggled her lips in thought. "Not leaving tracks would be easier if they just didn't walk on the ground. Eliminates the problem, altogether."

Matthieu stormed over to Tee. "Okay. And just *how* would they get around... fly?"

"Don't be silly. People can't fly," said Tee. "But, they could use long poles, or stilts—I don't know. There's a way, though."

Matthieu was taken aback by how Tee spoke to him.

She'd parried his frustration and talked to him like a peer, not a superior. He was about to yell at her to show some respect, but was interrupted.

"I've got it!" yelled Elly. She jumped up and down excitedly and tapped a tree.

Captain Charlebois frowned. "What, a tree? Seriously? Gabriel, I'm done—"

"*Look,*" said Elly, pointing at the tree's trunk. Then, right before their eyes, Elly climbed twenty feet up the tree, as if she were using a ladder. She disappeared into the forest canopy.

Matthieu was stunned.

"Oh, cool!" said Richy. He and Tee climbed up after Elly.

It took a moment for everyone else to see. Carved carefully into the trunk of the tree was a well-worn ladder. It had been gently carved into the tree, and then painted to make it blend in.

Captain Archambault walked over to his counterpart and slapped him on the shoulder. "Care to reconsider your opinion of these kids?" he asked, smiling proudly.

Matthieu turned to one of his men who stood about twenty feet away. "Hey, what do you see when you look at this tree from over there?"

The guardsman looked at the tree and shrugged. "Just a tree, sir."

"A tree, indeed," said Matthieu, grinning from ear to

ear. "Brilliant! Captain Archambault, I'm enough of a man to admit I was wrong, and I love it when I'm wrong like this. So! We're dealing with someone very smart."

Pierre ran his fingers over part of the carved-in ladder. "Those we're looking for might not be the ones who made this. This is old—I'd say more than thirty years, judging by the tree growth."

Gabriel stroked his mustache. "Maybe the Ginger Lady made it a long time ago? Or, more likely—"

"She simply knows about it," said Matthieu. "Perhaps the Ginger Lady has allies, and they told her about this, or built it for her. Perhaps this woman is tied to something bigger."

Captain Archambault looked around and wondered. "What if the bigger thing isn't around anymore? What if she's doing this on her own? Maybe she needs the money, or something else?"

Tee climbed down. "You won't believe what we found," she said. Looking up, she called, "Okay, pull it!"

There was a silent second after Elly and Richy pulled a rusty lever hidden up in the tree's canopy, but then came the sound of gears moving, and leaves rustling. Through the leaves, they could make out some metal parts moving across the canopy. It almost looked like a wave that passed from the tree Elly and Richy were in, over to a tree twenty feet away.

Everything went silent again. Pierre, Gabriel, and the guardsmen looked at the canopy, unsure there was anything different.

Captain Charlebois squinted, and pointed carefully. "Fascinating. At first, it looks all the same, but look, carefully, for the brass and silver colors... Some kind of platform?"

"You're right, Captain," said Tee. "It's a metal bridge that extends through the canopy. I'm guessing these zigzag through the forest in places, from large tree to large tree, and the reason we see the odd footprint is because these bridges aren't all close enough together."

Richy climbed partway down. "Tee, come up and see this," he said. "This thing has weights and stuff that remind me a lot of the treehouse mountain pulleys. Definitely older, though."

"Wait—before you go, tell me again what I'm looking at, Tee? I don't understand how this is possible," said Captain Archambault.

"Someone talented like my grandfather made this. We know of something else similar, but newer. Whoever designed or built this must have taught others."

"Wait, Tee—another question," said Gabriel.

"Sure," said Tee, containing her excitement.

"Could someone use this to—?"

Just then came the sound of the gears going again, and the leaves rustling. The wave that had extended out now moved in the opposite direction. After the sound stopped, no hint of shiny metal showed through the canopy.

"Guys! What happened?" yelled Tee.

Elly replied, "It retracted on its own! Richy... what's that? Hang on... Richy thinks it must have a timer of some kind, once there's no weight on the bridge. This is more sophisticated than we thought."

"Captain, were you going to ask—" said Tee.

Gabriel waved his question away. "Never mind. Go."

Captain Charlebois turned to Gabriel. "Bridges that disappear... hmm. The trees with the contraption are surrounded by red pines, so even in winter, it would seem invisible from the ground. And the ladder— invisible any time of year."

"People could be using this for all sorts of things," said Gabriel, amazed, "and right under our noses."

Pierre thought back to Solstice, and asked Gabriel, "Could these have been used to chase Mounira into the forest without leaving a trace?"

Tee briefly stopped her climb, having overheard Pierre's question. "Actually, Pierre, that makes sense. Maybe those same Red Hoods are the ones who took the children."

Captain Archambault sighed and turned to his colleague. "While you were away during Solstice, there was an incident. I don't know if you were briefed—so let me tell you about it. I'd forgotten until now."

As Tee climbed up the tree, she thought of Mounira,

who was spending the day with Tee's mom, doing some mother-daughter "girly" type things. Tee didn't mind, as she knew Mounira must be missing her own mom terribly. If anything, it was a relief for both Tee and her mom, as doing "girly" things was not something Tee usually enjoyed.

Suddenly, from a little further into the forest, came the sound of gears turning, and a bridge extending, followed by the sound of someone running over the metal bridge.

Tee, confused, looked at Richy and Elly.

"That's not us," said Elly.

Down below, Pierre yelled, "Hey, someone's coming!"

"Help me!" yelled a teenage boy. He ran toward the captains and guardsmen as fast as he could. "Whoever you are, help me!"

"Men, defend the boy!" ordered Captain Charlebois, unsheathing his sword and charging forward.

Tee pulled the lever to extend their tree-bridge while her friends pulled out their shock-sticks and started cranking the handles.

Pierre ran to the teenage boy, who promptly fell into Pierre's arms. The boy was exhausted. The captains and the guardsmen took up positions surrounding the two. Each guardsman had his sword drawn, and his other hand ready to draw his pistol.

"What's your name?" Pierre asked the boy.

"My name... is Franklin... Charles... David... Watt,"

whispered Franklin, almost out of breath. "I was held… prisoner."

"What was that?" yelled Captain Archambault over his shoulder.

"The boy says his name is Watt," said Pierre. He scooped up the boy, looked around, and wondered what was next.

"Watt!" yelled the Yellow Hoods, looking at each other.

Tee yelled down to the captains, "We've been looking for him! Watt!"

Captain Archambault looked at his counterpart. "The Solstice attack on Mounira, kidnapping children, and now this Watt boy? I suspect it's the same group."

"Agreed," said Captain Charlebois.

Just then, a tall red-hooded figure in black leather boots appeared at the other end of the tree-bridge.

"Looks like Watt was running for a reason," said Elly, twirling her shock-sticks and then charging forward.

Richy did a double take. "You're acting like Tee!" said Richy, running right up behind Elly.

"What can I say—she's a bad influence!" said Elly, switching to a battle cry as the red-hooded figure ran toward them.

Tee pulled out her slingshot and a couple of stones.

"This is going to be awkward—I didn't think this through," said Richy, realizing the narrow tree-bridge constrained them to a single file.

"Richy, no shocking me!" ordered Elly, stopping at the mid-point of the tree-bridge and waiting for their opponent.

The red-hooded figure pulled back his hood, revealing his light brown hair. He grabbed the staff from his back and slowly moved forward to meet Elly. "*Yellow* hoods? Seriously? Are you supposed to be kid copies of us?" he said, swinging at Elly.

"More like the other way around," said Elly, nearly landing a shocking blow on Saul.

Hans and Gretel, below, stopped their running and looked at the guardsmen and captains.

Pulling out his rapier, Hans yelled up to the trees. "Saul, we're going to need your help here, so whatever you're doing, hurry up!"

The guardsmen and captains started moving toward Hans and Gretel, who appeared to be just standing there, fifty yards away. Pierre headed back to the horses and sail-carts with Franklin.

Hans took a couple of swipes at the air to warm up.

One of the guardsmen slowed his advance and laughed.

"He's fighting no one—and still missing, with that flimsy sword," said another.

Hans smiled as the guards got to the perfect distance. "Firstly, it's called a rapier. And now, dear sister, if you'd do the honors?"

What had looked to the guardsmen like a walking stick, being partially hidden by Gretel's red cloak, became quite clearly a bow as she quickly raised it up for use. Her quiver was now visible over her left shoulder.

Immediately, one guard went down.

"One!" chirped Gretel.

"Mother did do *one* thing right," said Hans, running forward to engage the surprised adversaries.

"What's that?" yelled Gretel.

"Getting us those lessons so long ago!" he said, swinging at the air.

"Two!" yelled Gretel.

"She's an archer?" said Tee. "They're all bigger, older, and more deadly than we are." Tee loaded a stone and crept along the tree-bridge until she was above Gretel. Glancing to her friends, who were dodging and weaving Saul's attacks, Tee decided they could handle it. She looked back toward the ground, found a line of sight through the canopy, and took the shot, hitting the red-hooded head.

"Ouch!" yelled Gretel, letting loose an arrow into a tree, below. "Where's the little troll who threw that?"

"Uh oh," said Tee, trying to scurry away.

"There you are!" yelled Gretel, aiming up at the moving, yellow Tee.

"One!" yelled Hans, having made short work of the

guardsman who tried to take him on.

Gabriel and Matthieu started to pull back as the two remaining guardsmen went forward to challenge Hans.

Every time the guardsmen raised their pistols, Gretel raised her bow at them, and when they lowered their pistols, she lowered her bow. Hans giggled with delight.

Above, on the tree-bridge, Elly slipped and dropped one of her shock-sticks as Saul again narrowly missed hitting her in the head with his staff.

Richy pulled himself up onto the thin railing of the metal bridge and then sprang at Saul, armed shock-sticks in hand. Elly looked in disbelief as Richy jumped over her.

Saul let go of his staff and grabbed Richy's hands, falling backward with him and avoiding getting shocked.

"*Hotaru?*" said Saul. Having seen Richy's face, Saul let go of him, backed up, and stood. "Is—is that you, Hotaru?"

Richy, seemingly ignoring Saul, curled himself into a ball, and then yelled, "*Ready!*"

"*Lights out!*" said Elly, putting one foot on Richy's back, leaping, and jabbing her remaining, armed shock-stick into Saul's chest.

"I've got you now!" yelled Gretel below, loosing a second arrow at Tee, but narrowly missing. The canopy between her and her target presented a challenge.

"Bye-bye," said Tee, clicking the button to activate her

shock-stick, and then dropping it on Gretel. Fortunately, it made contact.

Hans finished off the last guardsman and wondered why his sister was no longer responding to his banter. He turned to see her lying on the ground, twitching. "What have you done?" he yelled, running over to her.

"Guys, we better get out of here, now!" said Tee to Elly and Richy. They dashed for the tree ladder and regrouped with the captains, Pierre, and Franklin.

"Best we get out of here," said Captain Archambault. "We've no idea if there are more of them coming."

CHAPTER TWENTY-FIVE

The Fare of Failure

The Red Hoods picked themselves up from the deserted battlefield and slinked off to recover in another part of the forest. The loss of Franklin angered them, and Hans took his frustration out on some travelers they robbed along the way. Afterward, they visited a small village, to fill their stomachs, and then headed home.

"Saul?" said Gretel as they extended one of the last tree-bridges on the way home. "What happened out there? You've been in your own little world ever since." Hans trailed behind, out of earshot.

"Nothing," replied Saul firmly. He couldn't forget Richy's face and it bothered him deeply. He couldn't remember how he knew the boy he'd called Hotaru. He felt like his memories had a wooden floor, and he'd somehow peeked underneath to rediscover a truth hiding there.

Gretel came down the tree first. While Saul and Hans descended, she motioned for them to remain silent, and pointed to the brown horse tied up near their run-down house, and the four children playing, unattended, in the yard.

"Do you think the captains came back with new guards and already found the house? We *were* only a half mile away," whispered Hans.

Gretel tied her hair into a neat ponytail again, using thin leather strips from her belt pouch. "I don't think so. First, they would've tried to hide their horses, and second —"

"There would be *more* than one horse. Also, they'd be all over the place, and noisy," added Saul. "Whoever this is, they're alone."

"You're right. Also, the kids wouldn't still be here," said Hans. "Those captains would've taken them away."

Gretel rubbed her chin. "Whoever it is, they probably left the children out and the horse in view to let us know they're here, waiting for us."

"Maybe it's Master—" started Saul.

Gretel shook her head. "We haven't had any training in years. Mother is broke, and I think she long ago used up every favor anyone ever owed her."

Saul thought for a moment. "Okay. So, what do we do?"

"You go in through the back door. I'll go in through the front door. Gretel?" said Hans.

Gretel nodded in agreement. "I know to what to do.

I'll find a spot for a clean shot through the window. First, though, we have to deal with the kids."

So far, they had managed to stay out of sight from the kids, but that wouldn't be possible as they approached the house.

Hans looked at his sister, knowing she wasn't going to like his suggestion. "How about you lead the kids away first?"

"Why me? Because I'm a girl?" replied Gretel indignantly.

"Don't you always correct us to say *woman*?" asked Saul.

Gretel's look could've burned him to the ground. *"Don't* get me started." She walked away in a huff.

Five minutes later, they were in position. Gretel gave the nod, and both men entered the home, from opposite ends.

"Mother!" screamed Hans.

"What's going on?" yelled Gretel, slinging her bow over her shoulder and rushing to the front door. She could hear Hans yelling and sobbing. Peeking in, she could see him holding Mother's limp body.

"She failed to keep her end of the deal," said the Hound calmly. He stood in the far corner, leaning against a dirty white wall. He was dressed in the same beige and brown leather coat, but this time he also wore large, metallic, gear-covered gloves.

Saul came in, glanced at Mother, and then at his siblings. "Is she *dead?*" he asked in disbelief.

"*You* killed her!" growled Hans, standing to face the Hound. Hans' tear-streaked face filled with rage.

Gretel started to giggle. "She's gone. She's really gone! We're free," she said, repeating it as she gazed upon the old lady's body.

Saul stood there, confused. His body was unwilling to take any action other than remain standing while his mind filled with conflicting emotions.

The Hound turned the dial on each forearm's control box to its first position. The fingers of the gloves started to snap and crackle with small electrical arcs. "I'm only here to talk—but I came *prepared*," he said firmly.

Hans pulled out his rapier and lunged at the Hound. Mother's death angered him, but he also wanted to beat a challenging opponent, to make up for the day's earlier defeat.

The Hound side-stepped Hans' clumsy attack, but nearly fell over due to the weight of the large battery hidden under his coat. "*Stop!* If I wanted you dead, you'd be dead already!"

He'd taken a calculated risk coming alone, never mind wearing the shock-gloves for the first time. He knew that if they were going to listen to him, they were going to have to see his confidence and what he could be capable of.

"Hans—wait!" cried Gretel as Hans lunged forward

again.

The Hound moved out of Hans' way and then hit him with a gloved hand. With a flash, Hans found himself on the far wall, dazed, while little arcs of electricity danced around him.

The Hound turned to Saul. "You need to make an important decision." He switched his gaze to Gretel. "Either I crank these gloves up, and you all die here, today, with that insane woman—or, you can join me and find new purpose in life. Choose!"

The orders that Marcus had given the Fare's enforcer were clear: either retrieve Franklin Watt, or the steam engine plans, or leave the Ginger Lady dead. Engaging the Red Hoods hadn't been mentioned, but the Hound wasn't one to waste an opportunity. He felt they could be useful, and figured that having his own small team maybe wasn't a bad idea—a team that Richelle would think was hers, but he would know was his.

Gretel looked down at the crumpled woman. "Did you kill her because she took the children before handing over Watt?"

The Hound decided to put all his cards on the table. "Yes, that, and the fact that you don't *have* the Watt boy, or his brass tube. My orders were clear."

"Oh," said Gretel. She looked at the dead woman and was getting angry at herself for starting to feel a sense of loss.

The Hound walked slowly toward the open front

door. "I waited for you three because you reminded me of myself, not so long ago. You're lost. You need purpose. You want to *matter*. Come with me and you'll matter."

Gretel and Saul looked at each other nervously.

Hans slowly got himself to his hands and knees. "Do we get toys like those? Because, if we do, I'm in," said Hans, trying to laugh.

"Wait, did you hear that?" said Saul.

"Come, now! Before they see my horse," said the Hound.

A guardsman repeated, "Over there! A building!"

"You were right, Captain—the children weren't far from the house," said Pierre.

"Sometimes, you don't want to be right," replied Captain Charlebois.

CHAPTER TWENTY-SIX

LOST BOYS

"You eat too fast," said Mounira, shaking her head at Franklin.

Franklin paused to glare at Mounira, and then continued to wolf down the breakfast-style late lunch that Jennifer and William had made. Once Franklin had walked through the door and into the wonderful aroma of pancakes, sausage, and other goodies, he couldn't focus on anything else. The parade of flavor was very much welcome.

"Franklin, when you were held captive, did you avoid eating so you could think straight?" asked Richy. "You mentioned the other kids and the Ginger, but not much about you."

Franklin put down his knife and fork and carefully wiped his mouth with a napkin. He was starving, but he still was a young man of distinction, with manners. "The Ginger Lady put that concoction in the food—bread and cookies, mostly. She must have put too much in mine since I got violently ill and passed out. That stuff was horrible—it made me tired as well as made thinking difficult. Once I had my senses back, I tried taking only water."

"Are you done?" asked Tee, gesturing her willingness to start collecting everyone's plates.

"Let me have a breather," said Franklin, eyeing the heaps of food still in front of him.

"Pardon?" said Tee, confused.

Franklin was slightly taken aback. Tee and everybody else spoke with only a slight accent, which he had assumed was merely a regional difference, but he hadn't expected any difference in vocabulary or idioms. "Um— give me a minute?" he offered as an alternative.

"Ah, okay. Everyone else?" asked Tee.

Elly got up and helped Tee carry the dishes to Jennifer and William, who were washing up.

Nikolas rubbed his full belly; he hadn't eaten like that in a while. Even on Solstice morning, he'd moderated his eating, but today was truly a one-of-a-kind celebration, or so he hoped. "Franklin, you have filled your stomach now, yes? Good. Now, we can talk of other matters."

Franklin sat up straight and glanced around. "Here?" he said, leaning forward, surprised.

"I see no problem. Do you?" said Nikolas.

"With... all of *them?*" said Franklin, pointing to Mounira and the Yellow Hoods. "I know *you* are a great inventor and a member of the Tub, but... them?"

Elly intentionally bumped into Franklin with her

arms full of dishes. "Before you say something insincere, I'll remind you—with all due respect—that *we* found you and saved you. You might want to reconsider what you're saying, *genius*."

Franklin realized Elly had a point: he was making assumptions based on the way they were dressed. Nikolas was dressed as a gentleman, and could have easily been a guest in the parlor of any noble's house in Inglea, but the rest were dressed as petty commoners. While Tee's mother had the decency to wear a dress, Tee and Elly were dressed like boys.

After a minute of silence, Franklin pointed at Mounira. "Well... *she* wasn't there, so why does she need to be part of this? She's a deep southerner, and you can't trust those people. I don't see why she should be here. How old is she, anyway—eight?"

Mounira was about to pounce on Franklin, but Tee placed a hand on Mounira's left shoulder.

"She's got more life experience than you have, even with your little adventure," said Tee sharply.

Franklin rolled his eyes. "Oh, please. Anyway, we men have business to attend to," he said. While he knew his father would disapprove of such rudeness, he knew that Inglean men behaved that way—and, therefore, he assumed it must be right.

"Listen," said Elly with a growl, her right index finger pointing at Franklin, "we're going to leave—*only* so that Mounira doesn't tear your head off."

"With one arm?" said Franklin, scoffing. "Please."

Elly grabbed her yellow cloak and ushered Mounira out.

Tee brought the last load of dishes to her parents. Then, just before she followed Elly and Mounira, she glared at Franklin and said, "Mounira could do that with her arm tied behind her back. You might have anger, but *she* has fury."

"Let's go see where Richy is," said Elly, outside. "He should've been here by now."

"I liked that fury bit," said Mounira as they walked off.

Inside, Nikolas turned to Franklin and spoke with a rare forcefulness that sent chills down Jennifer's spine. "Franklin, when you are in my presence, it is for *me* to determine who may hear what. The Yellow Hoods have proven themselves wise and capable beyond their years, and you should hold them in high regard for having saved your life. As for Mounira—if I deem her worthy of hearing something, then you will, as well.

"Lastly, if I hear one more word from you with any sense of that pig-headed, islander nonsense about women, or southerners, I'll walk you back into the clutches of those Red Hoods myself, yes? Is *this* clear?" finished Nikolas.

Franklin's brain tumbled through many thoughts while Nikolas spoke. At first, he wanted to argue and prove he was tough, but that melted away. Then, he thought about the preconceptions he'd already dispelled along his journey. His father and Nikolas shared similar viewpoints, yet he had easily ignored his father, and no one else around him had shared his father's opinions. Franklin wondered whether he would've listened better if his father had just used the same passion and conviction as Nikolas.

He looked up at the great inventor with new respect. Nikolas had barely raised his voice, yet it had had an impact like nothing Franklin had experienced before.

Nikolas' eyes narrowed, showing he was running out of patience.

Franklin nodded, "Yes, sir."

"I don't feel like I'm allowed to move," whispered William to Jennifer. "I never heard him talk like that."

Jennifer put the plate down that she'd been holding since her father had started. Leaning toward her husband, she replied, quietly, "I still remember the speech he gave me about needing to respect myself more. I'd been listening to some older girls in town and was repeating dumb stuff—you know, stuff like how the only smarts a girl needs is to trick a rich boy into marrying her, and whatnot."

William was shocked. "*You* said things like that?"

"Yup," said Jennifer, smiling sheepishly. "But not after that speech. And that one wasn't as bad as the one he gave my—" Jennifer cut herself off as Nikolas turned to look at them.

"Yes, papa?" she said, trying to hide any nervousness.

William just stood there, frozen.

Nikolas stood up and straightened his brown-and-red vest. "Would you allow... how do they say it? Master? Master Watt, here, to sleep at your home? I will take him for a walk first, but I don't believe he should"—he turned to glare at Franklin, who shrank away—"be a guest at my home—not yet."

"No problem," blurted William, his voice cracking in the middle.

———————

After walking a while with Nikolas, Franklin offered an apology. "I'm sorry for what I said."

Nikolas took a breath and looked at Franklin. He was a good-looking lad, full of passion, and he could see he was genuinely sorry. Nikolas rubbed his chin, thinking back to lessons he himself had needed to learn.

"You know," said Nikolas with a friendly tone, "your father was young when we met. He had many lessons to learn, too—as we all had. Your father once believed that people should be separated by status—by how much money they had, or made. He believed that people who were poor were just being lazy. All of that changed as he experienced the world." Nikolas could see Franklin's mouth agape. "Oh, you don't believe me?"

Franklin looked at the ground pensively. "It's just... I didn't know that about my father. I guess there are a lot of things I don't know."

Nikolas offered a gentle wave as they passed other people out for a stroll. "Good to see you," he said to them.

Franklin looked up at Nikolas' warm, bearded face. "I thought my dad was just wrong for saying the same stuff you said back there. Everyone else seems to say the opposite. I suppose sometimes you have to be the one reed that will not bend."

Nikolas messed Franklin's hair. "Now *that* is your father's expression. Tell me, do you feel status is important? Do you have any status *here?*" he asked.

"Of course—" replied Franklin instinctively.

"Really? Why?" asked Nikolas, folding his arms. "Who, here, do you believe has ever heard of the Watt family? And if they have, what influence on them do you think it has, hmm?"

"Um—" said Franklin, looking at the people walking by. "None, I guess."

"Your status is what you earn, what you achieve— and if you ever *rely* on it, it will likely fail you," said Nikolas.

They continued their walk in silence, during which Franklin looked at Nikolas several times. He remembered the stories his dad had told him about Mister Klaus. He'd always thought his father gushed about Nikolas, and now he wondered if, maybe, his father had actually been holding back.

"Oh!" said Franklin, straightening as if suddenly

shocked. "How could I forget! I need to tell you what I did with the plans for—"

Nikolas silenced him by stepping in front of him and placing his right hand on Franklin's chest.

A tall, elegantly dressed woman approached the two. Franklin could tell she wasn't from this region—her fancy clothes and jewelry stood out like a torch at midnight. She carried a silver walking stick topped with a gold head.

"Anna? What are you doing here?" asked Nikolas, surprised to see her. William's father, Sam Baker, occasionally showed up unannounced, and DeBoeuf, the third leader of the Tub, had once, too, as part of a disastrous surprise birthday party for Nikolas—but Anna had never come without first sending a letter declaring when she was coming, and for how long. She was big on protocol, and though they had both been born in the eastern kingdoms, each had kept different elements of the culture.

"Nikolas, who is this? Is this one of the Yellow Hoods?" asked Anna. "Actually, the clothes are ratty, but… Inglean. Is this the Watt boy?"

Anna tried to look around Nikolas at Franklin, but Nikolas kept in her way. Something didn't feel right to him.

Franklin, hating to be talked about as if he weren't there, peeked around and said, "My name is Franklin Charles David Watt. Who, may I ask, are you?"

Anna looked at Franklin, not sure for a moment whether or not to talk to him. She looked back to Nikolas. "Nikolas, we need to discuss something, and urgently. I was in the area when I caught wind of a meeting of the Fare. We need to make a plan and act against them," she said in her most commanding tone.

Nikolas' bad feeling grew. He turned to Franklin so that his back was to Anna. In a serious tone, he whispered, "Go. I want you to tell Tee and her friends the tale you were about to tell, yes?"

Franklin was briefly confused, and then realized what Nikolas meant. He nodded and ran off.

"Now, Anna, do you want to sit for a tea? I know a good café not far from here."

As Richy told the whole story, he could see the pain growing on the faces of his friends. He took a deep breath to hold back his tears and keep his emotions bottled up.

"Basically, my parents want to split up and they want to move to different cities because they're afraid of all the talk of war and stuff. Each assumed the other one was going to take me with them," said Richy, his face heavy with emotion.

Richy now also understood why Jennifer and William were always concerned about him, always inviting him to stay for a meal. What he'd just found weird before now had a meaning, and he struggled to think about how to explain to his friends the rest of what he'd learned.

"I can't believe that," said Elly, putting her arm around Richy in a big-sister fashion. "You *can't* leave—you're one of us!"

Mounira, angry on Richy's behalf, was almost growling. "You can declare yourself your own master, right?" she asked. "Your kingdom has that rule, does it not? It is the fantasy of kids at home. These parents of yours, they dishonor you. Rid yourself of them."

Tee paused, never having thought about that. "Yes, I think we do have that rule, though I haven't ever heard of anyone using it."

"Then it's decided!" said Mounira, looking up at the taller Yellow Hoods.

"I'm sure it can't be that easy," said Tee, gesturing for Mounira to calm down.

"There's something else, isn't there, Richy?" asked Elly, reading a hint from his face that only she could see.

Richy mulled over what, if anything, he was going to say. Everyone felt the long pause. "Well, they also tell me I'm adopted, and part of that whole Ginger Lady thing," he mumbled.

"What?!" Elly and Tee said in unison, each of them shocked at the revelation. Mounira tried to remember what Tee had told her about the Ginger Lady.

"You were just going to skip over that part, weren't you?" said Tee, shaking her head.

"Seriously?" said Elly.

"I don't want to talk about it," said Richy. "I'm tired and my head is really mixed up right now."

Just then, Franklin found the group of friends. "Um, hello!" he said, trying to be extra friendly. "Why are you all so glum?" he asked, despite the ice-cold stares.

"Right—listen," Franklin continued, "um—I'd like to apologize, first and foremost. Your—um—grandfather can be a bit intimidating and has made it extremely clear to me that how I behaved was... terrible, for lack of a better word." Franklin's discomfort with apologizing was emphasized by how he kept playing with his hands. "So, I'm sorry? I mean, I'm *sorry*. If it happens again, then—um—I give you full license to give me what for!" said Franklin, trying to laugh.

Mounira smiled and nudged Elly. Elly raised an eyebrow and asked, "What's *what for*?"

"Oh, for the love of—" said Franklin, burying his head in his hand for a second. "I'm sorry! There, I've said it. I can't say any more about it without, probably, making it worse. So there you have it. Said. Done. Time to move on."

"Not quite," said Tee. "Mounira, what do you think?"

Mounira looked at Franklin. Something in his face reminded her of how she felt, far away from home, far away from her parents, trying to figure out the local customs and habits. "Any more remarks you care to make about *girls*?" she asked sarcastically.

Franklin grimaced. "Where I come from, the girls I

know seem to want to be mothers, and marry a rich man. Why? I don't know, but my mom's like that. I suppose girls can be anything."

"You should meet Sergeant Archambault," said Elly.

Franklin didn't understand. "I already met Captain Archambault. Nice man, though a bit rotund. Has that mustache like a sleeping bear."

"No—she means *Sergeant* Archambault, also in the Minette guard. The captain's daughter," explained Tee.

Without thinking, Franklin said, "Ha! A woman guardsman." He then realized they were serious. He kicked himself for so quickly falling back into old habits. "Really?" he added.

Richy chuckled. "Yes. Things are different here—even when you compare us with Mineau. There's something distinct about the personality of this place."

Tee added, "*Sergeant* Archambault is the best shot with a rifle that you're ever likely to meet, and she's the only reason my grandfather wasn't killed months ago."

Franklin digested all he'd just heard. "I thought you folks were just different in that some of the women didn't wear dresses here."

"*You* can wear a dress, if you want," said Mounira, but the joke came off as more biting than funny.

Franklin glared before realizing how Mounira had meant it. "I also came here," he said, getting to his real purpose, "because Mister Klaus wanted me to—"

"Actually, that will need to wait," said Nikolas, surprising everyone. "Madame Kundle Maucher wants to talk with all of us—now."

CHAPTER TWENTY-SEVEN

MAUCHER OF PLANS

Anna had been waiting at the Green Goo tavern when Nikolas, Franklin, Mounira, and the Yellow Hoods arrived. They were surprised to see it was empty except for Anna and eight guardsmen.

"Where is everyone?" asked Franklin. "A place like this should be packed at this time of day."

"I cleared it out, including the proprietor, so we can be assured of secrecy," said Anna.

"The what?" asked Mounira.

"Owner," whispered Elly.

"Oh," nodded Mounira.

Nikolas glanced at the guardsmen. Their uniforms were out of place for Minette. He didn't approve of her decision to hire Mineau guards, but she had made it clear in their brief discussion—before he'd retrieved the kids— that she was calling the shots.

Nikolas had heard, second hand, that Anna had

experience leading battles and ambushes. He assumed she must know what she was doing. While Nikolas considered himself a good planner and strategist, he'd rarely used those skills. What he didn't know was that Anna had never actually done the things he'd heard about—rather, she'd always had someone handle such operations on her behalf—while she would end up taking the credit. This would be her first time doing everything herself.

Anna was pleased as she looked over everyone assembled. She felt right in thinking the military leaders who'd served under her through the years had been incompetent. *Planning is easy*, she thought.

"I'm glad you are all here," said Anna, with a smile and a hint of sincerity. Her hair, again, was perfect and done up. Her maroon blouse and silver-trimmed dress were fashionable, and expensive-looking.

She motioned everyone to gather around a large table as she unrolled a map that one of the guardsmen had just handed to her. "There's a meeting happening, tomorrow at noon, at *this* location," she said, pointing to a spot on the map. "It's just outside of Mineau, in the Red Forest."

Richy looked at the map. "Wouldn't that be Bergman's Failure?"

"What's that?" asked Franklin.

"A broken tower with a half castle wall. Bergman was this rich guy... long story," said Richy.

"That's an isolated area," Elly added, "That's not just

outside of Mineau—Mineau's over *there*. This is north of Mineau, almost directly east from Minette."

"Direct—if you could *fly*," snickered Mounira.

Anna forced a smile. "You know your geography. Good. Yes, there's a partially constructed tower, a landing and stairs to the tower, and part of what was to be the castle wall."

"Rampart," corrected Franklin. "According to the notes on that map, it's two walls with a walkway in the middle. That's called a rampart."

"I know what it's called," snapped Anna.

Nikolas waited for Anna to settle and then asked, "What is this meeting, tomorrow, about?"

Anna looked at him and hesitated. She straightened herself, touched her hair, and replied, "All that I can tell you is that it is *important*. We can end the Fare's activities if you all do your part properly."

Tee wasn't buying it. "Don't you think you should have professionals doing this? We're good, but we're kids. Doesn't that bother you?"

Nikolas kept his eyes trained on Anna—her every gesture, her every movement. He knew she was hiding something, and he detected layers to the deceit. Anna had lied to him before, under the guise of the greater good, but this time it felt different.

Anna glared at Tee. "I *would* use professionals, if there were such people around here, but sadly you lot are the best there is."

Elly was stunned. "What about—?"

Nikolas cut her off with a quick smile. "Thank you, Elly. I'm sure Anna has looked at all available options."

"Thank you, Nikolas. Listen to your betters, children," said Anna, shaking her head in frustration and grabbing the table's edge.

"Now, Anna, what do you expect, from all of us?" asked Nikolas, leaning back in his chair and folding his arms. Nikolas could play along, if for no other reason than respect for her position within the Tub.

Anna touched her hair and surveyed the map and everyone gathered. It was her job to get them to buy into the plan; she had to accept that. They didn't know her or her ways, and so she had to accept their rudeness, for now. "An important *person* from the Fare will be arriving there to meet a contact. If we seize the opportunity, we can capture him, and put an end to the hostilities—right there and then."

"He must be a very important person if that can happen," said a skeptical Franklin.

Ignoring Franklin, Anna pointed out positions on the map. "I want the Yellow Hoods up here in the tower, and I want the Watt boy—"

"I'm not a boy," protested Franklin.

Anna bit her tongue. "—*Watt*, here, to the south of the wall, with a couple of the guards. The other guards will be with me, just in front of the wall, here, to the east of it."

"What about me?" asked Mounira. She'd kept quiet during the talk of the Tub and the Fare, lacking context, but figured she could ask Tee or Anciano Klaus about it later.

Anna glared at Mounira. She hadn't even noticed the one-armed girl until now. "To be honest," she said sharply, "I have no use for three-quarters of a girl. Stay at home and play with dolls—whatever you wish. You have no value in this. I don't want you there."

Surprisingly, it was Franklin who grabbed Mounira's hand and held her back. She squeezed his hand hard, drawing down her anger, while almost bringing Franklin to tears, but he felt he deserved it. There was something about hearing similar words to what he'd said come from a leader of the Tub that struck him as deeply wrong. He'd never forget that moment.

It bothered Nikolas that Anna had been vague on some details, yet had been quite specific about where she wanted certain people. "And myself?" he asked, pointing out that Anna hadn't mentioned him yet.

"Oh," said Anna, again frustrated with her own miscalculation, "I'd like you... um... *here*, with me and the remainder of the guards."

A few minutes later, as Anna rolled up the map and thanked everyone for attending, she remembered one thing. "Excuse me, Yellow Hoods, do you have your wind-up Kundle... I mean shocking sticks? I've heard about them, and they sound very much based on my design. I'd like to ensure they are in… perfect working order, for tomorrow."

Before Richy reached into his yellow cloak's hidden pocket to take his shock-sticks out, he felt Tee grab his hand. She glanced to Elly, who then looked at Anna.

"We're not allowed to carry them when we're not on a mission. We're still kids, remember?" answered Elly, hoping her lie would work.

"Oh, of course," said Anna, happy to hear that there was some sense in the world. "Never mind."

Franklin, Mounira, and the Yellow Hoods quickly made their exit.

As Nikolas was about to leave, Anna motioned him back.

"Oh, Nikolas, one question," said Anna. "Are Mounira and Franklin going to be staying with William and Jennifer?" She couldn't imagine Nikolas allowing anyone to stay in his home; she certainly wouldn't allow it, if it was her.

Nikolas stroked his short beard, pretending to be lost in thought. "Sorry? Oh—yes," he said. "Yes. Is that everything?"

"Yes, thank you," said Anna, smiling tightly. "I'll see you and everyone in the morning."

Leaving the tavern, Nikolas walked home to get one of his specially made lanterns. He wound it up, turned it on, and went for a late evening walk.

An hour later, in the middle of the forest between Minette and Mineau, Nikolas knocked on the door of a cabin he'd only visited twice before.

"Hold on—whoever you are! If you're a thief, you might've had the decency to kill me in my sleep," said a gruff voice.

The door creaked open.

"Hello, Pierre," said Nikolas.

"Nikolas?" Pierre became distracted by Nikolas' lantern and its clicking, moving parts. It shone a beautiful blue light, unlike any he'd ever seen. "It's bright—but doesn't hurt my eyes. What *is* it?"

"Oh—an idea. One of those things I created recently, when I couldn't sleep," Nikolas replied.

"You can't be here to talk about the lantern, so come in," said Pierre, yawning. "I'll see if the fire is still warm and put the kettle on. So, what did you come to see me about?"

Nikolas sat in the chair Pierre offered, while Pierre sat on his bed. Nikolas looked about the sparsely decorated little cabin.

"Do you know the Cochon brothers?" he asked.

CHAPTER TWENTY-EIGHT
THE VISITOR

It was late evening. With his own plans set in motion for the morning, Nikolas walked home, struggling to make sense of Anna's behavior. Based on what he'd heard on his own, the Fare was stepping out of the shadows, and intending to hit the Tub where it was most vulnerable.

While it was possible that a high-ranking member of the Fare would come near Mineau, Nikolas couldn't figure out why nor how Anna would've come to know about it. And why was Anna so close to Mineau when she'd heard the news? He realized he didn't so much trust Anna, as he trusted her position in the Tub. He wished he could reach either DeBoeuf or Sam, but that would take weeks if not months—time he didn't have.

On arriving home, he checked on Mounira, who was fast asleep, and then gave Jennifer a kiss goodbye and thanked her for watching his little guest. Then, he walked into the kitchen to make some tea.

A short while later, there was an unexpected knock at the door. He pulled out his pocket watch and wondered who it could be at such a late hour.

Mounira awoke in the middle of the night to the sound of Nikolas talking with an unfamiliar woman. While she couldn't make out what the two were saying, she could judge from the tone that they knew each other. Her curiosity wouldn't let her go back to sleep. A couple of times, they laughed so heartily that Mounira couldn't help but laugh herself, and she buried her face in her pillow to muffle the sound.

When the front door closed, Mounira heard the sounds of the dishes being cleaned. She was about to drift off, expecting to hear Nikolas walk up the corridor from the kitchen to the bedrooms, when to her surprise, she heard him instead go down the stairs, to the landing. Then, she heard him go down *more* stairs. She sat up. "But... there aren't any more stairs," she whispered to herself.

Unable to contain her curiosity, she scampered out of bed and peeked around the corner. It sounded like Nikolas was, somehow, below her, but that was impossible—or was it?

She arrived at the kitchen, turned to her left, and went down the set of stairs to the landing. She looked back up at the stairs, and to the walls on either side. "Where did he go?" she wondered aloud.

Just as Mounira was about to go back to bed, she caught a glimpse of a blue light. Strangely, it was shining through part of the wall to the right of the stairs.

Mounira slowly shuffled her feet forward, through

the "wall," until she felt the end of the floor. "I'm in the wall?" she said to herself, wishing it were brighter. She sat down, closed her eyes, and went down the hidden steps as a small child would—on her bum.

At the bottom, she opened her eyes and looked back up. There were stairs leading up to the landing—no secret door, just simple stairs. "Hmm," she wondered, "I bet the passageway was painted so that it doesn't look like anything is there, just like in one of the royal castles back home. I can't believe I never noticed before."

She turned and continued to follow the blue light coming from a door, slightly ajar, at the end of a short corridor. She tiptoed up to it and peeked in.

The room had bookcases along the walls, a fireplace, a nice rug, a worn couch, and a decorative chair with an ottoman. Everything had an order and elegance to it— there were no piles of books—as if the room had a personality different from the rest of the house. Nikolas stood by the fireplace holding a small painting in his hands.

"She's grown into quite a woman. You'd approve, Isabella," he said, finishing his conversation with the painting. He kissed the top of the frame and placed it on the fireplace mantel.

Feeling something odd, Mounira scanned the room. "How is it so bright?" she whispered to herself. She could see no lamps, yet the room was properly lit, with no signs of shadows.

Nikolas walked to a bookcase near the door. Mounira curled up, closed her eyes, and froze. She was certain she wasn't supposed to be here and had no idea what he'd do if he discovered her.

Mounira opened her eyes again when she heard something thump on the well-worn couch. Nikolas was now at a bookcase at the other end of the room, pulling out a dark-green book just like the one he'd just dropped on the couch. He sat down with the two books.

"I guess he likes to read... two books at the same time?" said Mounira. Her one hand clung to the underside of the door, making sure it didn't sway open.

Nikolas held the first book up, twisted its spine, and caught the small metal rod that fell from it. He did the same thing with the other book.

"What are those?" whispered Mounira, nearly poking her head into the room.

With a metal rod in each hand, Nikolas started walking toward the middle of the rug. He held his arms out in front, pushing against an invisible force.

Finally, sweat now dripping off him, Nikolas managed to get his two fists to touch the middle of the rug. The look on his face told Mounira that whatever he had been pushing against was gone.

"I need to lower the field level," said Nikolas to himself. "I almost couldn't do it this time. The new generator is stronger than I expected. This is good, though."

Mounira was about to leave, thinking this was perhaps a strange exercise routine, when all of a sudden there was a series of loud clanks and clunks. She opened the door just a bit wider, ever so curious, when all of a sudden she saw the rug start lowering into the floor.

As Nikolas descended atop the rug, he noticed the open door. "Hmm—I thought I'd closed that."

He almost saw me! Mounira thought as she scampered up the stairs and back to bed.

CHAPTER TWENTY-NINE

JAMMED THOUGHTS

Tee walked out of her room and saw the vacant blankets and pillows by the fire. She wondered where Franklin might have wandered off to. From the lingering smells of breakfast, Tee knew that her parents were already up and likely gone.

She noticed Franklin at a bench in the backyard. He was drawing, and had an intense look on his face. She'd seen that look many times—the inventor's look. His eyes were wide, and his face contorted in a combination of pain and joy. It was the first time she'd seen any hint of him being an inventor's son.

After brushing her hair, she got dressed in a simple set of drawstring pants and a blouse, and then went to the kitchen to have homemade tomato jam on a slice of bread.

"Hmm… now where did they go?" said Tee, spotting the note from her dad. After reading it, she started on her breakfast. Tee expected her parents would be back for dinner, but wondered what kind of trouble they were checking out in Mineau. She turned to see Franklin still working diligently. Ready to satisfy her curiosity, Tee walked outside.

Franklin was nearly over top his drawing, as if he were trying to hide it from the sun, or dive into it.

"What is that?" asked Tee, without presuming anything—though she could make out what it likely was.

Franklin looked at Tee. "Thought you were going to scare the bee's knees off me?" he asked.

Tee didn't know how one would get *bee's knees* in the first place, but figured she knew what he meant. "Yes, I suppose."

Franklin was accustomed to dismissing people for being less smart, less educated, or less capable than he thought himself. He didn't like having his time wasted, and wasn't comfortable with sharing his works-in-progress—except with his father.

Tee was different, though. It was evident she *was* the granddaughter of one of the greatest minds of their time. Still, Franklin wasn't yet sure if he wanted to share his work—whether out of a misplaced sense of superiority, or else out of fear she'd find it trivial.

"Want some jam toast?" Tee offered, seeing a dilemma play out on the young man's face.

Franklin was confused. "But—it's not toast. *Toasted* implies heat was applied. That's simply sliced bread."

Tee looked at the half-eaten piece. "Yes, well—while that is true on *one* level, you *could* argue it has been heated to the exact temperature of the room, which means heat *was* applied. Heat does two things; one is add temporary warmth to the bread, and the other is render it less pliable, or more stiff—whichever way you want to think about it. Given that, isn't it *toast* once sliced?" replied Tee, grinning. She rarely spoke like that, but had heard her grandfather talk that way, all the time. Taking the last bite and licking her fingers, she gave Franklin her wide, brown eyes treatment, to see if he'd respond.

After awkward silence, Tee swallowed and said, "I'm getting another. Do you want one, yes or no?"

Franklin was still sitting back, thinking about what Tee had said. She'd earned at least enough respect for that, and, to his astonishment, he really couldn't find a way to refute her point. All he could think of would seem like nitpicking, and he felt that would ultimately only make him look like an idiot.

Franklin looked up at Tee, with her long, dark hair, and her huge, brown eyes and suddenly found himself feeling awkward, unable to talk. Part of his brain had just realized Tee was, in fact, a teenage girl. "Um—" he started, "ah—"

Tee smiled at the poor boy. "I'll take that as a *yes*. Back in a minute."

She was reminded of other boys in town who suffered similar problems around her and Elly. She'd suffered it *once* herself, when she'd met a friend's visiting cousin. Thankfully, Elly had been there to give her a quick elbow to the ribs and snap her out of it.

Tee returned and handed Franklin a piece of jam-covered bread on a plate. Franklin smiled, having by then rediscovered his ability to speak intelligently to a pretty girl.

Pointing at his drawing, he said, "Your grandfather had sent me a design for an armband. It was wonderfully useful. I've been trying to redesign it from memory, but there are a couple of things I haven't yet got right. The armband got me out of a pinch, so I'd like to make another."

"A pinch?" asked Tee, sitting beside him.

"Oh—a bind, or a bad situation. Don't you lot speak Inglesh?" asked Franklin, slightly annoyed at being called out regularly on what he considered common words or expressions.

Tee scanned his drawing, then answered, almost half-interested in the conversation. "We lot? No. We call it Frelish. *Inglesh* just sounds... stuffy. You're an islander, anyway. It's Inglesh today, Torvash tomorrow."

Franklin felt his national pride wounded. "Well, the island kingdom is called Inglea—most of the time. Well, some of the time. Okay, I think I see your point," he conceded.

"Well, right *now* you are in the kingdom of Freland," said Tee, taking her last bite. "We're the Frelish, regardless of who is in charge. We don't have royals who decide to freshen up the place with a zazzy new name."

There was a beautiful simplicity to it, thought Franklin. "Huh. Frelish it is, I guess."

"So," said Tee, leaning over the design, "you're trying to improve this?" She walked through some of the finer points with her finger.

"Yes," said Franklin, nervously.

"This, right here, is similar to the mechanism in my sail-cart. Come—let me show you. I think you'll appreciate some of the changes we made, and it may give you some ideas. Come on," said Tee, getting up.

Franklin looked at Tee and smiled. Maybe this smart, Frelish, peasant-looking girl wasn't so bad? Maybe.

CHAPTER THIRTY
INTERCEPTED

Nikolas looked at his watch. If he didn't leave now, he'd be late meeting Anna and the others at the crumbled tower. On the other hand, he wasn't comfortable leaving Mounira. He'd checked on her twice, and then left a note beside her bed. She'd never slept in this long, and while he was certain she could take care of herself, his paternal instincts didn't like the idea of waking her or leaving her alone.

Nikolas yawned. *I really should have gotten more sleep, but it was worth it,* he thought. *The output of the engine is five times better. What will Tee say when I show her?* Months ago, he'd shared his horseless cart prototype with Tee and her parents. Since that time, he'd worked in secret. Now he was ready to show Tee the next generation, in a form closer to her heart.

There was a knock at the door.

Nikolas looked at the door, frowning. He wasn't expecting anyone, and everyone he could think of was occupied with one endeavor or another. Cautiously, he opened the door.

"Hello, Nikolas," said Marcus Pieman. "Mind if I come in?"

Marcus' clean-shaven face was decorated with a leather eyepatch over the left eye. He wore a high-collar black coat with gold buttons, a flat white shirt, and brown pants. The style was different from anything Nikolas had seen before. Marcus' clothes somehow spoke of the future, while remaining connected with the present.

"Are these Richelle's designs?" asked Nikolas, gesturing to the clothes.

Marcus laughed. "Yes, what do you think?"

Nikolas nodded as he noted the stitching and angles. "Suits you. Different—yet speaks of the type of change you desire to bring about," answered Nikolas. "Now why are you holding what I can only guess is an ocular device?" he asked, gesturing to the curious-looking device with a leather strap that Marcus was holding.

"Well," said Marcus, chuckling humbly, "I didn't feel right wearing it when you opened the door. Funny, isn't it? I've worn it everywhere else on this trip. I'd love to show you what I've done with it. Apparently, it makes me the spitting image of Abeland."

Nikolas nodded, smiling at the mention of Abeland, whom he'd known since Abe was born. "Yes, it's funny who we are to others, and who we are to those who know us best. The device looks interesting," said Nikolas. "Well... I suppose I'm not intended to meet up with Anna and the others then, yes?"

Marcus looked sorrowful. "No—I'm afraid not, and I apologize for having to do this. I will need you to pack some bags, as you'll be coming with me. But, before we have to deal with that, may I come in for a bit?"

It became clear to Nikolas why so many things had felt wrong with Anna's plan. He'd miscalculated, judged poorly where to place his trust. Anna had been right— someone from the Fare *was* coming—but had she known who, or why? It was obvious there was no meeting of a contact, at least not another agent of the Fare. This had all been a ruse—or possibly something worse was afoot. Nikolas hoped the Yellow Hoods would be safe.

Rubbing his bald head, Nikolas finally said, "Yes, sorry, Marcus—come in. I've had a lot on my mind. I wasn't prepared to be social. You know how I am—when I am surprised."

"Yes, again, I apologize for that," said Marcus. "But, it is *good* to see you. It's been a long time."

Nikolas gave Marcus an affectionate light slap on the arm. "That, it has been. May I offer you some tea?"

Marcus stepped into the house. With genuine appreciation, he replied, "Yes, please. The stuff on the road has been dreadful—it's been only dust and fannings. We were in such a rush that I neglected to have my own teas packed. Perhaps I'm losing my mind in my old age."

"I very much doubt that," said Nikolas. He stiffened as he heard the distinct creak of a floorboard from outside Mounira's room. Marcus seemed to notice, too. "I can't remember, Marcus—have you been to this old, creaky house before?"

Marcus scanned about. He couldn't see concern on Nikolas' bearded face, nor obvious signs of anyone else—other than some shoes and clothes on a hook that he assumed belonged to Nikolas' granddaughter.

"No," said Marcus, "I don't believe I've been here. I did hear about it, though. By the way, you still look the *same* as when we had that painting done nearly forty years ago—just more gray."

"Please, Marcus, don't bring your political flattery here. We've always been honest with each other," said Nikolas. "Anna did the same thing. It took everything I had to be civil."

Marcus nodded, smiling with a touch of embarrassment. "It is a nice house. Honestly. I can see Isabella's hand in some elements. Oh, is that a *trompe-l'oeil*?" said Marcus, pointing at the specially painted stairs to the lower level, and referring to the technique that made it nearly invisible. "Nicely done. You've always been a man of subtlety. I miss that. Simon is so…"

"Challenging?" offered Nikolas as he walked up to the kitchen.

"Yes!" laughed Marcus. "Indeed. Simon is more than I can deal with, some days. Thank goodness for Richelle."

"How is your granddaughter?" asked Nikolas. The last time he'd seen Richelle, she'd been younger than Tee.

Marcus sat at the kitchen table. "She's well—excellent,

in fact. I've heard a good deal about yours, too. A mix of you and Sam, though I suspect some Isabella and Rosie, too.... By the way, Nikolas, you've got my assurance that no harm will come to your granddaughter today."

Nikolas placed the kettle on the wood stove and turned to lean on the counter. "I appreciate that. I *am* surprised, however, that you came all this way." Nikolas' mind raced, thinking of the ways that things could play out. He was certain Marcus was doing the same.

"Well, taking you *out of the game*, as you used to say, was in the plan—though not for a while yet. There was an opportunity that required us to move up our timetable," said Marcus openly. "Rather unexpected."

Nikolas got out the tea cups and saucers. "Anna, I presume."

Marcus hesitated, knowing that Abeland and Richelle would not approve his sharing of any information. If roles were reversed, he'd probably think the same—but this was Nikolas Klaus, the closest thing he had to a brother.

Nearby, Mounira nervously peeked out her bedroom window. She could see two guards in unfamiliar dark gray and purple uniforms walking about. They were armed with rifles and swords. When she heard the heavy laughter from the kitchen, she silently made her bed, removed all traces of herself from the room, and then hid under the bed.

CHAPTER THIRTY-ONE
CRUMBLING PLANS

The sky clouded over and became more and more menacing as the group journeyed down from Minette to Mineau, and then into the Red Forest. When they arrived at Bergman's Failure, the storm was only minutes away.

The Yellow Hoods jumped out of their sail-carts while Franklin, Anna, and the ten guardsmen dismounted their horses. They were at the northwestern edge of a huge clearing in the Red Forest.

Tee looked at the guardsmen with concern. She didn't like that two from the previous night had been replaced, and there were two new ones who looked clueless. The rest looked so nervous that she was afraid they would scream and run away if a leaf floated by unexpectedly.

The mossy, white stone tower stood a hundred feet tall, with a caved-in top. The rampart wall extended from it to the south, some thirty feet. The stairs from the tower's blocked door descended to the west and stopped at a small landing. From there, the stairs continued several steps to the south and joined the cobblestone path that led under the rampart. It looked like someone had started building the northeastern corner of a castle, and then had given up. Few knew the real story of Bergman, yet Tee did, and she feared they were about to share his fate and be betrayed.

Anna huddled with the guards, giving orders and talking through what she expected to happen.

"This place is more remote than I'd figured," said Franklin to the Yellow Hoods. He was worried. Unlike the Yellow Hoods, he'd never been in a fight, let alone a real battle. The idea of physical violence made him panicky.

Elly, her arms crossed, kept a watchful eye on Anna. "So *much* about this feels wrong. Don't you think we should've just abandoned the plan, Richy?"

"Huh?" he replied. Richy's mind was still a mess from his own news of the day before. "I don't know. Lala, what do you think?"

"Lala?" said Franklin, looking around. "Who's Lala?"

Tee chuckled. "It's my nickname. Before you start asking why, let's just focus. Okay?"

Franklin stopped himself from following up the point and waved for Tee to continue.

"We've trusted Anna this far. I think we have to see what happens, at least until my Grandpapa gets here. If things start to go wrong, we look after each other, and get out—together. No Bergman's fate for us, okay?"

Franklin looked at Richy and Elly—both had agreed

—while he wondered just who this Bergman fellow had been.

Anna marched their way, and they fell silent. "So, are my little troops ready?" she asked condescendingly. She was dressed in yet another expensive-looking outfit. It was an ankle-length, slightly puffy formal dress of black and gold, with a gold sash around the waist. It seemed highly impractical for the sort of mission they were supposedly on.

Richy, who'd been staring at the guards, turned to Anna. "Why are the guardsmen armed with only swords and flintlock *pistols*? We're out in the *open*. Shouldn't at least two or three have rifles?"

Anna glanced quickly at the guardsmen. "You don't understand tactics, child. Now all of you—get to your positions." She stomped off while muttering something to herself.

Two guardsmen remained with the sail-carts and tied the horses to some trees. Tee, Elly, and Richy headed for the tower's small landing. Franklin went with four guardsmen to the freestanding rock pile about fifty yards south of the tower. Anna and the remaining four guardsmen stood at the ready, just to the east of the rampart.

Anna stood proudly, chin up. She pulled out an ornate pocket watch from her dress' sash, and smiled. Everything was close enough to perfect. "They should be here any minute," Anna yelled to everyone.

"Anna, where's my grandfather?" Tee yelled back. "Isn't he supposed to be here?"

Keeping her back to Tee, and taking a couple of seconds to respond, Anna replied, "He said he'd be late. Don't worry about him."

"She's lying, Tee," said Elly, looking around. "We're exposed up here. Anyone to the south or west can see us. Maybe she wants us up here so that we can be seen?"

"I'm thinking the same thing," said Tee, ushering her friends to crouch down.

Richy scanned around. "You know—someone with a rifle could probably hit us from the forest, there," he said, pointing to the south. "Someone with skills like Egelina-Marie could *definitely* hit us from there."

"Let's get ready, guys," said Tee, pulling up her yellow hood. "Charge your shock-sticks."

"What about Franklin?" asked Elly, winding up the small handle on her shock-stick.

"Quiet!" yelled Anna. "A coach is approaching."

Four brown horses came into view, pulling a dark gray coach with gold trim. Two soldiers in dark gray and purple uniforms rode the lead horses, while four more soldiers were positioned at the corners of the coach.

Anna grinned as the coach came to a stop just a few yards in front of her. She'd taken a risk, as many great leaders had, and offered an olive branch to the enemy. She had argued against her fellow leaders of the Tub for the past two years about anything and everything related to the Fare. Now she was going to be able to show all of them just what she could accomplish when not leashed by their idiotic fears.

She figured it best to offer an opportunity to the Fare to return to the peace agreement that had been worked out, long ago. It would probably take money or some other incentive to get them to agree, but she figured it would be well worth the cost. Doing this would allow the Tub to regain its strength and resume managing the peace of all the kingdoms.

When she'd bumped into the Hound—by chance—at The Pointy Stick inn, she had found what she needed: a way in. She'd offered the Hound a deal. He'd asked for a couple of things, one of which she had thought odd, but didn't care enough to argue about. She'd agreed to make sure that the Yellow Hoods would be present at any meeting. Anna's own condition of the deal was that she would meet the Fare's leader, in person.

Anna was surprised and relieved when the Hound had found her a week ago to tell her exactly when and where they would meet her. She was told she was to include Nikolas in her planning, but that he would not be participating in the actual meet. The Fare was concerned he might influence things—and Anna understood completely. She was fine with it; it didn't matter—it was all for the greater good.

A Fare soldier hopped down from the front left of the

coach, and then opened its door. The Hound stepped out, wearing his brown leather long-coat and his metallic, gear-covered shock-gloves. He moved more comfortably with his gear—he'd been practicing with it every day since meeting with Hans, Saul, and Gretel.

The Hound was followed by a woman in a red hooded cloak. She wore a long dark brown jacket and pants. The lapel on her jacket was square, and distinctive. At her right, she wore a long, thin, white scabbard, and at her left, strapped to her leg, was what looked like a cannon of a pistol, with tubes that led under her cloak. She pulled back her hood, revealing her black hair tied in a neat, simple ponytail. She slowly surveyed her surroundings, finally settling her gaze on Anna.

Anna was appalled at the woman's attire; it was insulting for such a meeting. The woman looked like a strangely dressed man.

"Who are they?" asked Tee. "Is she another Red Hood?"

"She's not dressed like anyone I've ever seen before," said Elly.

"Maybe she's the queen of the Red Hoods? Look at the way she's carrying herself," said Richy. "Did you see how she looked at each of us? I almost *felt* her analyzing me."

"What's that guy wearing on his hands?" asked Elly, squinting.

Tee looked. "It's a weapon," she quickly answered.

"Look at how he's just standing there. He's ready for anything. See the way he's holding his gloved hands? They're his weapon."

"I wish I'd brought the telescope from the treehouse," said Richy.

Tee and Elly smiled at each other; their Richy was back, at least for now.

Franklin wondered what he'd got himself into. Part of him was fascinated with the technology worn by the man with the reddish-brown beard, while the rest of him was just short of running in circles in a stark-raving-loony panic. He had to distract himself. He looked at the four guards that stood with him, and noticed their hands were at their backs.

"They're not expecting trouble. This is bad," he whispered to himself.

"Who are you? And where is Marcus? I was told the leader of the Fare was a man named Marcus," snapped Anna. "Clearly, you aren't him, girl." Anna hated being toyed with.

Unfazed, the woman looked at Anna. She slowly pulled off her white gloves, while keeping her eyes on Anna. The woman held out her gloves and a soldier came, took them, and put them in the coach. The soldiers then took up their positions flanking her, and the Hound.

She offered an instant smile to Anna, which caused Anna's face to twitch in frustration. "My name is Lady Richelle Pieman, and this is my associate, the Hound."

Anna banged her cane on the cobblestones, popping out the two spikes from its head. Small electrical arcs danced between the spikes. "I didn't ask to meet with *you*, girl. I asked to speak to the leader of the Fare. This Marcus character. Now where is *he?*" demanded Anna, holding her cane menacingly. Something that Richelle had said nagged at Anna's mind.

Richelle turned her gaze to the Hound. "Is this the woman you met with? The *stick maker?*" she asked. She was certain her tone and word choice would get further under Anna's skin.

"Yes," confirmed the Hound, unconcerned with Anna's threatening stance. He was ready and eager to engage. Richelle had been happy with the allies he had arranged to join them.

The sky grew darker and the rain started to fall noisily. Franklin and the Yellow Hoods could no longer hear everything being said, but they could already tell from what they'd seen that the plan had derailed.

"So, *you* are the famous Anna Kundle Maucher? The maker of candles and sticks?" said Richelle, sounding uncertain. She channeled her frustration at Anna's disrespectful words and tone down to her toes, which curled so tightly the knuckles cracked. Richelle had built up her reputation to where she could walk into almost any royal court room, unannounced, and request a private audience with the king or queen.

"Yes! That's me," said Anna, hoping that things were

finally going to get back on track. There was something about Richelle's name that kept nagging at Anna—yet she'd never known anybody named Richelle. "Now, tell me—where is Marcus! We had an agreement."

Richelle's mouth twitched—she was at her limit of how much rudeness and anger she could absorb. Her left hand closed around the handle of her pistol.

"Don't threaten *me!*" barked Anna. *Now* what *did Richelle say her last name was?* Anna wondered.

"I call this my *hand-cannon*," said Richelle, biting her lip. "I designed it. I learned a lot—from my grandfather—about how to use metals and different elements of nature to effect the simplest of things. I learned the most amazing thing about air. I can kill without need of gunpowder, or bullets. It's nature's fury."

Anna's cane lowered a bit, and Richelle could see her shoulders slump slightly. Anna's left hand, which was holding the cane end closest to her, was starting to shake.

"I can see you've almost figured it out. I'll help you along. My family excels in the role of ambassador. We know how to absorb emotions, and absorb insults, and to store it all. We then boil it down, and shape that energy to our will, and from that we are building a new world order. That is who we Piemans are," said Richelle with an ear-to-ear grin.

Anna's eyes went wide. "Wait—Pieman... Marcus? But he's *dead*... that—" She had unconsciously lowered her cane to where it was pointing right at the ground.

"How—"

"This could have been such a nice, friendly chat," interrupted Richelle. In the blink of an eye, she dropped to one knee, held her hand-cannon with both hands, and then, with a blast, sent Anna flying backward.

Richelle turned to the Hound with a smirk on her face. "Some people are so *rude.*"

She holstered her hand-cannon and ordered her soldiers, "Signal everyone. Kill their guards if they are dumb enough to stay. Subdue the Yellow Hoods and bring me the Watt boy—but if you kill any of them, you and your family will share a worse fate."

"What just happened?" said Elly.

Suddenly, an arrow narrowly missed Richy's head.

"An archer—in the forest!" warned Tee.

"Scatter!" yelled Richy.

As the battle grew louder and the rain pounded down, Anna thought about how little she'd trusted those around her, and how much she'd acted out of fear and pride. She had unnecessarily risked all of their lives, and possibly doomed the Tub.

Just before she blacked out, she heard Tee scream for help.

CHAPTER THIRTY-TWO
ALLIES OLD AND NEW

Pierre had spent most of his morning searching Minette for the Cochon brothers and Egelina-Marie. As he was about to give up, he spotted them leaving a tavern at the end of a road. "I wouldn't have thought to look there," he said to himself. The habits of towners were still somewhat a mystery to him.

"Well," said Bakon, slapping his middle brother on the back, "you're an old man now, Squeals!"

"Can we sing happy birthday again?" asked Bore, always the big kid.

"No!" yelled the others in unison.

"You're a grown man, Bore—enough with the happy birthdays," said Squeals.

"Don't make me cuddle you and call you George!" said Bore, grabbing his older brother and giving him a play squeeze.

"Oh—hello, Monsieur de Montagne," said Squeals,

quickly getting out of his brother's grip.

"Have you been drinking?" asked Pierre, worried he might already have failed in his mission.

Bakon laughed. "Huh, no, no—it's morning. We just started the day with a great breakfast. It's Squeals' birthday, and this place has an amazing breakfast for special occasions, if you ask well enough in advance—*or* if you're Egelina-Marie and ask the night before," said Bakon, winking at her.

Egelina-Marie lost her relaxed pose and straightened up. "What's the matter, Monsieur de Montagne? Something's wrong."

"That's not just concern on your face," said Squeals. "Spill it."

Pierre was nervous. In all his years, he'd rarely been entrusted with a task so important. "Monsieur Klaus sent me to find you. The Yellow Hoods' lives might be in danger."

After relaying everything Nikolas had told him, Pierre studied their expressions. "I don't know what all of that means, but I know it's not good, and it's some distance away," he said.

Bakon rubbed his stubbly face. "It means we shouldn't've spent five minutes standing here!"

Egelina-Marie took charge. "Squeals, Bore—go to the house and get your flintlocks. Bakon, get some horses— *fast* ones. I'll get my stuff. Meet me at the southern exit of town."

"What should I do, Sergeant Archambault?" asked Pierre.

"Come with me. Go over everything you said, again," said Egelina-Marie. "We'll plan on the way. Bakon's right —we don't have much time."

———

Mounira hid, curled up in a tight little ball, under her bed. Quietly, she repeatedly mouthed the words she'd heard Nikolas reusing, hoping it was some kind of message. "Marcus, Pieman, old home, engine."

Every few minutes, panic started creeping in. At first, she fought it off by reminding herself that she had to save her friends, and Anciano Klaus. When that wasn't enough, she focused on a mental image of her father and mother, and thought about how much she wanted to see them again.

The next time panic came, nothing seemed to work. She wanted to run outside and reveal herself to the guards and the man who would take Nikolas away, just to be done with it. She was halfway out from under the bed when she caught herself and forced herself back under.

Mounira curled herself back up again into a tight ball, closed her eyes, and focused on the one thing she had left: her pain. Every moment of every day, she had worked at blocking out the pain from her right arm's stump. She imagined herself facing the evil pain monster, grabbing it, and pulling it into herself. The pain was so intense that she was certain she was going to pass out, but she didn't. When she opened her eyes, she was nearly soaked to the bone.

The front door closed, startling Mounira. She was about to crawl out from under the bed but heard a floorboard creak nearby. She watched well-worn, black leather boots walk into and around the room, leaving traces of grass and mud. Finally, the person turned and left. When the front door closed again, there was finality to it.

Mounira remained there, under the bed, a little longer. She had no idea what to do. With a deep, calming breath, she climbed out from under the bed and decided to brave the hallway. Shuffling her feet, she nervously made her way to the kitchen and timidly peeked around the corridor corner. Nothing was out of place in the kitchen—even the sink was empty.

She wondered if perhaps they'd washed the dishes and put them away, though she couldn't recall hearing that take place. She felt the side of the kettle; it was cool enough to the touch that she doubted whether they'd really made tea. Could she have fallen asleep and imagined everything?

Suddenly, the front door burst open. Mounira spun around and screamed at the top of her lungs. Standing there, arm up in the air, she yelled "I give up!"

A beige-hooded figure stepped in and closed the door.

"Sorry to scare you. I didn't realize anyone was here—and actually, the people who just took Nikolas must not have known you were here, either." The figure pulled back the beige hood, revealing short, blond hair and a striking, square-jawed woman.

Mounira, frozen with her arm still in the air, stared at the woman slowly ascending the stairs.

Gesturing for Mounira to remain calm, the woman said, "My name is Christina. I don't mean you any harm. By the way—I don't mean to be rude, but do you only have one arm? Your blouse sleeve seems empty… or might you have a crossbow or pistol hidden behind your back?" Christina raised her own hands to show she wasn't carrying a weapon.

Mounira smiled nervously and put her arm down. "No. I—ah—just have the one, since about half a year ago."

"Sorry to hear that," the woman said compassionately. She walked up to Mounira and crouched down to look her in the eyes. Christina was five-foot-eight, a good deal taller than Mounira's four feet and four inches.

Mounira examined Christina's clothes. She wore a white blouse and a simple, buttoned, dust-colored vest over top. Her leather pants were dark brown. Her boots were light brown, and appeared quite durable. A black belt held several pouches of various sizes, a strange-looking pistol, and a familiar eighteen-inch metal rod.

"Is that a shock-stick? Like the Yellow Hoods have?" asked Mounira, pointing to the metal rod.

Christina glanced down. "Yes, it is."

"You know Anciano Klaus, don't you?" said Mounira. "Were you here last night?"

Christina smiled. "Yes. Did you hear us? We tried to be quiet. I hadn't seen him in a couple of months and I had some things I needed to discuss with him. He was my father's best friend."

Mounira looked at Christina's arms; it looked like there was something under one of the blouse sleeves. "Are you an inventor, like him?"

Christina smiled and stroked Mounira's hair. "You're observant. I grew up inventing things with my father. We traveled a lot. Several times, we came here. I've known Nikolas for a long time—I was younger than you are when I first met him." Sadness crossed her face as she thought of her father.

"You have nice teeth, and I like your accent," said Mounira, smiling back. She let out a gargantuan sigh.

"Thank you," said Christina. "I came running here once I saw a coach departing with its windows covered. I recognized the colors as—"

Mounira blurted out the words she'd been trying to remember, "Marcus Pieman's old home engine!"

Christina was confused. "Wait—what? Was Marcus Pieman here?" she asked, standing up and looking worried. "Marcus Pieman? *Here?*"

Mounira nodded. "Yes. Who is he? And why did Anciano Klaus and he sound so friendly when they were talking to each other?"

Christina thought for a moment. "Are you *certain* it was Marcus Pieman? *Absolutely* certain?"

Mounira nodded vigorously. "Yes! Nikolas kept saying the other man's name and so I thought he was trying to signal something to me. He also had a funny way of saying the other words—*old home*, and *engine*."

Christina closed her eyes and tried to remember something. "Wait—um... Now how did my father used to do it... Tell me—which words are the ones that stand out when I say: The dog went *home* last Thursday, after *it* rained."

"*Home*, and *it*," answered Mounira.

"Great!" said Christina, grinning, though with tears in her eyes. She started looking around, for nothing in particular. "This is terrible. Your friends are in worse danger than Nikolas thought. We'll never get to them in time, even with my whirly-bird."

Mounira poked Christina to get her attention. "Maybe there's something in Anciano Klaus' secret lab, downstairs?"

Christina patted her on the head. "Oh? That's just a library," she said. "I've got to figure this out."

"*No*," said Mounira, with fiery eyes. "I mean the place

that the *rug* lowers into. There's got to be something in there?"

Christina analyzed Mounira's face. "Show me."

CHAPTER THIRTY-THREE
BATTLE OF THE HOODS

The Yellow Hoods scattered as the rain continued beating down. Richy ran toward the sail-carts and the two guardsmen there. Elly bolted off to join Franklin and the four guards by the southern rock pile. Tee ventured out onto the rampart.

Gretel emerged from the Red Forest, southeast of the rock pile. Hans, with his own escort of soldiers, engaged the guards protecting Elly and Franklin. Saul, with two soldiers, headed for Richy and the sail-carts. The trio proudly wore their red hooded cloaks.

Tee nestled into position and pulled out her slingshot and stones. She took aim at a soldier attacking Elly and Franklin. The rain made it challenging, but her third shot connected, distracting the soldier. Elly took advantage, and lit him up with a shock-stick.

"Crack shot, she is," said Franklin from behind Elly.

"That's my girl!" said Elly, dodging another soldier's sword.

"If he doesn't make short work of you," sneered Hans to Elly, referring to the soldier, "then I will—once I'm done with your guards."

"*Get him, Elly!*" Tee cheered into the loud rain. A glint of gold caught Tee's attention, and she turned to see that she was not alone on the rampart. A huge man in his long, brown leather coat and scary gloves stood there; water was pouring off him as if it were afraid to get him wet.

Before exacting revenge for his humiliation at the hands of the Yellow Hoods, months ago, he wanted Tee to know his name. "My name's the Hound," he said, looking down at her.

"Well—what *big gloves* you have, all the better to—" jested Tee, as she sprang up—but then lost her footing. As Tee slipped over the wall's edge, her slingshot's leather strap got caught between two of the rampart's stones. She clung to it, tightly, with both hands.

The Hound shook his head. "Huh—you are *unbelievably* lucky. This time, though, luck *isn't* going to save you. I'm going to have all your yellow hoods hung on a wall."

Just as the Hound reached down to grab Tee, a shot rang out that startled him. The Hound slipped and banged his head on the rampart stones. Stunned for a moment, he lay there.

Still dangling, Tee said, "You need to work on your follow-through, especially after that bit about my luck. Of course, any time you'd like to get up and, ah, help me up, I'd appreciate it." Inside, she bordered on terrified.

Elly glanced over to Richelle whom, to Elly's surprise, was still standing in the rain, some fifty feet away, with her hood up. Richelle hadn't retreated to the dry comfort of her coach but instead remained on the battlefield. She watched her soldiers finish loading Anna's body into the coach.

"Another one down," said Hans, finishing with the last guard. He stared menacingly at Elly and Franklin.

Elly and Franklin recoiled in fear.

"Get the Watt boy," commanded Hans to his remaining soldier.

Franklin turned to run, but slipped. The brawny soldier scooped him up.

Hans pointed his rapier at the ground and gave Elly a smug look. "Care to surrender? We're not supposed to hurt you, but *accidents* do happen."

"Run, Elly!" yelled Franklin, struggling hard, yet unable to get loose from the soldier.

Elly changed her grip on her remaining, fully-charged shock-stick and clicked its activation button. She took a step toward Hans, who leapt backward, and then threw her shock-stick at the soldier. Just before it made contact, Franklin used the back of his head to knock the soldier in the chin, causing him to lose his grip on Franklin. The soldier never knew what hit him.

Hans raised his blade. "I don't mind two-on-one, but you're all out of shock-sticks, aren't you? So—what are you going to do now, against my blade?" He slashed at the air with his rapier.

Elly pulled two older shock-sticks from her cloak. She'd charged and packed them earlier, just in case. Eyes trained on Hans, Elly said, "Franklin, go to the sail-carts —now."

Hans smiled sinisterly. "Ooh—some spare toys? Does this get any better? Let's dance!" he said, lunging forward. He wished Elly would put up a good fight before her defeat. His challenge would be remembering *not* to kill her. How he hated rules.

Tee felt the slingshot's strap slip slightly, and looked down at the cobblestone landing, twenty feet below. "Guys?"

Richy finally accepted that the sail-carts weren't going to be of any use—the sails were too wet to use in the rain. He felt guilty for abandoning his friends for a pointless endeavor.

"Richy!" yelled Bakon through the storm. The Cochon brothers, with Pierre and Egelina-Marie, exited the Red Forest, and quickly dismounted from their horses.

Richy's blue eyes shone with hope, and he started talking a mile a minute. "*Guys!* We need help! They have soldiers, and I think Anna's dead! And they have this Red Hood lady that we've never seen before—and the other

Red Hoods are here, too!"

"Wow—you've been busy," said Bakon, looking around.

"Okay—I think I got all that," said Egelina-Marie. "Pierre, Bakon—you guys rush on ahead. We're going to make some noise to draw some of their forces here."

Richy snapped his fingers, having remembered something he left out. "Oh, and they've got a guy with these *huge* metal gloves, with electricity jumping around!"

"Got it!" said Bakon, getting back on his horse. Bore and Squeals quickly helped Pierre get back up onto his.

"You're doing well for a guy who never rides," said Egelina-Marie to Pierre.

"The pain in my backside, I can ignore for now! I've never felt so alive!" said Pierre, laughing.

Bakon looked at Pierre. "Like before, just a little nudge to the ribs is all she needs." A moment later, they were bolting down the battlefield.

Egelina-Marie turned to Bore. "Tie up our horses like the others."

"Got it!" replied Bore, sounding almost like Bakon. Egelina-Marie smiled.

"Squeals, Richy, cover your ears," Egelina-Marie said as she raised her rifle. "I'm going to get us some attention."

CHAPTER THIRTY-FOUR

THE YELLOW HOOD

With a series of clanks and clunks, Christina and Mounira found themselves lowering through the floor, on the rug of Nikolas' downstairs library, and into his hidden lab.

Christina grinned and shook her head in disbelief, looking at Mounira. "You know, people *suspected* he had at least one place like this. I can't believe you discovered this secret," said Christina, wiping the sweat from her brow and putting down the small metal rods.

"Was getting those metal things to the middle of the rug really that tough?" asked Mounira.

"You have no idea," said Christina.

"What were you pushing against?" asked Mounira.

"Must be some type of magnetic field. I know the theory, but I've never heard of anyone creating one." Christina could see the confusion on Mounira's face. "If I hadn't learned about magnetic fields from Nikolas himself and discussed it with two other master inventors, I'd have no clue, either. Nikolas is way, *way* ahead of his time."

As the platform stopped lowering, they gazed around

in astonishment.

"This place is huge," said Mounira, turning around and around in awe.

Christina stepped off the rug. "I'm—… speechless."

They had been lowered into the middle of a grand laboratory, with artificial lighting similar to the library above. In the lab were geared machines in various states on two workbenches: one in front of them, and one behind them. Machinery and contraptions stood in chalked-out areas to their left and right. There were bookcases and wooden cabinets behind the tables, and things hanging from the ceiling in the distance.

"This lab must be at least the size of the house," said Mounira.

"Unbelievable. How did he build this place?" said Christina. "I mean—people had to have helped him, but *who*? I can't imagine how this was all kept a secret."

As Christina wandered about, Mounira climbed up onto a stool at one of the long workbenches and marveled at the clockwork machinery before her. There was care and deliberateness in how everything was laid out, as if Nikolas had taken the device apart to adjust something, but hadn't yet had the time to finish.

"What's this supposed to be?" asked Mounira, gesturing to what lay in front of her.

Christina turned on her heels. "Hmm—let's have a look," she said, walking over. She pulled out a pair of spectacles from a belt pouch and started inspecting the pieces. After a minute of mumbling to herself, she removed her glasses, and then wondered aloud, "Odd. *This* is definitely a joint, but it only bends one hundred and eighty degrees. Hmm... I wonder why he limited it. Then there's this additional joint, here, where he hadn't finished something yet. There are these small tubes, and —" Christina scratched her head.

"I can't read his writing," said Mounira, inspecting the plans elsewhere on the huge worktable. "I think these are the drawings for that thing. Is this even Frelish?"

Christina moved over to have a closer look. "Those are indeed the plans. My father Christophe, Nikolas, and a couple of other master inventors developed a secret shorthand for their plans. They wanted a standard, so they could collaborate, but they only taught a few how to read it. I remember when my father got the others to agree that he could teach me—it was a great honor. I'm officially a junior master inventor."

"*Junior* master?" asked Mounira, making a funny face. "Isn't that like being a small giant?"

"Something like that," chuckled Christina, still looking over the plans. "Some people would be offended at age thirty five of being called a *junior* anything, but not me. Maybe this is the year I shake off that part of the title... who knows?"

"Now, hang on a second," said Christina, restarting her analysis of the design. "Well, it *is*. Oh my—" Her eyes welled up with tears.

"What is it?" asked Mounira, looking back and forth between Christina and the huge design diagram sheets. "What *is* it?"

Christina, a tear now running down her face, looked at Mounira and smiled. "Nikolas was—ah—trying to build you an arm."

The young girl—who'd been fighting to make a place for herself and yet not be in anyone's way—was stunned. "I... I don't understand."

Christina laughed, releasing some of her emotion. She wiped her eyes with her sleeve and took a breath. "See this, on the drawing? It would have gone here, on this joint. There's an impossibly small engine that would have gone here. This... *all* of it... it's some kind of clockwork arm. I've never seen anything like it."

Mounira choked up. "He was building an *arm?* How can anyone build an *arm?*" She looked at Christina in disbelief. "For *me?*"

"Do you know another one-armed girl in his life?" asked Christina.

"But—but I'm no one! I'm just—" said Mounira, her eyes now shedding droplets of their own.

"Well—you're *not* no one," Christina said, rubbing Mounira's back. "I can't read some of the code here, but it seems like he's been working on this for a while."

Mounira started to wonder, but then a thought came racing, screaming, back to the front of her mind. *"The Yellow Hoods!"* she exclaimed. She and Christina had been too easily distracted by the wondrous contents of the secret lab, but her friends remained in danger.

"Oh—right!" acknowledged Christina, pulling back her blouse sleeve and glancing at a thin armband machine she wore underneath. She flipped a part of it. "We've only got fifty minutes until noon."

"What's that?" asked Mounira.

"Later! We do need to focus. Recognize anything else here?" said Christina. "Anything, on the off chance, that would be fast?"

Mounira looked around. "In the corner over there— *that* looks like a sail-cart, but it's glowing blue, and doesn't have a mast."

"What's a sail-cart?" asked Christina.

"Anciano Klaus made a few for the Yellow Hoods. It's like a mini-horse coach, but it uses the wind, not horses."

Christina ran to the sail-cart. "Blue… what did he say about *blue* last night?… Ah! The horseless cart! But he made it sound like he was *years* away from making anything like this…" she said, pulling off some panels to look it over.

"This is incredible! Okay, this connects to… hmm, right, and this…" Christina's eyes sparkled with ideas. "It's too small for *me* to fit in there. Do you think you can drive it? I know how it works."

"To save my friends? I can do anything," said Mounira, though unsure of what she was getting herself into.

"We'll need to make a couple of quick changes. But first, I need to get something from the big shed outside."

Christina soon returned with a huge, bulging bag with curved, wide blades sticking out. She found Mounira sitting in the cart, simulating what she'd seen the Yellow Hoods do.

"Figured it out yet?" asked Christina.

"There are things in here I haven't seen before," said Mounira. "I think *this* switch makes it go, and then this stick here maybe controls the speed?"

Christina nodded approvingly. "Sounds like a good guess."

Mounira noticed the bag. "What's that?"

Christina smiled. "This is my masterpiece—I call it a whirly-bird. Judging from what I saw when I looked at the panels, I should be able to rig the two together. Probably best to put this at the back."

"Where are you going to sit?" asked Mounira.

"You'll see. And—trust me—there's a reason I asked if you can drive it. I'm going to be busy in the back," she said. "Oh, one more thing—here," said Christina, pulling something yellow from out of the bag.

Mounira shook it out. It was a yellow cloak with a hood, identical to the ones that Tee, Elly, and Richy wore!

"Where did you *get* this?" Mounira asked. She was amazed with the fabric, so light, and yet incredibly strong.

Christina started unloading her bag. "I make those."

CHAPTER THIRTY-FIVE

FALL OF THE MOUNTAIN STONE

"Guys! Don't leave me hanging! I need help!" yelled Tee, seeing the Hound get on all fours, after his fall, and shake his head clear.

A moment later, the Hound stood, did a quick check of the control boxes on his forearms, and then turned up the dials. His shock-gloves started to crackle with electricity.

Tee shot a glance around to look for her fellow Yellow Hoods, almost losing her grip in the process. She could only see Elly, who was busy avoiding a red-hooded swordsman's blade.

"Lights out, kid," said the Hound. Electricity danced from finger to finger.

Tee took a deep breath. She could only think of one option, and it was risky. She freed one hand to delve into her yellow cloak's hidden pockets. Pulling out a shock-stick, she pressed its activation button while staring into the Hound's eyes. He hesitated.

"You've enjoyed this before, haven't you?" Tee said menacingly. She wasn't sure if she was willing to risk the fall to the cobblestone below.

Tee's pinky finger slipped off the end of her slingshot. She could feel the other fingers slipping, too. Then, a glint of steel from an arrow aimed at her from less than twenty feet away caught her eye. "The archer!" said Tee, trying to glance around without risking the fall. "What's that sound?" she said, noticing something cutting through the softening rain.

Gretel, her aim steady, slowly drew back her bowstring. She didn't mind taking her time to get the shot right—she would make it count, and have her revenge for their earlier encounter.

Suddenly, Tee's grip gave way, and she fell.

"Goodbye, little yellow birdy!" said Gretel, laughing as she adjusted and then loosed the arrow.

Tee felt herself suddenly snatched out of the air and held tight. The rider quickly brought the horse to a stop with his other hand, and loosened his grip around Tee.

Opening her clenched-shut eyes, Tee looked at who'd saved her. "Pierre!" she yelled triumphantly.

"Got you," he said. Pierre coughed, and then slid off the horse, falling to the ground.

Tee looked down at Pierre and could see the tail of an arrow on one side of his rib cage, and the arrow head poking out the other side.

Gretel was stunned. "Where did *he* come from?"

Tee slid off the horse and grabbed Pierre by his coat collar. "No, Pierre. No! No dying! You *can't* die on me!" she pleaded.

Pierre blinked his eyes repeatedly, as if trying to clear a growing fog. "Saved you, like you... saved me," he said weakly. He thought of the dire lynx, and realized that death hadn't been coming for him then, but rather giving him a warning—a warning to make good use of the time he had left. He smiled at Tee. "*I did,*" he mouthed.

Tee hugged Pierre tightly, washing away his fear. He wished he could tell her how much the three of them meant to him, and the purpose they'd given to his life. He used his last ounce of strength to give Tee a gentle tap, hoping his tap could—somehow—communicate all of that. Then, Tee felt Pierre's body go limp.

She looked at his unblinking eyes and knew he was gone. "No! No! Pierre! *No!*" she screamed angrily, her tears streaming down on him and replacing the rain that had stopped.

Elly and Hans both turned to look, as did Bakon and the Hound, now engaged in combat.

Just moments before, Bakon had slid off his own horse, blocking the Hound's path as he'd arrived at the bottom of the tower's stairs. "That was supposed to be *me,*" said Bakon. "But he wanted to save her. He—"

"He must have been important to you," said the Hound, placing his shock-glove on Bakon's shoulder.

"*Unhh!*" Bakon grunted with clenched teeth. The electricity made his muscles contract so quickly and intensely he thought his bones would break. He dropped to the ground, writhing in pain, and blacked out.

The Hound looked around. Gretel and six soldiers were with Richelle, and Hans, meanwhile, could handle one little girl. He decided to go help Saul.

Hans, ready to say something witty, turned back to face Elly. She tossed one old shock-stick to his left, forcing him the other way, and then jabbed her remaining one straight into his ribs. Sparks flew, and Hans dropped to his knees, clutching his chest.

"*Ow!* That really hurt!" he yelled. "What's with all the shocking lately? I'm getting tired of it!"

"Huh, it worked!" said Elly, giving Hans a good kick to the ribs to top it off.

"*Ahh!*" screamed Tee in rage.

Elly turned to see Tee charging with shock-sticks in hand directly toward Gretel.

The first of Richelle's soldiers ran to intercept Tee. She dropped to her knees and hit him with both shock-sticks against the inside of his right knee, felling him swiftly.

She sprang back to her feet in an instant, preparing for the second soldier as he came at her with sword out. The world slowed down for Tee as she analyzed his movements and instinctively adjusted her speed and direction.

As the soldier pulled back his sword and prepared to lunge, Tee stepped up onto his forward-bent knee, let go of her shock-sticks, grabbed his head firmly with both hands, slid over his shoulder, and then flipped him over with all her weight. As he landed with a thud, she picked up her shock-sticks, whacked him hard in the head, and continued her run forward.

Gretel's bow arm started to shake as she fired an arrow and missed Tee. There was something in Tee's burning eyes and berserker fury that had horrible memories pounding at the gates of Gretel's mind. She felt her arms go weak, and then felt powerless. She suddenly hated the feeling of her wet clothes, and the world. Unable to take it, Gretel dropped her bow and bolted for the safety of the forest.

All the while, Richelle had been watching Tee keenly. "Impressive," she said with genuine admiration.

Tee stopped chasing Gretel and scanned around, locking on to Richelle and her four remaining soldiers. "*Aahh!!*" she screamed, running at them. "*This is* your *fault!*"

As the soldiers hesitantly stepped forward, Richelle laughed. "Please—*don't* humiliate yourselves. *I'll* handle her. Get that other one," she said, pointing to Elly.

"Tee, what are you doing?!" yelled Elly, realizing her only choice was to run back to Richy and the others. She'd never seen Tee like this, and feared that this time Tee was going to get herself killed.

CHAPTER THIRTY-SIX

ROCKETING AHEAD

"I don't think this was a great idea!" yelled Mounira to Christina. The two shot down the road in the modified sail-cart as if they'd been fired from a cannon. Christina rode at the back, in a seat sporting a mast and folded-down, curved blades that looked like petals from a giant flower.

"We're *almost* going fast enough, Mounira. Push the speed stick into its last position! Let's see what this *rocket-cart* can do!" said Christina.

Mounira steered cautiously, shocked at how her slightest move resulted in a big change in direction. "This is crazy! We're going too *fast!* I can't let go of the steering wheel in order to change gear!"

"Maybe you shouldn't have slammed it into third gear to start with," said Christina, laughing. "How would Richy do it? He's the expert, right? I heard he can do all kinds of crazy—*hey*, watch out!" Christina pointed to a rapidly approaching bend in the road.

Mounira pulled on the steering wheel; the rocket-cart narrowly missed a horse and cart as it hugged the winding road. "It's hard to think right now!" she yelled back. She'd never done anything so foolish or exciting.

Christina glanced at her armband clock and turned some pieces. "Okay—we need to be airborne in less than four minutes, if we're going to make it in time!"

"Air—*what?!*" said Mounira, turning back to look at Christina.

"Eyes on the road!" ordered Christina. She had to admit this was a ludicrous plan, but it was the only one with a chance.

"You didn't mention flying! That's impossible!" yelled Mounira.

"Ha! That's what they all say—even when I use my whirly-bird right in front of them. Let's see just how much I learned, and if I hooked it up right," said Christina. "*Tree!*" she yelled, flinching as Mounira maneuvered the cart just in time. Given how close that was, Christina cringed as she said, "We need the extra speed *now*, Mounira. Now or never!"

Mounira swallowed. "I—I can't!" she said, afraid to let go of the steering wheel.

Christina dropped her big-sister tone and slipped into her natural voice, that of a leader of a resistance movement. "*This* is what being a Yellow Hood means. *This* is the type of hero that you are inside. *Lose the fear!* Pull out that locked-up fury and *focus*. Your friends have been betrayed! Nikolas has been taken! We're the *only* ones that can help. *Do it!*"

Mounira breathed in deeply. Letting out the breath, she used her knees to grip the steering wheel, then freed-up her hand to shift the gear into its last position, and just barely grabbed the steering wheel before the rocket-cart shot them forward, faster than ever.

For the next two minutes, they raced down the mountain in relative silence. Christina worked furiously to get everything ready, while giving Mounira the occasional direction.

"Wait—is that Tee's house coming up? Do you need me to stop?" asked Mounira hopefully.

"*Stop?* No—it's time for the leap of faith. *Keep it steady!*" ordered Christina, readying herself.

Mounira's eyes went wide with panic as they shot past the house. "Wait—the *cliff?!*" screamed Mounira.

As soon as the rocket-cart was airborne, Christina pushed a pedal, which released wings under the rocket-cart and unfurled the whirly-bird's blades. "Now—let's see if this will start mid-air."

Mounira closed her eyes and whispered prayers. A strange, loud sound sputtered, then kicked in, vibrating the rocket-cart. After what seemed like a while, she opened an eye. "Are we falling to our deaths?"

"Nope!" exclaimed Christina triumphantly.

Mounira opened the other eye and looked at the spinning blades—a blur. "It's working!" she screamed. She looked down at the trees below. "We're flying!"

Christina wiped her forehead, turned the mast controls, and checked some gauges. "Now I just need to make sure this doesn't fall apart, and we're good," she muttered to herself.

"Wait—what?" said Mounira.

"Pay no attention to the lady in the back," said Christina, laughing.

———————

As Squeals was felled by the Hound's shocking punch, Bore yelled and charged at him like a wild animal, knocking down two Fare soldiers that stood in his way. The Hound was ready, though, and a moment later Bore found himself screaming.

The Hound's eyes grew wide with surprise as Bore fell to one knee, but then appeared to be getting back up with stubborn determination. He cranked his shock-gloves up to maximum and placed his other hand on Bore. The fury in Bore's eyes began to shake the Hound's confidence until, finally, Bore's eyes rolled and he fell over.

Taking a breath to steady himself, the Hound looked to the group gathered near the horses and sail-carts, some hundred yards away.

With Egelina-Marie's pistol jammed and her rifle out of ammunition, she was forced to resort to her sword to deal with the Fare soldiers.

Franklin watched from behind a tree, amazed at the group's bravery, wishing he could be like them. He couldn't believe the conviction on Elly's face as she came into view; he'd never seen someone so young look so menacing.

The last Fare soldier exchanged blows with Egelina-Marie. As Egelina-Marie prepared to lunge, she slipped. The soldier tried to take advantage of her fall, but she recovered gracefully and got him right through the chest instead.

Saul and Richy stood, weapons in hand, staring each other down. Richy had a growing feeling that the Red Hood in front of him was familiar, but he wasn't willing to admit it.

"Hotaru—stop protecting those people! Come back to your *family*. Come back to us!" said Saul. "Drop those sticks and come *home*." Saul still couldn't remember the details behind how he knew Richy, but he knew that if he couldn't get Richy to surrender, he might be able to get him to lower his guard enough to take him out.

The Hound arrived and stood beside Saul. "Ready to give up, yet?" he asked of their adversaries. "Your entourage has fallen." The Hound gestured to the dead guardsmen, and the fallen Cochon brothers.

Egelina-Marie, Elly, and Richy quickly shared a look —they were in this until the end. Franklin had a death grip on the tree trunk. He couldn't believe what he was witnessing.

At the other side of the battlefield, Tee finally reached Richelle.

"Pierre's death is *your* fault!" Tee yelled, tears still streaming down her face.

Richelle lowered her stance as she prepared for Tee. She quickly took two small wooden planks out from under her cloak and started parrying Tee's blows expertly. "My responsibility in his death is indirect, at best." She could feel the pain in Tee's voice, empathizing with how Tee felt, but remaining focused. Richelle felt like she was fighting a younger version of herself. The rage was familiar.

"You're an innovative fighter when you're angry," Richelle said. "Evidently, it sharpens your mind. But you're getting tired—and sloppy." Richelle spun Tee around and shoved her away with her foot. "You're going to get yourself killed, if you don't stop."

They fought in silence for another minute, Tee never managing to land a blow. She started to breathe hard. She hated it, but Richelle was right—the rage that had fueled her was draining away, and her body was feeling heavy.

"You've gone further with your training than I'd have guessed," said Richelle. Tee lunged at her again, only to be flipped squarely onto her back. "Come see me in a couple of years. I'm interested to see what two granddaughters of world-changers would be like, whether as friends, or enemies. Now, go—before I change my mind. Go and bury your friend."

Richelle started walking toward her coach. Tee, thinking she sensed an opportunity, charged and leapt at

Richelle with her shock-sticks, hoping to finally land a blow.

In a flash of swirling red cloak, Richelle jumped backward, drew her cannon pistol, held it with both hands, and shot Tee backward into the air like a rag-doll.

"*Tee!*" screamed Elly.

"What's that?" said Richy, pointing off in the distance.

Saul immediately turned to look.

The Hound shook his head. He was about to criticize Saul for being gullible, but then heard something strange from behind. The odd sound grew louder and more unnerving, until finally he couldn't help himself. He turned around.

A bizarre contraption was coming towards them, flying above the trees at the southwest, shaking wildly. It came down to the ground in a series of drops and pauses, all the while continuing straight toward them, moving so fast that hardly any of them had time to react.

"Look out!" screamed Mounira as she and Christina jumped out of the crippled rocket-cart and rolled to the ground. The rocket-cart crashed forcefully into the Hound, sending him flying back.

CHAPTER THIRTY-SEVEN
FOREIGN ELEMENT

"We've got to get *Tee!*" said Elly, turning to run, but then stopping in her tracks.

"What's the worry?" asked a weary, approaching Tee. She had a black eye, blood on her chin, and walked with a slight limp, but was otherwise fine.

Elly jumped with joy. "*Lala!* But—I saw you thrown through the air when Richelle shot you!" she said, as tears of joy rolled down. She pounced on Tee and hugged her tightly.

Tee winced as Elly rocked her back and forth with an emotional hug. "Elly... you're... *crushing* me... *ugh*—dying," Tee joked.

"Sorry," said Elly, backing off, and wiping her tears.

"Wait—if *you're* fine," said Richy, "then Anna could be fine, too, right?"

Tee looked back across the battlefield. "Maybe—but they took Anna."

"What happened?" asked Egelina-Marie.

Tee looked back at the coach as it pulled away. "That

unusual, huge pistol of Richelle's shoots air. When it hit me, I felt like a leaf in the wind. The pistol connects to something on her back, hidden under her cloak. I saw it just as she spun around to shoot me."

"Whoa," said Richy. "An *air* gun. Wait… so Richelle came here *not* intending to kill us?"

The Yellow Hoods and Franklin looked at each other.

"She also had wooden paddles to block my blows. If she'd used a sword or anything else—" said Tee, bothered by what it meant.

"Don't say it!" yelled Elly, shoving Tee.

Franklin shook his head. "Bad guys who came but didn't want us dead? I don't get it."

"Tee," said Mounira, meekly, "I'm—I'm glad you're safe, but—"

"Mounira—nice cloak!" interrupted Tee. "Where did you get it?"

She looked at Christina. "She gave it to me. I'll—I'll take it off now."

Richy gently took Mounira's hand. "*No way* are you taking that off! You flew that… *thing*, and you hit the crazy bad guy with it. That's *crazy* awesome. You're one of us now."

Mounira blushed. "Thanks—but, Tee, I've *got* to tell you something."

"You look worried. What's wrong?" Tee asked.

"Marcus Pieman took your grandfather! Marcus—

he's the leader of the Fare. I was hiding in the house and heard it all. I—I didn't do anything except listen... I'm sorry," said Mounira, looking at the ground.

Tee suppressed her immediate feeling of surprise as she absorbed the mix of emotions on Mounira's face. "Hey," she said, lifting Mounira's chin, "you got his *name*. That will help us find him, and get my Grandpapa back. If they'd captured you too, then we'd know nothing. We *will* get him back."

"Count us in," said Bakon, as he and his brothers staggered over, shaking off the lingering effects of the Hound's shock-gloves. Their faces and hair were mud-covered.

"Don't get too close to me looking like *that*," said Egelina-Marie to Bakon, causing him to blush.

Franklin turned to Christina. "Um... silly question—and please don't misunderstand it as a lack of appreciation for you saving us—but whom might you be, then?"

Mounira answered, proud of her new big-sister figure. "This is Christina Creangle. She's the genius that made us fly!"

Christina laughed. "Well, there's more to it than that, but let's just say—"

Suddenly, they heard four gunshots from across the battlefield.

"Who's shooting?" asked Bore, looking around

annoyed.

"*Get down!*" said Squeals, pulling Bore to the wet, muddy ground.

"Over there—near where the coach was—more soldiers," said Bakon. "Eg, can you see if they're Fare?"

Egelina-Marie crouched and looked, "They *aren't* Fare… and they aren't Frelish, either. There are about a dozen men. I'm guessing they were firing at the departing coach and Fare soldiers. I'm stumped on where they're from and what they're doing here."

Mounira started breathing quickly. "We're being invaded—just like home," she whispered.

Franklin still couldn't believe that the little eleven-year-old, one-armed girl had helped save the day. "Mounira—" he started, but then paused; he hadn't done anything like this before. "It's going to be okay. They'll figure out what we need to do," he said, gesturing to the team around them.

"Eg—was it?" said Christina, making her way over to the trees. "I think we need to split up and meet back at Nikolas' place. Do you know the downstairs room at his house?"

"Agreed—but *what* downstairs room?" replied Egelina-Marie. She was collecting the pistols from the fallen guardsmen and handing them out to the Cochon brothers and Christina.

"Guys, they're coming!" said Richy.

The group quickly moved into the trees, pulling the sail-carts and leading the horses along.

"Give me a minute," said Egelina-Marie. She held out a pistol, took aim, fired one shot, dropped the pistol, and then used her spare similarly. Two soldiers, a hundred yards away, fell dead.

"Wow," said Christina. "Impressive."

"A shame they aren't repeating pistols or at least have extra ammunition... Seems Anna hired the cheap guys," said Eg, shaking her head.

Richy looked to Christina. "I'll go with them," he said. "Monsieur Klaus showed us that room once, a couple of months ago. It's where we're supposed to go if things ever go badly."

"Great," said Christina. "We'll meet you there in six hours."

"Bakon, boys—you good with that?" asked Egelina-Marie. The Cochon brothers nodded.

"Elly, you okay?" said Tee. Elly didn't respond but sported a goofy grin. Tee followed Elly's gaze and found she was staring at Christina. Tee gave Elly a quick elbow to the ribs.

Elly gave Tee a frown.

Tee's face then fell. "*Pierre!* We can't leave his body out there. We *can't.*"

Bakon nodded. "Agreed. We need to give him a proper resting place. I also have some frustration I need to let out"— Bakon cracked his knuckles —"and I think these soldiers may be willing to help me with that."

"Okay—we'll take care of Pierre. You guys go," said Egelina-Marie. "Those soldiers will be on top of us shortly."

Richy excitedly said, "We can use the tree-bridges to get around them. But—" he turned to Bakon, "I need *you* to promise me something."

"What, kid?" said Bakon, confused, while keeping an eye out for the soldiers who were finishing up checking their two fallen comrades.

"I need you to take me back to the Ginger Lady's house today. *Promise* me," said Richy, grabbing Bakon's shoulder, making Bakon look him in the eyes. For the first time, Bakon saw the kind of pain in Richy's eyes that Bakon had thought no one else could ever understand.

"We misfits stick together, kid. I promise," said Bakon.

CHAPTER THIRTY-EIGHT

GINGER SECRETS

Bakon pushed the front door to the Ginger Lady's rotten house; the door fell off its rusted hinges and to the ground. Bakon peeked inside, and then shook his head. He wasn't sure Richy would be able to handle it. The kid had been through a lot today, and now he wanted to do this?

Only hours had passed since they'd battled the Fare, dealt with the foreign soldiers, and retrieved Pierre's body. After finding a memorable, peaceful place near a stream in the forest—a place where they could properly say goodbye to Pierre—they had tried talking Richy out of coming here, but he'd insisted.

Bakon looked back to Richy. "I think—"

"*No*—we're going in," insisted Richy, again. His voice trembled, and his eyes were watery. Since learning about his connection to this place, Richy had been having nightmares. He'd grown up hearing scary tales about the Ginger house and the Ginger Lady. Like any child, he'd reached an age where he saw the tales for what they were supposed to be—a story to warn children. Yet, once he'd heard he was one of those children, the stories took on new meaning.

"I... I have to get rid of these nightmares," said Richy. "I can't hold it all in anymore."

Bakon bit his lip and just nodded in understanding. He stepped into the house carefully. "Man, this place stinks!" he exclaimed, covering his mouth and nose with his shirt. "Be careful—I think somebody went to the bathroom right there. *Geez.*"

Steeling himself, Richy walked in. He flinched each time the wooden floorboards creaked.

Bakon checked the bedrooms and returned. "Nothing in there except a bed in one, and rotten straw mattresses in the other. The stairs to the second floor are all broken and boarded up."

"There's no upstairs in my nightmares—they're mostly in here, in this room," said Richy. "There's something here—I *know* there is."

"What are we looking for?" asked Bakon, softly. Bakon walked around, staring in disbelief at the rotten furniture. "I've never seen anything like this." Doors were missing from some of the kitchen cupboards, while some hung from broken hinges.

Richy squatted down and touched the floor with a shaking hand. He gazed around, taking in every emotionally prickly detail. "I recognize that window," he said, standing and taking a step towards it. "In one of my dreams, I saw something—I don't know what—but then the monsters in the shadows got angry and I screamed myself awake."

Bakon scanned around. "I can't see anything that stands out." Looking back at Richy, he could see the boy might be starting to lose it.

"Why was I here? *Why?*" said Richy, tears dropping. "Why? Why?—"

"Hey!" said Bakon, snapping his fingers to get Richy's attention. "Kid, trust me—I have all the sympathy in the world for you, and you're an amazing kid, but we *don't* have time for a meltdown. So pull it together! *You can do this.* Okay?"

Richy gazed back, seemingly only half there.

Bakon stomped in frustration, cracking some of the floorboards. "It's just—I'm—I'm no good at this!" he yelled, stomping again even harder. Bakon wished he could explain to Richy his *own* nightmares, how he and his brothers had been abandoned as children, but he just couldn't find the words. He hated situations like this— they made him feel helpless, like the day he and his brothers had been abandoned. He couldn't take seeing his own pain reflected back at him in Richy's eyes. He wanted to rip that feeling apart.

"What's that?" said Richy, pointing at something showing through a broken floorboard under Bakon's feet.

Bakon got on all fours and quickly removed the broken pieces of floor, revealing some large books. He picked one up carefully and opened it. He took a minute to scan a couple of pages. "I don't believe it. These are accounting ledgers."

"Accounting… for *what?*" said Richy, trying to look, though Bakon wouldn't let him.

"Of… *kids,*" said Bakon. He closed the ledger. "Richy, the people who care for you up in Minette—*they* are your parents; your family. Whatever happened in the past is in the past."

Richy's hands stopped shaking. His eyes shifted from fear, to anger. "Those people in Minette? They *aren't* my parents. They don't even *want* me. Each of them thought the *other* would take me when they split up. What kinds of parents think that? They aren't my family!"

Bakon's hands were open, as if he was trying to catch something that he couldn't see. "Look… I don't know what to say about *them,* but I know that Tee, Elly, and the others—even me and my brothers—*we're* your family too. All this stuff here—" said Bakon, gesturing to the ledgers, "—is just going to eat away at you if you let it."

"*I need to know,*" implored Richy, looking Bakon in the eyes.

"*Okay,* okay. Sit down," said Bakon, opening the ledger and showing it to Richy.

Richy looked at the page, but it didn't make sense. "How can you read this?" he asked.

Bakon gave him a sad smile. "You know how the Klaus family took us in when we were young… and helped us? At least—as much as we'd let them?"

"Yeah," said Richy. "I heard that you, Squeals, and Bore were found in town, near the market. You were just seven or eight."

"Seven. Anyway, we never made it easy on them, but they didn't mind," said Bakon. "One of the amazing things about Isabella was that she made sure we got lessons, like her own kids. We didn't have to do all the same ones, but one that Isabella insisted I finish was accounting. I never thought I'd understand it, but she never let me give up—she somehow knew I could finish it, if only I'd keep at it."

The two spent the next half hour breaking up more floorboards, pulling out journals, and leafing through them independently—after Bakon had showed Richy what to look for.

"I think—" said Richy, getting choked up and closing the ledger he was holding, "I think I'm in this one. I can't look."

Bakon put down the ledger he was holding and took Richy's. "Let me have a look."

Richy started pacing about nervously.

Bakon took his time to digest the entries and notes, flipping back and forth to confirm his understanding. He watched Richy pace, and wondered how he'd take it. Would he hold on to the world he knew, or would he abandon it to hunt down the past?

Richy locked his fear-filled eyes on Bakon.

"Come here, kid," said Bakon. Richy plunked himself down and let out a big breath. He fidgeted with his hands. Bakon held open the ledger between them.

"Right here, it shows that you were bought. There are some interesting notes I'll get to in a minute, but from everything else we've seen, the Ginger Lady didn't *buy* children. She *sold* children, *received* children, and *stole* them—but you're the only one she appears to have bought... ever."

"Why?" asked Richy. "That makes no sense."

Bakon shrugged. "I can't find *why* she bought you, or to whom she was planning on selling you. I *do* know that you were here, and for two months. That was when, according to the notes, her second house—wait... you said you remembered *this* house?"

"Yes," said Richy. "Why?"

Bakon re-read the entries and was disturbed by his realization. "Someone warned her that Lieutenants Archambault and Charlebois were coming, and she put you in the other house, with most of the other kids. Her angry notes here describe someone forcing her to do that as part of a deal. Perhaps the other house was a setup, intended to be found by the Lieutenants."

"But who might warn and help the Ginger Lady?" asked Richy.

Bakon shook his head. "All I know is that the rest of this stuff says that you and several other kids were lost to her, and she'd only be allowed to keep three."

Richy nodded as he processed what Bakon was telling him. "What's that picture, just here?" he said, pointing to an odd little drawing in the ledger.

"I don't know… it kind of looks like a firefly," said Bakon. "It only shows up on the entry where she bought you. I checked the rest in this book, and I didn't see it in any of the other books, either. Did you?"

"No," said Richy. He took the ledger and studied its plain, black cover. It looked so unassuming, so harmless, and yet it was filled with horrible tales. Richy thought for a moment. Finally, he handed it back to Bakon. "I'll remember that picture, but I don't want this. You once said we misfits need to stick together, and that you guys are my family. Well, you're right—I don't care where I came from. I know who I *am*. Maybe what that Red Hood called me, Hotaru… maybe that's just how I said 'who are you?' when I was here. I was three, so it could mean anything. I think I can let all of this go. I won't let it haunt me." He looked at his trembling hand and made a steady fist from it.

Bakon was impressed. He took the ledger from Richy and placed it on the pile with the others. He heard something, and looked out the window. "Eg and my brothers have returned from their scouting."

"Hey, Bakon?" said Richy, gazing up at the rough-looking man.

"Yeah, kid?"

"Thanks, really," said Richy, giving Bakon a hug.

Bakon tapped him on the back. "You're welcome, kid."

As they walked out, something nagged at Bakon.

"You boys all done?" asked Egelina-Marie, from up on her horse.

"Yeah, we are—pretty much," said Bakon, in thought. "You know—why don't you four head out? There are a couple of things here I'd like to double-check."

There was something in Bakon's tone that Egelina-Marie hadn't heard before. She glanced at his brothers to see what they'd say.

"Fine with me—just don't be too late," said Squeals, unconcerned. "It's still my birthday. We've got to finish our celebrating."

Bakon gave Squeals a practiced smiled and an affectionate slap on the arm. "Don't you worry—I'll be ready for it!"

Squeals was happy for a moment, but then his look changed. He'd seen Bakon do that to other people, and to Bore, but never to him. Something didn't feel right.

"I'll catch up to you guys before you know it. Brisk, here—" said Bakon, giving his borrowed horse a tap on the neck, "—will have me blazing past you in no time."

"Okay... bye, then," said Egelina-Marie as she, Squeals, and Bore got their horses moving again. Richy got into his sail-cart and followed.

Two hours later, Egelina-Marie and Richy returned to the Ginger house. Bakon's horse was gone.

Richy hopped out of his sail-cart. "This is silly. He probably just went another way."

Egelina-Marie dismounted, scanning around. "As a guardsman, never mind as my father's daughter, you learn to trust your gut. My gut tells me he was hiding something."

"Should we have left Squeals and Bore behind in Mineau?" asked Richy. "They might have been able to help. It didn't feel right lying to them."

Egelina-Marie shook her head. "Honestly? I don't know. My gut told me that *they* shouldn't be here." She paused. "Can you figure out in which direction Bakon's horse might have gone?"

Richy started examining the surroundings, as Pierre had taught him. "There are hoof prints, here, that lead… eastward. Why would he go east?"

Egelina-Marie shook her head in wonder. "He should've headed west. Does it look like he turned his horse around?"

After continuing for twenty yards, Richy stopped. "No. He got his horse really moving by this point. What's east of here?"

Eg looked around, and then at the decrepit house. "I think the only place for answers is in that house."

Richy looked at the house, too. It seemed to already

be losing its power over him.

Egelina-Marie walked over and into the house, then came right back out, holding her hand over her mouth. "Ugh—I don't think I've ever smelled anything like in *there*."

"I'll go. I can tell you if anything's different from when I was here with Bakon."

A couple of minutes later, Richy returned holding a ledger. "Compared to when I was here earlier, there were more of these scattered all over."

"What made you grab that specific one?" asked Egelina-Marie, taking the old book from Richy and leafing through it.

"It was thrown against a wall, and a side table was broken, just over it. I don't remember that being there when I left."

Eg flipped through each page until she noticed two with smudged ink marks. She touched the spots. "They're still wet," she said, thinking. "I think something here made Bakon... cry."

"He can't cry—he's too tough," said Richy, defending his idol.

Egelina-Marie closed the ledger and closely looked at the ledger's spine, and then the cover that was damaged at the edges. "I think he dug his fingers into this book, before he threw it. He must have been quite angry." She opened it back up to the wet page. "I can't read this.

Here. Can you?"

"Bakon did show me how," said Richy, taking the ledger. "These are the dates, here, and this is where the kids are listed. She used this symbol here to indicate a boy, and another for a girl. She wrote the ages here. This symbol means the entry is canceled. Like these ones, here. I guess she never got the kids."

Egelina-Marie looked at the information again and got all choked up. "Oh, my—the date. The… oh… those ages—"

"What? What is it?"

"*They're* in the book… the Cochon brothers."

Richy's eyes went wide. "Wait…" Richy handed the ledger back to Egelina-Marie and ran inside. "There was something else out of place!"

He returned with a crumpled piece of a paper, handing it over to Egelina-Marie. "Can you read it? I just… I can't look, but I saw writing." The fear he'd felt earlier had returned. He closed his eyes as Egelina-Marie read it out, her voice trembling.

"Thank you for agreeing to take the boys. Your services came highly recommended, and I hope you are able to reunite them with extended family. You should have received my fiancée's payment with this letter. I was nanny to these boys since each was born, and I have cared for them since their family was killed. I will deliver them in the next four weeks. They are three, five, and seven years of age. It is with a heavy heart that I bid them goodbye, but I have little choice. Please take care of Boris, Sevilin, and Beldon Pieman, my three little piggies."

Richy turned to Egelina-Marie. "But, that means—" he started, in a panicky voice.

Egelina-Marie motioned for Richy to calm down and wait. She gently folded the letter and placed it in her pocket. Her voice was controlled as she said, "Richy, I'm going after him—"

"And I'm coming with you," said Richy decisively. "Bakon and you are family to me. I'm coming."

Egelina-Marie looked at the young, determined Yellow Hood and thought about it. She knew if she tried to send him home by himself, he could run into soldiers or worse. She also knew that Richy's tracking skills might make all the difference in finding Bakon—and the sooner they went after him, the fresher the trail would be. Yet, if they didn't head back, no one would know where they'd have went.

CHAPTER THIRTY-NINE

KNOCK, KNOCK

Christina stopped her pacing and checked her armband, again. "They're five hours late, and counting," she said, yawning. They'd already ventured to the kitchen, taken naps, woken up, and started all over again.

Christina and Mounira had been tempted to take everyone down to the hidden lab just for something to do, but they thought that might be a bad idea. There was no question of being able to trust Tee and Elly with the secret, but they weren't yet completely sure about Franklin.

Franklin was asleep on the floor with a book over his face. Mounira was reading on the couch. Tee and Elly, meanwhile, were playing cards on the floor by the fireplace.

"Are they ever late like this?" Christina asked again, to no one in particular.

Tee looked up, her face still heavy with the burden of having lost Pierre, and feeling responsible for it. She kept telling herself that her grandfather would be fine, at least for a while. "Christina, I know you're worried. We're worried too. Like I said earlier, the Cochon brothers can be late, but Egelina-Marie never seems to be. But I'm thinking more and more that something bad happened."

"I'm starting to think that's the *only* possibility," said Christina, looking into the crackling fire.

"What will we do when they get here?" asked Elly, too tired to remember the earlier discussion. Like Tee, she was still distracted by Pierre's death and Nikolas' abduction.

"Once they're here, we'll make our way to Tee's parents and bring them up to speed."

"*If* my parents are back," added Tee. "Given that they weren't there when we passed by, I have a feeling they aren't going to be back until tomorrow. It might be like... a big date night." She shuddered.

"Eww," said Elly.

"I *know!*" said Tee.

Christina continued to reiterate the plan, to kill time. "After they arrive, we'll split into two groups—one group going north to get the plans that Franklin—"

"We know," interrupted Elly. "The plans he hid under a bed in Herve. The other group will start figuring out where Marcus Pieman might have taken Nikolas."

"Someone's been listening," said Mounira, from behind a huge book.

"What is it, Mounira?" asked Christina, pushing down the book and revealing the worried little face behind it. "You've had that look since we got here. Whenever I talk about the plan, it seems to get worse."

Mounira hesitated. She wanted to say it was nothing, but she couldn't, this time. "The soldiers that showed up earlier today—the ones that came after the Red Hoods ran away—I've seen that before. My father and I saw it happen in the second town we had fled to. Ever since we came back here, today, I've been afraid the war that infected my homeland would spread right to our door." She pulled her book back up.

Elly went over, placed her arms around Mounira, and gave her a squeeze. "You're our little sister now," said Elly, "and we're *not* going to let anything happen to you. Not even, say, let you be dragged, screaming, up a mountain by a wooden bar." Elly smiled.

Mounira laughed and then tried to glare at Elly. "That *wasn't* very funny."

"Actually, it was *hilarious*," said Elly. "But it won't happen again… soon. I promise."

"Yeah—she'll do something *else*," said Tee, laughing.

"*Hey!*" Elly objected.

"Don't worry, Elly. I'm already plotting my revenge," said Mounira.

Elly smiled and nodded. "Good—glad to hear it."

Just then came a loud banging at the front door, and some yelling. Everyone froze.

Christina's heart sank. She'd heard that kind of

banging before—it was never good. "Mounira, wake Franklin. Tee, go and peek at who it is. Elly, you back her up. *Do not* engage. Peek, and return. Got it?" she whispered.

The duo nodded, pulled down their hoods, and slinked off.

Christina turned to Mounira and Franklin. "Gather *every* trace of us up," she said, marching over to get the first of the green-covered books holding a metal rod for opening the hidden lab.

A minute later, Tee and Elly returned. More banging and yelling came from the door.

"Who are they?" asked Christina, worried.

"Soldiers," said Tee nervously. "Lots."

Mounira grabbed Christina's hand and squeezed.

"We're going to be okay," said Christina nervously, turning the spine of the second book and catching the metal rod that slid out. She hoped the new plan she was formulating would work—their lives depended upon it.

CHAPTER FORTY

SECOND CHANCE

Jerome ran into his apartment and slammed the heavy oak door behind him, leaning back against it to catch his breath. He'd just run several blocks, and up three flights of stairs, in a panic. He wondered if his father or grandfather had ever stood where he was, now, worried like this. The apartment, and the Deuxième Chance café, had both been in the family for generations, yet he was sure they'd never witnessed anything like he had.

"Are you okay, Jerome?" called out a concerned, weary voice from one of the three adjacent rooms.

"You won't believe it! There are *foreign soldiers* outside!" Jerome replied, beads of his sweat falling to the worn, wide-plank wooden floor.

"Hmm. What are foreign soldiers doing in Mineau?" A grunt of pain followed the question. "I'm almost up."

"Let me help you," said Jerome, rushing to his friend's assistance. "You should be careful when getting up."

Jerome's friend, black stubble on his face, smiled back with gentle green eyes. His poorly-cut short hair, a favor from Jerome, was a mess, but he'd made the best of it. "You are very kind, but I need to learn to stand on my own," the man said, chuckling. Jerome helped him stand, and gave him a cane for each hand. "You have been *too* kind, these past months. First, your aunt cared for me, having found me beaten and broken by that roadside, and then, after her passing, you took me in. I do owe you and your family a great debt."

"I can't imagine what it would've been like to be robbed, run over by a wagon, and left for dead," said Jerome sympathetically.

Jerome's friend waved off his concern. "I don't like to think about it. I have a *new* lease on life—and I'm thankful for that."

Jerome gave a distracted smile. He peeked out the window, to the street below.

His friend stumbled forward. The well-worn robes made him look almost like a beige-hooded beggar. His legs, which had been broken, were still bound with wood as they continued to heal, and so he moved slowly, stiffly. "What do you see?" he asked, trying to have a look, but almost falling over.

"What concerns me is what I *don't* see," replied Jerome.

"What's that?"

"I don't see any of our kingdom's soldiers, nor our town's guardsmen. I see people, in small groups, running around. Some are fleeing, while some look like they're preparing to fight. But where are *our* soldiers? Our guards?"

His friend sighed deeply, knowingly. "Jerome, the Tub's influence here must have fallen. I heard this had happened in a couple of the southern kingdoms."

Jerome paused. "Huh? Wait—Andre, how do you know about the Tub?" he asked, surprised at his friend.

Andre chuckled, his jaw clicking slightly as he did. "Oh—I've learned *many* things in my life. I know of the Tub, and the Fare... and the *games* they play." He hobbled over to a chair, while Jerome sat on the floor by the window.

"My advice, Jerome, is that we wait this out, here in this apartment. We stay away from the windows when we see trouble. We're high enough up that we ought to be fine. We should *only* leave once all seems calm."

Jerome nodded his agreement while staring out the window, watching the occasional foreign soldier fire at a running citizen. He'd never seen *anything* like it.

The next morning, Jerome nudged Andre awake. Andre had fallen asleep in his chair.

"Huh?" said Andre, rubbing his eyes and stretching. "Oh—I feel absolutely stiff. When did I fall asleep?"

Jerome handed him some tea and buttered bread. "After the cannons stopped. You missed some fighting nearby. One fighter had a crossbow with different kinds of bolts—one had exploded, and another one had a rope on it. Strange," said Jerome, pausing. "I need to go see what has become of my café."

Andre took a sip of his tea and placed it on the floor, groaning as he did so. "Before you say anything about leaving me here, forget it—I'm coming with you. You can't go out there alone. If there's trouble, you need a distraction to allow you to get away. I owe you that much, at least," said Andre, making Jerome laugh as he helped Andre up.

The streets were eerily empty and quiet. It felt alien to Jerome, who had lived in Mineau all of his life. He walked slowly, to allow Andre to keep pace. They passed a couple of small buildings that had burned. Several windows along the way had been smashed, and left-behind items were scattered in the streets. Jerome was thankful there were no bodies to be seen.

"Maybe it wasn't so bad," he said, mostly to himself.

Andre hobbled along with his two canes. While strong enough to walk without them, he didn't want to test himself. As his body healed, so did his spirit, and his sense of self. His mind had been almost as damaged as his body, and his friendship with Jerome had helped immeasurably.

Oddly, Andre walked along without concern for what he saw. He wanted to share in the pain he could see Jerome going through, but he was numb to it. None of this meant anything to him. As long as his life wasn't in danger, Andre didn't care.

Finally, they turned the corner and on to the street

where the café was located. Things were worse here than they'd been led to believe. A military cannon, one of its large, wooden wheels broken, lay in the middle of the road. Many buildings nearby had burned down or were severely damaged. There were dead bodies here and there.

Jerome gazed in disbelief, panning from one side, to the other, and then locking on. "No, no, no—*No!*" he screamed, running down the street to the burned timber remains of the café that had been in his family for generations.

As Andre caught up, he started to feel genuinely bad for Jerome. He wasn't heartless—just selective, perhaps, in what he cared about—and he did care about Jerome.

Jerome was on his knees, clutching at the ashes, mumbling. Andre couldn't understand a word, but he knew the pain the man suffered.

Then, a glint of something caught Andre's eye. It was buried under rubble, where the office had been. It seemed to call to him. At first, he tried to dismiss it; *just junk*, he thought, but it nagged at him. He couldn't resist. He staggered over, letting go of his canes, and fell into the ashes and charred wood. He moved the debris until he beheld a tarnished, yet intact brass tube.

Andre's eyes were wide in wonder at his find. He unscrewed the brass top and removed the plans it contained. As he studied what he'd found, a giggle started to ripple through him. The giggle became a laugh, and the laugh twisted into a dark, sinister laugh.

Jerome looked to his friend, who was stuffing the plans back into the tube. "That tube! I'd forgotten about that. It belongs to Monsieur Klaus—he forgot it here, at Solstice. I suppose we should get it back to him, somehow."

Andre tore off his wooden leg braces, steadied himself, and stood up straight, grinning at his achievement. "Oh—*that's* certainly not going to happen," said Andre, sounding different.

Jerome got up and wiped his face on his sleeve. "Huh? What is it, and why were you laughing like that?"

Andre's sinister, green-eyed gaze pierced Jerome. Andre looked like a man transformed, with a menacing grin from ear-to-ear.

"Andre?" asked Jerome, afraid.

Andre put the tattered strap of the tube over his shoulder and looked at Jerome. "Jerome, please consider your life as payment for your kindness. Leave, now," he commanded. He closed his eyes and could feel the transformation complete.

"Andre—what's *in* there?" asked Jerome, backing up. His friend seemed somehow taller, straighter, and—menacing.

"Redemption," he replied, opening his eyes and sporting a sinister smile. "And who is Andre? My name... is *LeLoup*."

THANK YOU
FOR READING THIS BOOK

Reviews are powerful things. In addition to sharing your thoughts and feelings about the book, your review lets the rest of the world know that there are people reading the book.

Many people don't realize that without enough reviews, indie authors are excluded from marketing and newsletter opportunities that could otherwise help them get the word out.

So, if you have an opportunity, I would greatly appreciate it!

Don't know how to write a review? Check out **AdamDreece.com/WriteAReview**. Where should you post it? Your favorite online retailer's site and GoodReads.com would be a great start!

Thank you,
Adam

ABOUT THE AUTHOR

Starting The Yellow Hoods was one of the best decisions I've ever made. In taking a leap of faith and kicking off my indie author career, I ended 25 years of doing nothing with my writing, and transformed that *one day I'll be an author* thinking into *now what?*

The first world I remember creating and sharing with others was as a little jean-jacket wearing five year old at a park. I described for my friends, Tatiana and Simon, the imaginary realm we suddenly found ourselves in. We ran around using our fingers to shoot lasers and jumped on our Big Wheels to fly off through space.

I live in Calgary, Alberta, Canada with my awesome wife, amazing kids, and lots and lots of sticky notes and notebooks.

I blog about writing, life and more at **AdamDreece.com**.
Join me on Twitter **@adamdreece**, on
Facebook at **AdamDreeceAuthor** or
send me an email **Adam.Dreece@ADZOPublishing.com**

ADAM DREECE BOOKS

"This excellent offering of science fiction will keep readers obsessively turning the pages from the very beginning all the way through to the very end."
–Tracy A. Fischer, Readers' Favorite

Niko Rafaelo - a brilliant and driven inventor- is determined to flip the late 21st century on its head with a new take on a banned technology, nanobots.

The Man of Cloud 9
ISBN: 978-0-9948184-3-0

"Harry Potter meets Die Hard"
–M. Bybee, WereBook.org

"Madmax meets Lord of the Rings"
–Goodreads.com

A world once at the height of magical technology and social order has collapsed. How and why are the least of the wizard killer's worries.

The Wizard Killer
ISBN: 978-0-9948184-5-4

ADAM DREECE BOOKS

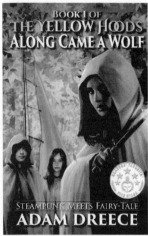

Along Came a Wolf
ISBN: 978-0-9881013-0-2

Breadcrumb Trail
ISBN: 978-0-9881013-3-3

All the King's-Men
ISBN: 978-0-9881013-6-4

Beauties of the Beast
ISBN: 978-0-9948184-0-9

Watch for Book 5, coming Spring 2017

ENVIRONMENTAL BENEFITS STATEMENT

ADZO Publishing saved the following resources by printing the pages of this book on chlorine free paper made with 100% post-consumer waste.

TREES	WATER	ENERGY	SOLID WASTE	GREENHOUSE GASES
10	**4,790**	**5**	**321**	**884**
FULLY GROWN	GALLONS	MILLION BTUs	POUNDS	POUNDS

Environmental impact estimates were made using the Environmental Paper Network Paper Calculator 3.2. For more information visit www.papercalculator.org.